THE
BLUE
WOMEN

Celebrating
30 Years of Publishing
in India

PRAISE FOR ANUKRTI UPADHYAY

Kintsugi

'I was mesmerized by the quiet beauty of this novel. With a tender yet unflinching gaze, Anukrti Upadhyay tells us the stories of extraordinary young women who craft for themselves the lives that they desire, memorable characters who are shaped, but never defined, by their grief and heartbreak. *Kintsugi* is about many things – devotion, loyalty, ambition, and desire – but most of all, it is a novel about resilience and courage.'

— AMRITA MAHALE, author of *Milk Teeth*

'I loved *Kintsugi* ... How the characters' connections/conjunctions never felt forced, kept surprising me; how the sentences weren't overwritten or straining for poetry, but also never bland or banal.'

— DEBORAH SMITH, translator of *The Vegetarian* by Han Kang

'The finest novel I read in 2020 ... It gladdened my heart.'
— KEKI DARUWALLA

'Delightful ... there's a certain quality to her writing that is both deep and light, very like the artistry of the jewellers that are the heart of this piece of writing.'

— OMAIR AHMAD

'*Kintsugi* is a delicate work about the many ways the heart remakes itself, that like an ornament slowly being chiselled and laid takes time to reveal its final shape. Yet by its end ... its artistry is evident, and despite its title, seamlessly expressed.'
— SHARANYA MANIVANNAN, author of
The High Priestess Never Marries

'What a book! Mesmerizing ... delicate and deep.'
— SHOBHAA DE

'Each character's individual presence is like a piece of life that comes together, melded gracefully by Upadhyay's writing. Her prose, spare and simple, takes shape delicately...'
— *Asian Review of Books*

'A little gem ... Upadhyay's writing has restraint, poise and an understated charm, with no room for superfluity.'
— *Hindustan Times*

'A rich, character-driven story that flows more or less linearly, and with a quiet beauty of language that seeks to work in aid of telling the story without drawing attention to itself. Read it for a little healing in these anxious times.'

— *Mint*

'In *Kintsugi*, the author shows the extraordinary strength inherent in the lives of ordinary people if only they had the courage to tap into it without fear ... A novel that echoes with loneliness, loss, longing, and unfulfilled promises.'

– *Open*

'The stories exist in a quiet zone ... there is more unsaid than said ... yet we are drawn into the lives of these six people almost immediately. And we are shown again and again, just how the human heart and its longings remain the same from person to person ... Easily one of the best books [of] 2020.'

– *The New Indian Express*

'A beautifully crafted novel based on the central idea of "kintsugi" or the skill of joining fragmented bits with precious artistry, the quiet flow of emotions is richly nuanced. While the novel reads easily due to an engrossing plot line, the complex narrative is woven with finesse to leave no loose ends. The author builds a web of life that is authentic to the cultures but transcends them to reach towards a universal humanism. A remarkable feat in imaginative extension and also firmly grounded on cultural reality, this book holds a wide appeal for a global literary audience.'

— THE SUSHILA DEVI AWARD 2021 JURY

Daura and Bhaunri

'Anukrti Upadhyay's novels are small wonders – transporting you to old worlds and new. I was transfixed by her language, sharp yet pliable, her attention to detail, and her ability to conjure the lost, the spoken, the less tangible, keeping always close the mystery at the heart of loving a person, a place.'

– JANICE PARIAT, author of *Everything the Light Touches*

'Tales within tales ... [*Daura and Bhaunri*] stand firmly on foundations slippery with all things human – love, raw jealousy, anger, a kalavant's music ... The novels are lifted by their language and characters; the former blends authentic terms with the telling and the latter never serve as caricatures ... In both, there is an understanding of patriarchy and the rising above of it in satisfactory telling ... Among the heat and dust, millet and anklets, clay griddle and flute, here are militant brides and princesses no human eye can see.'

– SHINIE ANTONY, *The New Indian Express*

'Simple, charming and poetic ... rich in imagery and lyrical prose.'

– *Hindustan Times*

'Luminous ... The magical and the mundane come together beautifully in Anukrti Upadhyay's novellas.'

– *Mint*

THE BLUE WOMEN

Stories

ANUKRTI UPADHYAY

FOURTH ESTATE · *New Delhi*

First published in India by Fourth Estate 2023
An imprint of HarperCollins *Publishers*
4th Floor, Tower A, Building No. 10, DLF Cyber City,
DLF Phase II, Gurugram, Haryana – 122002
www.harpercollins.co.in

2 4 6 8 10 9 7 5 3 1

Copyright © Anukrti Upadhyay 2023

P-ISBN: 978-93-5629-116-4
E-ISBN: 978-93-5629-120-1

This is a work of fiction and all characters and incidents described in this book are the product of the author's imagination. Any resemblance to actual persons, living or dead, is entirely coincidental.

Anukrti Upadhyay asserts the moral right
to be identified as the author of this work.

All rights reserved. No part of this publication may be reproduced, stored in a retrieval system, or transmitted, in any form or by any means, electronic, mechanical, photocopying, recording or otherwise, without the prior permission of the publishers.

Typeset in 10.5/15 Scala at
Manipal Technologies Limited, Manipal

Printed and bound at
Thomson Press (India) Ltd

Rough cotton, skeins of silk
Gold threads
All are from your box of wonders

CONTENTS

The Blue Women   1

Dhani   27

Made in Heaven   46

Mauna   72

Shawarma   94

Sona   107

Insecta   135

The Dragon in the Garden   151

Janaki and the Bat   178

The Big Toe   201

The Queen of Mahim   217

The Satsuma Plant   247

Acknowledgements   262

THE BLUE WOMEN

It was 3 a.m. In the surrounding predawn darkness, the brightly lit airport was like a ship alight in a dark, waveless ocean. The air bore the exhilarating early-morning smell as yet untouched by the day's inevitable pollution. I checked again the receipt the man at the prepaid taxi counter had handed me. The number matched the plate of a neat sedan in parking bay number seven. There was no one in the car.

'You are for Pune, sir? Did you book at the prepaid counter?' A woman stood beside me. She was dark-skinned and big-boned, her beige salwar-kameez dulled by the dazzling white lights. I nodded, craning my neck for the driver. I had meetings in the morning and wanted to be on my way.

'Could you show the receipt please, sir?' I handed the piece of paper to her. 'Is this your luggage, sir?' She clicked the electronic key and opened the car's boot.

I looked at her, puzzled. Then the penny dropped. 'You are driving me to Pune?'

'Yes, sir.' She smiled. 'You can check my driving licence if you like.' She pointed to the laminated bit of paper displayed on the dashboard beside a small Ganpati idol. 'I have been driving for ten years. Over a hundred trips to Pune and not a single accident. You will be safe with me, sir.' Shamefaced, I picked up my suitcase and stowed it in the open boot.

The car sped out of the airport and onto a broad expressway. 'We will take the NH4 to Pune, sir. I am not sure how familiar you are with the route but to reach the Pune highway, it would be quicker to cut through Dharavi and get to the Eastern Expressway. If you prefer another route, please tell me now.' I mumbled my acquiescence and leaned back in the seat. 'It will take around three hours to reach Pune. We have started early, so there won't be any traffic problems here or in Pune. Let me know if you'd like to stretch your legs or have a cup of tea. There are quite a few places along the way. It would not add more than thirty minutes to your travel time. And no extra charges.' I heard the smile in her voice.

'Thank you,' I said, and added, 'It is very brave of you to drive from Mumbai to Pune at this hour.'

'It is very brave of you too.' Her voice quivered with mirth.

'I am sure you understand what I mean – this is not the safest of jobs for a woman.'

'You are right, sir. But then, is there any job that is really safe for women?'

Her tone was polite, conversational, but for a reason I couldn't immediately pinpoint, I felt annoyed. 'There are jobs, and then there are jobs. Can you truthfully say you haven't had bad experiences in this line of work?'

'Bad experiences because I drive a taxi or because I am a woman who drives a taxi?' she challenged.

'Both,' I said. 'I hope you don't mind my saying so.'

'I don't, sir, if you don't mind it yourself.'

I sat up straight and looked carefully at her. I couldn't see her face; the rear-view mirror reflected only the straggling slums of Dharavi, grey in the grey light of dawn. She sat at ease, her broad shoulders relaxed, her powerful-looking hands resting on the steering wheel with assurance. There were traces of red nail-paint on the nails and green glass bangles tinkled at her wrists. Her hair was neatly plaited, not a strand out of place, a string of mogra flowers, wilting but still fragrant, attached to her braid with a black hairpin.

'I am truly sorry...' I began.

'Don't be, sir. These are not unusual comments or questions. I get them all the time. People assume that a woman driving a taxi is bound to have certain kinds of experiences. On my part, I have had some remarkable experiences, good and bad. I would think any woman who steps out into the world to earn her living would tell you the same.'

I nodded. All sorts of people book prepaid taxis. I could imagine men of the undesirable kind becoming troublesome, even dangerous. 'I understand. You can't be too careful. Can't the taxi company assign you families or perhaps only women passengers and allow you to drive during the day instead of at this hour?' I asked.

'No one has forced me to do this shift, sir. I chose it myself. In fact, these days I mostly do night shifts. The pay is better.'

'Isn't it unsafe to drive strangers late at night?'

'We have been trained to deal with trouble.' She flexed her shoulders.

'How about your family? You have children? Who looks after them when you are away at night?'

'There is more looking after to be done during the day than at night, sir. If I am away during the day, who would cook their meals and be home when they return from school? Who would keep them out of trouble and make them do their homework? I am only driving early morning today because it is a school holiday and they are with their grandmother in the village.'

'And your husband? Doesn't he worry about your driving late at night?' It sounded wrong even as I said it.

Her shoulders rose and fell as she breathed deeply. 'Doesn't your wife worry about you travelling alone at night?'

The car's air-conditioner hummed and vibrated in the ensuing silence. 'I am very sorry,' I said finally. 'I seem to be saying one wrong thing after another. Yes, my wife used to worry about my travelling alone until she herself undertook a journey alone to an unknown place. Who can tell whether she still worries about me there...' I remembered my wife's last days in the hospital, her body a mass of pain, all humanity extinguished, only a flicker remaining, somehow, which kindled upon seeing me – I, who loathed the disease for devouring her and, sometimes, her, for not giving in, just giving in and letting go.

'May your wife's soul be at peace, sir. I am sorry I spoke sharply just now when you asked about my husband. The fact is, I don't know where he is. The last time I saw him was years ago. I was eight months pregnant with my third, and he was leering at me from the mouth of the dry ditch he had pushed me into.'

I was aghast. 'I am so sorry...'

'It's all right, sir. I survived, and believe it or not, the baby in my womb lived too. That drunkard never showed his face near me again, he just left me with three children to feed. Things soon got tough for me. I had to sell everything – clothes, bedding, pots and pans. When there was nothing left to sell and I began thinking of the bottomless sea as the solution to my problems, I had my first stroke of luck. A neighbour's pregnant wife left for the village for her delivery and he needed someone to do his housework. He taught driving at a driving school and offered to teach me in exchange for cooking and cleaning for him. My folks back in the village didn't like the idea of my washing another man's clothes or sitting beside him in a car and learning to drive. But they weren't the ones feeding my children, so I didn't care about what they felt. I had no problems in learning to drive; I picked up the tricks of the trade easily too. I was always good with machines, even as a girl I could mend things – fix fans, hand pumps, things like that – and I quickly became handy with changing tyres, replacing oil, doing small repairs. I passed my driving test in the very first attempt and got a commercial driver's licence. A couple of days after I got my licence, I had my second stroke of luck. The local goon, who owned a few taxis, thrashed and threw out one of his drivers for cheating. I went to him with my three hungry kids, my story of hardships and my new driving licence. He hired me on the spot, and gave me fuel money too, which was great as I was completely broke. From that day onwards, a little over a month after my neighbour offered to teach me driving, I found myself behind the wheel of a newish taxi, eight hours a day, learning my way around busy city streets. I thought finally my days of trouble were over. I even began making plans to save and buy a room in the slum, and someday, my own taxi. But I had relaxed too soon, for this was the time the first blue woman boarded my taxi.' She paused.

'Blue woman?' I echoed, wondering whether it was some obscure religious sect or the name of a girl band.

She was silent for a moment. 'I am sorry, that just slipped out. I have never spoken about the blue women with my passengers. I worry it might make them nervous.'

This, of course, only had the effect of increasing my curiosity. 'With this preface, how do you expect me to not want to know more about them? If you really did not want me to be curious, you should have simply said they were students of a famous girls' school or members of a dance troupe. I would have believed you readily and asked no further questions.'

She laughed. It was a quiet laugh. I saw it rather than heard it – her shoulders shook gently and the green bangles on her wrists danced. 'I was never any good at making things up, sir. I couldn't even make up stories to tell my children when they were little. So for me, telling the truth is the only way; imagination – I leave for those superior to me!' I smiled at her subtlety.

'I don't want to make a mystery of it,' she said. 'If you really wish to hear about it, I have no issues telling you. But before I do so, I would like to tell you something about myself because it is important for you to know the kind of woman I am before I go any further. Hardships are not new for me, I was born in a village that saw many droughts. Every monsoon, women performed rituals for plentiful rains and prayed that the crops won't fail, that their men would not need to leave for the city to carry loads or work as masons to make ends meet. I saw no point in the rituals, in being yoked to a plough like an ox or in breaking coconuts and anointing fields with handfuls of sindoor to appease the rain god. Instead, I helped weed the fields and mend the water channels, and when the crops did fail, I collected firewood and fodder for the cattle. Please don't take this to mean that I don't believe in the gods. It is just that I have never had any patience with imagining things. I had had an early introduction to reality, and reality has always been sufficient for me. As a little girl, instead of playing with rag dolls or clay puppets, I looked after my little sister and I did it better than my mother. I fed her sugared water while my mother was away in the fields and carried her everywhere on my back – to the railway tracks to collect the coal that fell from the freight trains, to the pond to fetch water, even to the school whenever I could sneak some time from the chores. But I never once took her to the ojha to be cleansed of evil spirits with a straw broom. I was no different when I had my own children. I refused to paint black spots on their cheeks to ward off an imaginary evil eye or pray to the goddess of pox for their health. Instead, I stood in long queues at the hospital to get them vaccinated and stayed up nights nursing them when they fell ill. The way I see it, there is enough trouble, why bother with imagining more? This is the type of woman I am – an ordinary, practical-minded woman, not someone with a hyperactive imagination. It is important that this is clear before I proceed further with my story.'

'I think you are quite an extraordinary woman,' I replied. 'You are very strong.'

'Yes, I am strong,' she agreed, 'but that is nothing extraordinary. All the women in my family, my village and neighbourhood, all those that I know in this city, are strong. They have no choice – they have children and good-for-nothing husbands. But that really is not the point.'

'I understand your point,' I said. 'I believe you are practical-minded and truthful, and do not like to imagine things. Whatever you tell me, rest assured, I will not doubt its veracity.'

'Thank you,' she said. 'Sometime after I began driving a taxi,' she continued, 'I called my little sister from the village to live with me. She was a young woman now and a great help to me in every way. She was more like my own daughter. She had always wanted to learn the beauty trade. After coming to the city, she enrolled in a diploma course at a nearby institute and did very well there. She was so good that later, they waived half her fee. Anyway, I was very careful about her; she was young, and this was the first time for her in a big city filled with strangers instead of kinsfolk. Every morning after I sent my children to school, I walked her to the bus stop. Only after she boarded the bus would I pick up my taxi at the taxi stand and begin my shift for the day. Those days, I drove the taxi from early in the morning until 3 p.m. in the afternoon so I could be home by the time my children returned from school. Though new, I was good at my work.

My fare and fuel accounts were always accurate, and any scratches on the taxi were because I could only control my taxi and not the rest of the traffic. After my shift ended, I would hand the taxi to the next driver, render my accounts and pay the daily rental to the swaggering young man from the neighbourhood who managed the fleet of taxis for the owner. I exchanged banter with him as he looked through my accounts. You see, I was still a young woman then and sometimes enjoyed talking to a young man who understood the kind of day I had had – irate cops, traffic jams, noise, arguments about fares or right-of-way, and so on. On my way home, I would stop at a grocery store and buy the simple ingredients I needed for preparing the evening meal – some split yellow lentil, a little turmeric and cumin, some onions, a few green chillies, and on feast days, jaggery and peanuts and sesame and nutmeg. When I returned, I would find my children playing in the alley in front of the house. There were drains overflowing with washing-up water and sewage on both sides of the narrow alley, and the stone-slabs covering them were broken and slippery. Every day I worried they'd slip and crack their heads, or worse still, would fall in bad company. Petty thieves and glue sniffers abounded in the slum I lived in then. But I could not keep them indoors all the time. We had a single ten feet by ten feet room; we cooked and ate and slept in it. On Sundays, I bathed the children there too, and my little sister washed her hair there instead of at the public tap in the alley. After coming home, I'd give the children some tea and snack – roasted chickpeas or puffed rice garnished with coriander, or occasionally, if I had made good money, seera made from flour, sugar and toop. I would then sit them down to do their homework and prepare the evening meal, set the pulses to boil, knead the dough or cook some rice, slice onions and green chillies. On days I picked up a few long-distance fares, I bought potatoes or beans and cooked them with garlic and red chillies. It all depended on how much I made after paying the taxi's rent and fuel money. My little sister helped me clean the house, wash clothes, hang the children's uniforms to air and make sure they packed their bags. This is how a typical day would pass, busy enough but nothing exciting, no different from that of any other woman in my neighbourhood. Money was scarce – there were my wages and my little sister got some money for working as a trainee. Thankfully, my mother sent rice and millet from the village, and the children got a free meal at their school.

'One late April afternoon, the humidity was very high. A heat haze hung over the sea, and inside the taxi was like being in a sweaty, sticky embrace. We who live in this city know the stifling feeling on days when the very tar on the road begins to melt, when everything is unbearable and everyone angry and impatient. It was that kind of day. A young woman, dressed in shirt and trousers, flagged down my taxi. Though there was a traffic cop on the curb and the road was busy with moving traffic, I stopped. I could see she was harried. Her eyes wore that familiar tight look of a person in a hurry to be elsewhere. I guessed she worked in an office and was late returning from lunch. She opened the rear door and sat down heavily, leaning back into the seat and letting out a deep sigh. She asked to be dropped at one of the large mid-town office complexes. I joined the queue of vehicles at the big traffic junction at Haji Ali going towards the other side. Crossing it usually means waiting for the lights to change a few times. The congealed mass of vehicles at the junction seems as wide as the sea that rolls just beyond the low parapet. As the engine idled, I adjusted the rear-view mirror and noticed a kind of blue glow reflected in it. I was surprised and moved the mirror about until it showed my passenger. The sight caused me to almost faint. Instead of the young woman who had just boarded my taxi, there was a blue woman in the passenger seat. Her body glowed, as if she were lit from inside by a blue flame. There was a large wound on her head, half her forehead had caved in, and there were bruises on both her eyes. My head jerked around like a puppet's on a string. There was the woman, her twisted, broken body sprawled across the rear seat, blue like the throat of the God of Destruction. The wound on her head was bleeding, her face was twisted in pain. She was dressed in a torn and stained salwar-kameez, and a soiled dupatta was stuffed in her crushed mouth. I screamed in terror. Instantly the blue light and the battered body disappeared. The midday sun blazed through the windscreen flooding the taxi with its harsh glare and the young woman squinted at me with suspicion. Was there anything wrong, she asked in the sharp voice women acquire to keep all sorts of trouble at bay. My heart pounded worse than the last fast train and I hardly knew what to say. I muttered something about the car behind being too close. The woman didn't say anything, but in the rear-view mirror I saw her look doubtfully at me and slide her hand on to the door handle. I stuck my head out the window on the pretext of checking the car behind and gulped the smoke-filled air. I dropped her at the office complex and, while she rooted about in her purse for the exact change, I examined her closely. She was neither tall nor short, neither fair nor dark. Her hair was tied in a neat ponytail, her large eyes were outlined with precise strokes of kohl and she wore a name tag around her neck. There was not a scratch on her anywhere. After she left, I parked the taxi under a tree and rooted around in the back of the vehicle, reaching into the recesses of the seat, peering into the footwell. I am not sure what I was looking for. All through that day and the next few days, the thought of the blue woman haunted me. I was sure I had not imagined her, but I could not make head or tail of what I had seen in the back of my taxi.

'A couple of weeks later, I saw her again.'

I sat up. 'You saw the young woman again or the vision?' I asked.

'Well, I saw a photo in the newspaper. After my shifts, I used to leaf through the newspapers while waiting for the young account-keeper to tally the day's accounts. He had an easy life, that man. He took in all sorts of newspapers and magazines, mostly those with half-clad women and stories of gruesome murders, to while away time. The photo of the blue woman was on the front page of a city newspaper, only she wasn't blue. But in every other respect, she was exactly the way I had seen her in the back of my taxi – the terrible wound, the bruised face, the battered body and gagged mouth. She was found the night before, covered in blood and dead, not far from the office I had dropped her at. You would, of course, understand that I was shaken by the whole thing. The entire evening, I could think of nothing else. I wondered whether I should tell the police about my vision, but what could I say? That I saw the dead woman in a blue vision a couple of weeks ago? What use would that be, even assuming they believed me? It might even get me into trouble, and then where would my sister and my children be? In the end, I decided not to say anything to anyone. As it is, I had enough troubles of my own at that time. A good-for-nothing from the neighbourhood had been hanging around my sister for some time and I could see my sister was beginning to take an interest too. The good-for-nothing did nothing except ride a loud motorbike through the slum, day and night, and wear his hair like the heroes in the movies my sister had acquired a taste for. Now, it wasn't as if I was too old to see his appeal, but I was old enough to also see that trouble was written all over him. An added complication was that the good-for-nothing was distantly related to the goon whose taxi I drove. I had to be careful, and anyway, I knew saying anything to my sister would probably achieve the exact opposite result. So, I increased my vigilance, dropped in at her institute whenever I was in the vicinity and made sure she stayed indoors when home.

'Shortly after I saw the photo of the young woman in the newspaper, the second blue woman appeared. This one was older, middle-aged, an ordinary housewife. She boarded my taxi near the big bus stop at the vegetable market in Dadar and was carrying a bagful of vegetables. She didn't take long to turn blue. As soon as she pulled the door close, the blue light filled the taxi. There were welts around her neck, her eyes protruded out of her head, her tongue stuck out, her body was stiff. It was a truly horrific sight. My hands wobbled on the steering wheel, and I had to stop the taxi by the roadside. Perspiration fell from me like rain, and I trembled as though I was struck by the worst rain-fever. "Are you okay?" my passenger asked. She had such a kind voice, a mother's voice who suppresses a smile even as she scolds her unruly child and lets him have an extra sweet later. "I am fine, just this heat and the glare of the sun," I lied. "I can understand," she said in her soft voice and gave me an orange to suck. "I suffer from the heat too. That is why I flagged your taxi. The bus was too long coming and the sun was giving me a bad headache." While I drove her to her destination, she told me about herself. Nothing unusual, just ordinary marital misery. Four children, and an alcoholic womanizer for a husband. Mine was, too, I told her. Why don't you leave him, I asked. "How can I?" she said. "It's not easy to leave." She was right, of course. It isn't easy. I was lucky that mine left me, otherwise I would be sewing sequins on dresses until I was blind or washing utensils and swabbing floors, only for him to grab the money I earned and beat me every night by way of thanks. "He is a policeman, no one would pay heed even if I complained. I just have to hold on somehow until my children grow up," she sighed. I couldn't blame her for not being able to see beyond her children. Most women can't. I dropped her at the police quarters where she lived. That gave me a bit of comfort. I thought at least she would be safe in the police compound. I gave her a discount on the fare. I knew I would have to make up for the discount somehow. The account-keeper, though agreeable enough and lately a bit too free with his attentions, was strict about the money owed to the goon.'

'Was he troubling you, the account-keeper?' I asked.

She laughed her silent laugh again. 'Nothing worth mentioning, sir, it was just a lot of drama. He'd clutch at his heart and speak filmi dialogues – he wished he was the motor I drove, he envied the sun because it could touch me – that kind of nonsense. Still, his foolishness made my day interesting. Once or twice, he waylaid me in a quiet alley as I walked home, pressed up against me, tried to kiss and fondle, but he stopped the moment he saw that I was really angry. Despite all his swagger, there was no real harm in him. The fact is, his wife had left him for another and his pride as a man was wounded, so he played the lover boy with every woman he met.

'But this isn't about the account-keeper,' she said. 'A few days later, I decided to check on the woman I had dropped at the police quarters. You see, the second blue woman coming on top of the photograph in the newspaper had unsettled me. So one day, I skipped lunch and drove to the police quarters. Her house was locked. I knocked at the neighbour's door. They told me she had committed suicide. Hung herself from the ceiling fan with a nylon clothesline. It was several hours before she was found, they told me; her body was stiff, her eyes starting from her head, her tongue bitten through. "How did you know her?" they asked. "Are you related to her?"

I couldn't speak, I was crying so hard. I don't know how I managed to complete my shift that day. The account-keeper was concerned when he saw me. Had I suffered a heatstroke, he asked, or did someone dare misbehave with me? He felt my forehead and got me a lemon soda. I thanked him and said I had a bit of a headache, that was all. You see, I couldn't tell him about the blue women. If he knew, he would be duty-bound to tell the owner, and I would lose my job. Who would allow someone who had visions of blue women to drive a taxi? Still, I couldn't keep it all to myself. I felt I had to tell someone, talk about why it was happening, what it all meant. So the day after I learned about the second blue woman's suicide, I told my little sister. I poured everything out to her while the children slept under the pale, flickering light of the weak electric bulb. I made her swear on our mother that she would not tell anyone. She was both horrified and intrigued, just as I expect you are, sir. What does the blue glow mean, she asked, and why only women? "I don't know any more than you do," I said. "I just hope it stops, or one of these days I will have an accident." She was very worried for me, so I said to her, "I am very troubled. Won't you be sensible, my little doll, and keep away from the good-for-nothing for now, at least until you finish your diploma and find a good job? Once you are more settled, we can talk again." My little sister promised, and she was as good as her word.

'The children's summer holidays had begun, and I decided to send them and my sister to the village to spend the months before the rains in my mother's home. A few days before they were to leave for the village, I was flagged down by a smartly dressed lady. She wore a tunic the colour of a cat's eyes and heels which were not meant for walking. There was an expensive-looking car by the roadside, smoke pouring from under its hood. A couple of men were bent over it. She climbed into my taxi and told the men to call her once the car was fixed. Then she turned to me and gave me the address of a famous old club in the rich part of the city. Despite being such a smart lady, she chatted with me. She complimented me on my driving, on the neatness of the taxi, and asked all sorts of questions about me and my life. We had just stopped at a traffic light when I happened to glance at her in the rear-view mirror. One moment she was smiling and typing something into her phone and everything was normal and the next there was the accursed blue glow in the taxi, emitting from her puffed up body, swollen out of shape, battered and bruised, not a shred of humanity left. I sat paralysed I was so shocked. The traffic signal changed, the cars behind me honked sharply, and I somehow managed to ease into first gear. My skin crawled with horror, and I did not dare look into the rear-view mirror again. At her destination, she paid the fare and refused the change I held out. Instead, she handed me her business card. "Come see me next week before I leave for Goa," she said. "I am a documentary filmmaker and you have given me a great idea!" I felt panic surge inside me, I did not know what to say, what to do. I wanted to warn her against going to Goa, to not go near the sea at any cost for, you see, the blue woman I had seen in the back this time was a drowned corpse. Meanwhile, she waved at me and disappeared into the old club.

'The rest of my day passed in a haze, but I was careful to disguise my anxiety from the account-keeper. I did not want him to think I was sickly. In trying to conceal my agitation, I went to the other extreme and was so spirited that he felt encouraged enough to grab and kiss me. I was annoyed with myself for not seeing this coming. The door of his little tin port-a-cabin was broken and hung from one hinge, and something of this sort was bound to attract gossip. I slapped him half-heartedly and walked out. That night, I told my little sister about the drowned blue woman. She listened carefully. She is a smart girl, my sister, and she suggested that I write to the lady. "Since she has given you her address, it would be a simple matter of writing a note and delivering it to her office," she said. "You can warn her and explain what you saw. I am sure she would understand." I thought that was a good idea, and we composed the letter together. We decided to write about the other blue women and their fate, and to appeal to her to take my vision seriously, to take precautions against drowning, perhaps not go to the seaside at all. My sister wrote it out in her neat handwriting. I am going on and on, sir. If you feel bored or sleepy, please tell me.'

'No,' I said, 'I have been utterly engrossed. Your story is fascinating. Please go on.'

'The next day my fares took me to the other end of the town, far from the city centre where the lady's office was. The day after, I refused fares unless they were heading towards the city centre. Towards the end of my shift, I found myself in the vicinity. Her office was on the fourth floor of a newly painted old building; the stonework was picked out in white paint and the window frames were black and shiny. Her name was on a pearly white plate outside. A smart, young man was seated on a sofa, tapping away at a computer, his bare feet propped on a black table shaped like an anvil. I explained that I had met the lady and she had asked me to come see her in a few days. "I have something important to tell her," I said and held out the letter. The young man raised an eyebrow and pointed to a low table, green like a soldier's uniform and, of all things, shaped like a wave. "Leave the note there. She will see it when she comes in," he said. I placed the note in the first trough of the wave, weighed it down with one of the pebbles, green like the table, that were lying heaped in a glass bowl, and left.

'Over the next few days, I got busy with preparations for my family's village trip. There were gifts to be bought, money to be arranged for deepening the borewell, the children to be told to do their holiday homework, and my little sister to be reminded to supervise them in the village and not let them run wild in the afternoon heat. But I kept an eye on the city newspapers and was relieved that there were no reports about drowning-deaths. A couple of days after my family left, I had a slow shift and decided to visit the smart lady. The office was as before – the white nameplate, the black table shaped like an anvil, the young man. He was standing on one bare foot, the other resting on the wall behind him, talking into his mobile phone. I waited for him to finish and then told him that I had come to keep my appointment with the lady. He looked at me, and I saw his eyes were red and he was unshaven. "She is dead, drowned in Goa," he said flatly. My legs collapsed under me. Until that moment I was so sure I had saved her, that I had defeated the blue vision. The young man helped me to a seat and got me some water. That's when I saw the note I had left for the lady, lying untouched in the first trough of the wave-table. I picked it up. "She left in a hurry. I thought it could wait." He choked up. Back in my taxi, I struggled to control myself, but I was shaking so violently that the tea I bought from a passing tea boy spilled all over me. Eventually I managed to drive the taxi back to the stand, handed over the rent money and my fuel book to the next driver, and requested him to give them to the account-keeper. I told him I was feeling unwell, and it was true – I was soaked in sweat and my teeth chattered uncontrollably.

'Reaching my room, I warmed some water on the small stove on which I did most of my cooking. Then I took a bath inside the room instead of going to the public washroom at the end of the alley. I soaped my body and washed my hair and scrubbed my hands and feet. After putting on my clothes and swabbing and drying the floor, I unrolled one of the mattresses stowed in the loft and lay down. The heat in my body had abated, but I felt a sickness inside me, a kind of aversion towards my own self. The fatal blue women floated before my eyes, gory, rigid, dead. I shuddered with horror, my own flesh repelled me. I don't know how long I lay like that. It was evening when I was roused by a knock on the door. At first, I ignored it, but the knocking only grew louder.

Reluctantly, I got up and opened the door halfway. The account-keeper stood in the alley. "I came to check on you. Are you okay?" I nodded. "I have got you something to eat. I know your children and sister are away, and there is no one to give you any food," he said, holding out a bundle wrapped in newspaper towards me. I opened the door and let him in. What else could I have done? I couldn't touch the food, my flesh crept with horror of myself, and there he stood with his simple needs, alive and whole, unaware of death and decay. I let him hold me, caress me over my clothes, kiss me clumsily. After his fumblings were over, I lay next to him, his body against mine. We were almost of equal height. He held me and cried, whispering about his loneliness, the bastard his wife left him for, the children he'd never had. I could feel my body through his hands as they grasped me, and my horror slowly ebbed away. After all, I was only a medium, I had no active role to play in anything. I soon got rid of him, but until my family returned from the village, he continued to pester me.'

'But you were lonely yourself,' I said. 'You didn't think of taking up with him?'

'With him? Never,' she said. 'If I had found him an exciting lover, it might have been different, but he was clumsy, inept, quickly spent, and all I could muster for him was pity. Anyway, I had no time for all that. I had to think things over and take important decisions.'

'What decisions?'

'Decisions about what I should do about the blue women. You see, I couldn't go on like that. I had to do something to stop the blue women from haunting my taxi. So I decided to avoid taking female passengers and found a job with a long-distance car company. No city-driving for me. I have driven inter-city ever since.' She fell silent.

'What happened next?'

'Next? There isn't much left,' she replied. 'My story, like our journey, is drawing to an end. You will soon reach your destination. We are already in the outskirts of Pune.'

I was surprised. 'How is that possible? You said it would take three hours.'

'And it has!' She sounded amused.

I looked out the window. The rocky ghats had given way to a straggling cityscape. There were apartment blocks scattered on both sides of the road; and restaurants and hotels, too. The day looked fresh and a large, orange-coloured sun hung just above the raggedy mountains. Coarse-leaved dwarf mango trees, African tulip trees bearing bunches of vermillion flowers and sunshine trees sending forth sprays of yellow blossoms flashed past. How could the story be over when none of the questions were answered?

'Let's stop for a cup of tea. You must be tired after the long drive,' I stalled.

'My throat is somewhat dry, and I never say no to a cup of tea,' she said and slowed the sedan, bringing it to a halt before a neat-looking restaurant by the roadside. There were tables and chairs set under a large tamarind tree, and a couple of puppies, dirty brown but still charming as only small animals can be, loitered about. I asked the boy who was dusting tables to bring some tea, and whatever was hot and freshly cooked.

'Kande-pohe,' she interjected, 'topped with fresh kotambir. I can smell the onion-peanut-curry leaf garnish from here. Also a packet of biscuits for the puppies. Those puppies do not seem to have a mother around.'

'Neither does that boy,' I commented, as the boy retreated. He was skinny. The shoulders of his shirt hung low over his elbows and the hem fell below his knees.

'Oh, he has a mother all right.' She settled back into her chair.

'How could you be so sure?'

'You can see for yourself, sir. His face and hands are clean, and his hair oiled and neatly parted. His shirt is clean too. He has a mother, or at the very least, a grandmother.'

The boy brought our tea and snack. She tore open the packet of biscuits and breaking them into bits, threw them to the puppies. The little creatures yapped and swarmed around her feet, wagging their small, curved tails. I observed her carefully. The first impression of strength and neatness I had when I saw her at the airport was reinforced. She had large eyes set wide apart and her face was not unpleasing. The loose tunic she had on fell comfortably around her large bosom and broad hips. Her arms were muscled, and veins stood out on her wrists where the glass bangles gently jostled.

'So, what happened next?' I repeated my question. 'Did you never see another blue woman ever again?'

She raised the teacup to her mouth and hesitated.

'You did, didn't you?' I said.

'I did,' she conceded, 'once, but this was not like the other occasions. This happened right after my children and my little sister returned from the village and shortly before I took the new job. The good-for-nothing was making a nuisance of himself, saying he wanted to marry my sister, trying to make her run away with him. He found out about the account-keeper and me and thought he could hold that over me, the fool. I, of course, told the account-keeper, and he thrashed the good-for-nothing. You would think a person would give up after this. Not him. He bought a country-made revolver and brandished it around. My little sister, though smart in other ways, is rather foolish about people. She got it into her head that he would shoot himself if she did not agree to marry him. By this time, she had completed her diploma and had taken a job with one of those home-beauty service companies. I was not in favour of this job, her going from house to house dragging heavy cases filled with bottles and tubes and machines to beautify idle women; it seemed less respectable than working in a salon. But she liked it, and because of her job, it was difficult for me to keep track of her. I was sure she was meeting the good-for-nothing every day.'

She emptied her cup, and I asked the boy to bring another.

'You must be wondering what all this has to do with the blue women. Well, my little sister used to travel to her appointments by trains, taxis, autos, depending upon the location. Whenever I was headed in the same direction as her, I gave her a lift. One day, during the time all the mess with the good-for-nothing was going on, she was riding in the back of my taxi, and believe it or not, at one of the traffic lights, there was the cursed blue glow and there was my little sister, bullet wounds to her stomach, her mouth open in a scream of agony. I felt the nausea surge in my throat and screamed her name. I heard her frightened voice stammering, what happened, what happened, and the horrid sight was gone. She was no longer blue, no longer bleeding slowly to death. I told her what I had seen. "I am sure the good-for-nothing is planning to do something drastic," I said. "You must listen to me, my vahini, my little sister, you must quit this job tomorrow and leave for the village directly. Stay there for the remainder of the summer. Let me see how things go here. When I think the time is right, I will call you back." My sister was scared. She agreed and left the next day. That was the last blue woman I ever saw, and I am glad that there have been no more.' She pulled out a paper napkin from the plastic napkin holder, wiped her mouth, and shaking the crumbs from her tunic, rose. 'We must be going, sir. The morning rush hour is terrible, you wouldn't want to get stuck in a jam.'

I paid the bill, gave some money to the little boy in the oversized shirt and followed her to the car.

'So, no more blue women after that,' I said after a while.

'None at all, sir,' she said, 'not a single one.'

'Have you ever wondered why you never had visions about blue men?'

'I have asked myself many questions,' she said in response. 'Why did I see those specific blue women? What was I supposed to do upon seeing them? But I have found no answers.'

We were in the city now and speeding through broad, treelined roads.

'Perhaps the purpose of those visions was for you to save your sister from that murderous fellow,' I said.

'Perhaps,' she agreed. 'My sister is now married to a boy from our village whom I always liked for her. She works in a proper salon now. She doesn't need to go to people's homes like a common servant.'

'And that good-for-nothing?' I asked. 'You said he was connected to the goon in your locality. He didn't kick up a fuss?'

The car turned into a pair of wide gates and rumbled over a gravel path. For the second time that morning, she hesitated. 'He did trouble me,' she said slowly.

'I thought as much,' I said, a note of satisfaction creeping into my voice. 'What did he do?' I asked.

'He shot himself with that cursed revolver in front of our house. Made a hash of the job too, the fool. Shot himself in the stomach ... They took him to the hospital, bleeding and screaming in pain.'

She brought the car to a stop in front of a glass façade.

'We have reached your hotel, sir,' she said.

DHANI

T HE WOMAN LOOKED up and smiled. The small silver rings in her nostrils trembled, her face gleamed like new leaves.

'Damn crowded here today, no? Sit, if you like.' She shifted to make room on the metal seat, painted grey like the monsoon sky.

She was right about the crowd, except it wasn't just today that the restaurant was crowded. It was crowded every single day. It was the busiest restaurant on the Bombay side of the Bombay–Pune highway. I should know, I make this trip every weekend and am familiar with every restaurant, tea stall and food cart along the highway. However, this isn't about me. This is about the woman with the twin nose rings who was looking up at me, her head tilted to one side, her bright eyes seeming brighter against the monsoon day dim with clouds, and offering me perhaps the only available seat in the restaurant. Still, I hesitated. I had good reason for doing so. This woman was a complete stranger, and I try my best to avoid engaging with strangers. If truth be told, I avoid engaging with those known to me as well, but like I said, this isn't about me. I looked around once again – not a vacant seat in sight. The seat opposite hers was firmly claimed, too, a backpack, a biker's helmet and a heavy-looking document holder heaped on it. I decided to accept her invitation. Not because she was smiling in a way as to fill the entire field of sight, like a dominant note claims the entire ear drum. No, not at all. My reasons for accepting the seat were practical and had nothing to do with her. Firstly, I had been jostled in the crowd while carrying the food tray; as a result, the sambar in my tray had sloshed over the idlis and I wanted to eat them before they soaked any more of the liquid and disintegrated. Secondly, when on a journey, I am not one to dawdle over food, or anything else, on the way. I believe that one should not linger, there is no point in drawing the journey out. Finish and get it over with, that's how I think.

I set my food tray down on the table. 'If you are sure this isn't an inconvenience...' I began.

'What inconvenience? We are here to eat. It isn't as if either of us is planning to spend the rest of the monsoon here!' She laughed.

I pulled a couple of tissues from the plastic tissue box and looked sideways at her while wiping the cutlery. Not because I didn't wish to meet her eyes, which I admit had a way of looking at one that was too direct, but because that's the only way to look at someone seated next to you. How can you see someone alongside you squarely? For that you have to face them. Anyway, I do not want to keep explaining myself. That's one of the reasons I avoid engaging with people, and in any case, as I have mentioned already, this isn't about me.

The woman was dressed in a dark vest and a pair of jeans. I noticed she held herself very straight. She had good ears. They seemed larger than average – though the reason for that could be that her hair was cut very short, exposing her ears entirely – but they were otherwise quite a handsome pair of ears, pale and translucent, shaped like shells, with their lobes free and well-proportioned. From where I sat, I could see the delicate whorl of bones leading to the smooth, flushed tunnel within. She had shown good sense in not disfiguring them with piercings. I can never understand why people stick bits of metal into their ears, as if they can somehow improve their perfect, flawless shape. As you may have guessed, ears are my particular speciality. I am a technician to an audiologist, and in my line of work, I examine many pairs of ears in a day. However, I can't say I get to see such young and healthy-looking ones very often. I mostly have to deal with aged ears, wrinkled and marked with liver spots, slack and veined, unable to perform their function efficiently, as if the sounds and words of a lifetime have accumulated inside the ear canal, encrusted the membrane, benumbed the nerve endings. Of course, I am aware that's not the case; I am a trained audio technician after all. But despite my training, I approach ears with a sense of mystery. They are such sensitive organs, intricately, even secretively, shaped – cartilage, bones, membranes all arranged in a fine, impeccable balance. I often wonder how my patients bear my examining their ears with such composure, allowing me to probe, poke, peer at the dark, hidden places inside. And yet, all of them do so without even a murmur of protest. There they sit in the cushioned examination chair, tuck their hair back, tilt their necks and offer me their ears eagerly, like someone holding out their hand to a palmist, unafraid of the past and the future that could be read in it. Anyway, and I repeat, this isn't about me. All I want to say is that there is a certain kind of pleasure in seeing a pair of well-shaped ears such as the woman with the nose rings possessed, and it is for this reason that she interested me.

I picked up my spoon and hesitated. It was true that I didn't know her, and yet, she had shared her seat with me. It felt awkward to eat while she sat meal-less, her arms resting on the table, fingers drumming softly upon the metal top, and even more awkward to offer her food from my tray. I wondered what to do. Should I ask her whether she'd like to try an idli and wave to a waiter to bring an empty bowl so I could share one from my tray, or would it be better to offer to order a separate plate of idlis for her? I sat there, wavering, spoon in hand. My mother gets annoyed at my silent ditherings. He has got a borrowed mouth which he must return, she says caustically; that's why he is afraid to use it. Before I could make up my mind, a man carrying two trays laden with food came over. He was one of those well-built men who wear shirts that are ridiculously tight across the chest and short in the arms, to show off pads and mounds of muscles.

'Here, I think I got everything that you wanted. Nice and hot – kotambir vada, kande pohe, seera,' he said and placed the trays before her.

'Everything I wanted?' She was looking up at him, smiling.

The man slapped his forehead. 'I forgot the vada pav!' he said and darted away.

The smile remained fixed on her mouth as she followed him with her eyes. I pressed an idli with my spoon; sambar had seeped into it, it broke into three pieces.

I ate in silence. Some people are proud of their ability to converse, I am proud of my ability to be silent. I prefer silence to the chatter people fill it with. You would, too, if you spent entire days in an audiometry lab listening to sounds at different frequencies and pitches and shouting instructions into deaf ears. Still, it is true that sitting next to that silently smiling woman, I felt an urge to talk. Though, what can one say to a stranger beyond the commonplaces? I chewed the unuttered, meaningless words with a mouthful of soggy idli. Outside, the clouds had thickened. I have often noticed that the blue-grey light of a monsoon day softens the most mundane and ugly of objects it falls upon. The tarred road, the dustbin shaped like cartoon cats, a lone, straggly tree trapped in concrete – everything acquires a mellow magic.

The man returned. This time he held two paper plates piled with steaming hot vada-pav, the pav-buns sliced and stuffed with crisply fried potato balls, liberally sprinkled with powdered red chilli and coconut. The savoury fragrance made my mouth water.

'There,' he said, placing the plates on the table, 'now I really have got everything.' He pushed the helmet, backpack and document folder aside, and sat opposite the woman.

'Everything?' The woman's smile never wavered. 'This restaurant has everything? Everything I wish for?'

'You want something else? They have more options.' The man made to rise.

As I have said, the two of them were strangers to me, their business was none of mine, and yet, I was present there, co-opted as a witness. Breaking my own rule, I spoke to them. 'Perhaps they don't have everything, but they definitely have an extensive menu and they make everything fresh here. Their vada-pav is better than the stale, oily ones we get in Bambai.'

The man looked at me. 'You are absolutely right. Best food on the highway. We've come here after a long while and nothing's changed.'

'We have come here after a long while and everything's changed,' the woman intoned.

They looked at each other, smiling, but their smiles were entirely different. Her's was bright and sharp, drawn deliberately like the curved blade of a katar; his emerged flickeringly like a doubtful firefly. I am not explaining this well for I know nothing about smiles, I only understand sounds. Thankfully, they are less complicated than smiles and such like – they enter the dark tunnels of your ears, make their way to your brain and you know what they are, whether a loud whistle or a soft murmur. There's no endless wondering whether they mean one thing or another, and if you find yourself wondering, it is time you came to the audiometry lab and got your ears looked into.

'Nothing needs to change, Dhani,' the man said earnestly. 'Everything could go back to the way it was. None of this is irreversible.'

The woman's smile deepened. 'We are still trying to figure out all that has changed, and by the time we do, everything would have changed all over again. That's the way things are.' She mixed a spoonful of seera with rice flakes fragrant with turmeric and coriander.

'You keep saying so, but tell me what has changed? We are here together, and like always, you are eating sweet mixed with savoury.'

'But the flavours – they are all different.'

The man leaned back. 'It is just a notion you've got hold of, Dhani...' He broke a piece of the kotambir vada and chewed the coriander-encrusted savoury.

They had forgotten my presence. It began to rain. First, large, heavy drops pierced the watery, blue-grey light like so many glass bullets, then the rain set in in earnest and fell in wind-waved grey sheets. It fell with equal fervour over the patchy concrete of the highway, the straggly tree, the mist-veiled mountains. Each time the glass door opened to admit groups of dripping, laughing travellers, the rushing, beating sound of rain filled the restaurant.

The man broke off another piece of the thick fritter. His eyes rested on me absently.

'You come here often?' he asked.

'Yes, every week.' This is another of the reasons I avoid talking to people. They begin with asking questions – where do you live, what do you do, how many in your family, and next you know, they have taken a flying leap from enquiring to giving advice about how you should organize your life. I have heard every kind of advice from strangers encountered as fleetingly as bird-shadows over grass, the gist of which always is that I shouldn't be living the way I am:

'You should bring your mother and sister to Bombay to live with you.'

'You should return to Pune to be with them, that's your duty as a son.'

'You should move to the south, there are big hospitals there.'

'You should go north, the weather is better there.'

'Wherever you go, just don't think of leaving your own country. You'll regret it one day.'

'What will you earn here? Go abroad and make some money while you are still young...'

I have to admit, though, that the man, whatever be his faults in choice of clothes, wasn't nosy.

'We are making a trip to Pune after a while,' he said slowly, his eyes still resting on me absently, the forgotten fritter crumbling slowly between his heedless fingers.

I felt obliged to say something. 'You've chosen the perfect time of the year to do so. Monsoons are best experienced in the ghats. The greenery and the waterfalls will all vanish in a month or two. But for now, the ghats are beautiful.'

The woman rested her spoon on the rim of the paper plate. 'We are not going for the beauty of the monsoons.'

'Oh ... you are visiting relatives perhaps...'

'Unhnn,' the woman shook her head. 'No.'

'Dhani...' the man pleaded.

The woman turned her head, her eyes falling on his like a shining blade. 'We are returning to Pune to get a divorce,' she said.

I was taken aback. In all of my thirty-three years, I had never once come across a situation like this. Uncertain, I looked down at my wilting dosa, crumbling idlis and cooling sambar. It was difficult to go on eating mundanely after the woman's momentous announcement. A server in a blue uniform stopped by and proffered a tray of tea in clay tumblers and filter coffee in stainless steel glasses. They chose the tea – I could smell the sugar it was laden with. Before I could make up my mind, the server moved to the next table.

'Here's a real change' – the man sipped his tea – 'waiters in uniform.'

'The staff seems new, too, and the owner, the old man who used to sit behind the cash register, is no longer there. Perhaps he sold the restaurant,' the woman suggested. 'That's a kind of divorce too, isn't it?' she added, still smiling her bright, flinty smile. I felt tired just watching that smile.

'It was all her idea.' The man looked at me apologetically. 'I mean, getting a divorce...'

'Getting married was my idea too.'

The restaurant was filled with the dull drone of conversations and the muffled sound of rain coming down with a detached ferocity. I felt tired of those sounds too. The whole situation had begun to annoy me.

'We are making you feel very uncomfortable, aren't we?' the woman too turned her gaze towards me.

'There's nothing to all this, really,' the man reassured, 'just one of her notions. I have known Dhani for the last ten years, right from the day we joined the architecture school. She just runs away with an idea from time to time ... There's nothing to it all.'

The woman raised her brows. 'There's nothing to us getting divorced?'

'You know what I mean ... There was really nothing, at least, not from my side ... If you thought ... you could have always said something, Dhani ... You still can, you know...'

The woman watched him in silence.

'Dhani's always been like this. First, she insisted we move because of the frogs and now this divorce...' The man shrugged his muscular shoulders, the shirt straining at the seams.

'Hello, you are the one who had a problem with the frogs!'

He shrugged again. 'It was a really nice flat too. Very conveniently located, train station ten minutes away, no water or electricity disruption issues, and to top it all, very reasonable rent. But then you came up with the frogs.'

'I didn't come up with the frogs, they were just there. And you were queasy about the frogs, not me.'

'I wouldn't even have noticed them if you hadn't pointed them out. We could have stayed on in that flat and everything would have been fine.'

The woman arched her neck and laughed. The twin silver rings in her nostrils glinted, her ears flushed. When she stopped laughing, she looked at me. 'We have thoroughly confused you, haven't we?'

I confess I felt a tad lost, the way I had felt when I saw an audiogram for the first time. To me, the fine, rising, peaking and dipping lines and numbers on the x and y axis made no sense, but the doctor who had studied innumerable audiograms and all the known maladies of the ear had taken one look at them and said with assurance that it was noise-induced hearing loss, the cochlea was impacted and sounds at higher frequencies would pose a challenge. What I mean to say is that those two could follow the lines and curves of each other's thoughts, which, naturally, I couldn't, for example all that talk about frogs in a flat.

'I understand the difficulty of finding a reasonably priced flat near a train station. If you find one, you should stay put. However, this is your private matter. Perhaps I should move to another table—' I made to rise, though the restaurant was even more crowded than before. The unstoppable rain had driven travellers into its shelter, and groups of people stood around balancing plates of food in their hands, talking, eating, waiting.

'Not at all,' said the woman shaking her head vigorously. 'If you get up, someone else will sit here. This place is bursting with people. Anyway, nothing's private any longer. Everything has been filed in the family court and anyone can pay the court fee and look it all up.'

The man let out a deep breath. 'Once something gets into her head...'

'The frogs were in my head?' She gulped her cooling tea and shifted slightly in her seat to face me. 'Let me tell you about the frogs, then you can decide for yourself.'

The man withdrew the arm he had placed along the back of the seat and leaned forward. 'Dhani, be reasonable. He could be in a hurry, he might need to reach somewhere.'

'So are we, but it is raining like crazy. Besides,' she tilted her head and looked at me, 'you don't look like you are in a hurry. Or are you?' She was smiling again, the ear turned towards me was tinted a delicate ruby.

'I am in no hurry,' I answered glancing towards the man. His eyes were fixed on the woman. I was not planning upon leaving until the rain let up and this wasn't because of the woman, or her scimitar smile, or her flushed ear. It was because of the rules at the audio lab I worked at. I had learned early on in the job to be careful about my health. Most of our patients are elderly, prone to catching any microbe lingering in the sequestered lab environment, so anyone with even the slightest cold or cough is immediately shifted to quality-control duty in the factory where the hearing aids are machined. Factory duty is tough – commuting for hours on bumpy roads amidst intrepid truck drivers casually speeding up, missing you by a hair's breadth. Add to it eight-hour shifts, punching your card even for toilet breaks, and everyone from the foreman to the supervisor asking you when you planned to get married. It was far better to stay put to avoid getting drenched in the rain and listen to the story about the mysterious frogs.

'It isn't the Ramayan that it would take hours to tell,' the woman said, biting into a green chilli. 'This happened about a year ago when we moved from Pune to Bombay. If you've ever lived in Pune, you'd know what that means.'

I nodded. I had lived in Pune until three years ago and had no desire to move back there to live in the house my father had built, now sinking deeper and deeper into shade as buildings rose higher and higher around it. Still, every time I entered the quiet lane with the old trees, I felt a strange quickening inside me. An inexplicable desire to toss my bag over the gate and vault after it, whistling, like I used to do years ago, would rise within me.

'And I had always lived in Pune, literally my entire life. Mummy-Daddy, my sisters, my friends, everyone's in Pune—'

'But you never cared much for Pune,' the man interrupted. 'You used to complain how narrow and limiting it was. One time you even wanted to go to Australia.'

'Yes, for a year. To do a course in environmental architecture, not to live there. Anyway, you'd chickened out.'

'We had just begun working then, Dhani. We had no money to speak of. We were learning the ropes, learning to be real architects. We weren't even married.' The man looked at me and shook his head. 'You see what I mean when I say she gets these ideas. For a whole six months she was wild about going to Australia, and two years later, she didn't want to leave Pune and move to Bombay.'

'So we didn't go to Australia to study because we weren't married, and moved to Bombay to work because we were,' the woman continued as if she hadn't been interrupted. 'And in the interim, we learned being real architects by copying Hong Kong offices, New York apartments and holiday homes in the south of Spain. If you see an ugly, shiny, tall building in Hinjewadi or Yerwada or anywhere else in Pune, there's a ninety per cent probability that we designed it. We had learned all about green buildings, harmonious landscaping, local material, climate-conscious designing back at the school, and what did we end up building? Glass, chrome and pre-fab eyesores that guzzled energy. That's what we did for four years.'

'You exaggerate, Dhani. Our designs had technical excellence, design integrity. They are appreciated, the buildings we built are useful. It's only towards the end that the job became frustrating. Too many projects didn't take off. The whole Pune construction scene was tapering off. We'd work hard on site-surveys, sweat over AutoCAD, and then something would go wrong – either the financing fell through, or the land had wrong Vaastu.'

'Actually, that was the only saving grace. Imagine, if every monstrosity we ever designed was uglifying the city right now.'

'You mustn't think that we did bad work,' the man spoke earnestly. 'This is just Dhani's way of exaggerating everything. We are very good architects.'

'We are very good architects who design very bad buildings.' The woman stirred the green chutney with the little finger of her right hand.

'We were so good that we got better jobs with large firms in Bombay.' The man's tone remained even.

'You got the job in Bombay because you applied for it and ditched the plan to set up in partnership with Prakash and others. And I got a job because I had no choice.'

At last, the man looked at her. 'That's hardly fair, Dhani. You knew I was applying. We didn't burst our asses in architecture school to play at mindful designing and ethical construction with friends. What would we have achieved by working with Prakash and his gang? They hated every developer in and around Pune. Who would have given us work? We were lucky to get out, lucky to find good jobs.'

The woman wiped her finger with a napkin. The green from the chutney made a dark stain on the soft, white paper. 'So that's how we came to Bombay – because we were lucky.'

The man sighed. 'Yes, and because we were lucky, we found a perfect flat. It was owned by an alum, a very successful one, and was close to my work. There was a market and a temple nearby too, and the cherry on top was that the landlord was a very decent man. He didn't even ask us to put up a deposit.'

'That was because you volunteered me to tutor his daughter,' the woman said.

'What was wrong with that, Dhani? Ria's a sweet girl and you enjoyed coaching juniors at our college.'

'Because they wanted to learn. It wasn't that I would be talking about Antoni Gaudí's design scheme, and they'd ask why I was wearing red nail polish with my blue kurta.'

'Now you are exaggerating again,' the man challenged. 'You used to be kinder to the juniors, used to cut them so much slack. Besides, Ria isn't like that at all.'

'Why don't you say how she is then?'

The man flushed. 'I am not saying she is brilliant like you...'

'Neither am I.' The woman flashed. 'Anyway,' she turned to me, 'we'd been in that flat for a few months when one morning I step into the bathroom and there's a kind of movement, you know, the kind that you don't quite see but sort of notice from the corner of your eye? At first, I think maybe my eyes are playing a trick. Sometimes, just after you wake up, you get these visual illusions, don't you? You see patches of colour or the outlines of objects seem wavy.'

Though I know nothing about eyes, I agreed with her. Often patients complain of a harsh ringing or a persistent drip-drip or some other sound amid the soundproof silence of the audio lab. If ears can play such tricks, who was to say that eyes don't?

'I switch on the lights and there's a frog in the corner, no bigger than a coin and a neutral beige in colour. I look carefully and there are several of them – under the window sill, in the corner by the shower, even in the small basket I stored soaps and shampoos in.' The woman turned her head slowly and looked at the man. He was leaning back, arms folded. 'Once our eyes got accustomed to spotting them, we saw them everywhere in that one-BHK flat. We found them in the shoes we had just stepped out of, among the freshly folded clothes, in the unwashed utensils in the sink ... they were literally everywhere. Perhaps they'd always been there, only we hadn't learned to see them.' She rested her chin on her two hands wrapped around each other, but her eyes remained on the man, their lids trembling slightly every now and then, like fish tangled in a web.

'I have seen frogs in my stairwell in monsoons,' I offered as the silence stretched out. 'Our yard turns into a swamp when it rains.'

The woman shook her head. Her breast heaved in a long breath.

'This was in December. And there wasn't a leaf of grass to be seen anywhere in the building; even the potted plants were plastic. The nearest tree was an hour's journey by train.' She smiled slightly. 'Come to think of it, it could easily pass for one of the buildings we designed – concrete compound and flaring façade studded with large metal discs that had no purpose unless you can call reflecting sunrays and starting an occasional garbage fire in the dry season one!'

'It was a new, well-built apartment complex,' the man said. He was collecting the crumbs of the kotambir vada and building a fragile, mini tower on his paper plate. 'No one else had faced any problem there. Our landlord got a pest exterminator to come in, but he couldn't do anything to solve our problem.'

The woman shrugged her bare shoulders. 'It wasn't a problem that could be solved. I thought I was okay with the frogs at first, but it was exhausting to always be on the watch for them...'

'I was just tired of everyone talking about them.' I was startled by the harshness in the man's voice. 'Wherever I went, it was always the frogs: Are you still facing the problem? It's been a long while, why don't you do something to solve it? Everywhere I went, the problem stuck to me like a poster. It became impossible for me to relax. I don't know whether anyone can understand what I mean...' the man trailed off.

I understood them perfectly. Although I had never faced an infestation of tiny frogs like them, I, too, had felt the nagging discomfort they spoke about. The first place I worked at after completing my technical training, I had felt a similar sense of unease. The work was all right and the salary was fine too. The doctor I worked with was young and newly qualified and knew all about the latest technologies and machines. The only issue was that he had a strange lisp, which caused his 's's and 'sh's to emerge with a hiss that echoed ominously. The stark silence of the audio lab, protected from all external sounds by careful soundproofing, susurrated with those hissed 's's. Every time he tuned a machine correctly, his celebratory 'Yesss!' uncoiled like a long snake in the sterile space of the lab. Often while working with complete concentration, his hisses startled me like a jolt of electricity. Gradually, it came to a point where I was always on the alert for those sibilant 's's, my neck, shoulders and back tense, my ears straining after the smallest sound he made. I found myself unable to relax anywhere; even my dreams resounded with his hissed words. After a few months, I had to quit the job. I could not endure it any longer.

'I understand,' I assured them.

'I understand too,' the woman echoed. She leaned forward, reaching out and touching the man on the shoulder lightly, briefly, before dropping her arm on to the table.

The man looked at her intently, his puzzled eyes raked her, his hands hovered over hers. 'You do, Dhani? Really? Then why all this, all this...' he threw an arm out, unable to capture his confusion.

The woman stood up and stretched her arms, her body undulating like a wave. 'Chal,' she looked down at me, 'we will make a move. The rain's stopped.'

'But...'

'We are getting late for the court. Today's the final hearing.'

The man rose. He looked lost, confused.

'Please excuse me,' I said, unable to contain my curiosity. They paused and turned towards me in unison. 'Do you know what happened to those frogs? Are they still infesting that flat, or were they finally gotten rid of?'

There was a moment's silence.

'We have no idea,' the woman said shortly.

MADE IN HEAVEN

THE PHONE FLASHED a third time. It distracted Pankaj momentarily from his presentation. He disconnected it discreetly and carried on. This presentation was the culmination of an intense and much-debated business proposal of his. The bank had finally approved the digital business platform. This was his moment of triumph, his winning lap – presenting the business plan and projections for the coming years to the senior management and the Board. After the presentation and question–answer session, which went smoothly, he chatted with the senior management team over sandwiches and coffee. He knew the importance of this kind of networking. This was his opportunity to ensure that he personally connected with the board members and they identified him with the business, as its leader. While making conversation with the board members, some of them in India for the first time, and advising them on places to see and eat at, Pankaj wondered why Jyoti di was calling him.

Jyoti di was more Ujla's mother than her elder sister. Ten years older than her, Jyoti di had practically raised Ujla after they lost both their parents in an accident. Jyoti di was in college at that time. There was no one to turn to, and she had left her degree in commerce mid-way to work in a stockbroker's office. Later, of course, the insurance money had come through. Jyoti di had finished her degree while continuing to work at the stockbroker's office.

'Jyoti di always said to me, you are the one with the blessing of learning. I don't want to waste money on my mediocrity...' Ujla had told Pankaj once. 'She even told Animey jiju that I would always come first, and he should marry her only if he was okay with that.'

Pankaj was surprised. 'The relationship of a husband and a wife is the primary relationship. Everyone else, however important, must be secondary. I can't understand why Mr Dey agreed to that.'

'Perhaps because she came first for him?' Ujla had said. Those were early days of their marriage, and despite being academically brilliant, Ujla was still impractical.

Pankaj and Ujla had connected through a matrimonial site. They were an almost perfect match. Pankaj wanted an intelligent woman with Indian values, and Ujla, despite her Master's degree in Biomedical Sciences from the US, was just the right person. The first time they had met at a bar near his office. Ujla had come dressed in a salwar-kameez, her wavy hair tied back. She had sipped at iced water all evening. Later, she had confessed to Pankaj that she had been impressed by his knowledge of business and economy, and the ease with which he reeled off figures that seemed esoteric to her – annual electricity production, value of rice-exports, number of free-range cattle.

Jyoti di never made a secret of her reservations about Pankaj. 'Marriages are difficult and complex. Don't be in a hurry, Ujla. I don't believe in the made-in-heaven stuff. I am the last person to say you should not have practical considerations, but don't marry just for practical considerations,' she said to Ujla when Pankaj had come to be introduced.

Pankaj had looked around at the small flat, a typical two-bedroom-hall-kitchen in the suburbs. He understood Jyoti di's discomfort. As Pankaj's wife, Ujla would move far above Jyoti di in terms of social strata. He was the youngest vice president in his bank and had bought his own flat in the town. He was going places, he knew that.

Jyoti di continued to hold him at a distance even after their marriage. Things came to a bit of a head when a couple of years after they were married, Pankaj was offered a two-year stint in Singapore. Jyoti di was bitterly opposed to Ujla leaving her doctoral work mid-way to accompany him. 'Why did you put in so much effort to win gold medals and research grants if you just wanted to trail behind a man? You could have done that without all those years of hard work.'

Pankaj had rationalized the outburst to Ujla. 'It is just Jyoti di's own frustration for not being able to study further. She wants to live through you, which is not fair. We have our own life now. We have to plan a family.'

It is true that Ujla had initially objected to moving to Singapore and had suggested that she join Pankaj after a year during which she expected to complete the laboratory tests she was conducting or at least arrive at an advanced enough stage to work on the findings at one of the laboratories in Singapore. But Pankaj had been firm. 'This is a non-negotiable for me. Long-distance marriages don't work. I have needs. I want you with me. Your work is not time-bound, you can resume it in two years' time. This move is crucial for my career.'

Ujla had eventually agreed as Pankaj knew she would. She was always sensible, and also, Pankaj secretly thought, unimaginative, particularly in bed. She was compliant but not enthusiastic. Pankaj had realized this early in their marriage, in fact, the very first time they were intimate on their wedding night. Ujla was running a slight temperature as a result of the late-night wedding ceremony that had been held in an open-air venue. Pankaj had opted for the venue because the marriage hall suggested by Jyoti di was too small to hold his guests. The night had been cold, and the ceremonial fire before which Ujla and he were seated, holding hands decorously, her left palm in his right, wasn't enough to keep them warm. Later, Pankaj had held her feverish body in his arms and had found her remarkably ignorant even for a virgin. That she was a virgin, he knew before their marriage. He had asked her as much, and had been pleased by the blush that coloured her face and ears. But he had thought that being a science post-graduate, she would at least know the physical mechanics. She didn't, and Pankaj had had to guide her.

The Singapore stint proved to be very successful. The assignment stretched out to five years, and Pankaj was promoted twice. They eventually returned when Pankaj's father became too frail to live by himself. In the initial days in Singapore, Ujla had retained her connection with academic research and even managed to do a project or two, but with Advait's arrival, they had agreed she should focus on him. During the last two years in Singapore, she gave up her research work altogether. Instead, she did a course in early childhood development and devoted herself to Advait. Pankaj joked that she needed a degree even for motherhood.

Upon their return, Ujla found it difficult to resume her research work. The field had advanced in the five years she had been away, and she eventually settled on a new topic. It was good in a way, Pankaj felt. It helped her develop a broader view of the subject. But the research work and temporary teaching assignment at the university, and caring for Advait and Pankaj's father left Ujla exhausted. At night when Pankaj reached for her, she would be too tired and sleepy to respond.

'You must slow down, Ujla,' Pankaj told her one night as he caressed her reluctant body. 'We can't let your work come between us. Advait is our priority. Besides, he is going on four. We need to think of another child before it is late.'

His own busy, travel-intensive schedule at work left Pankaj little time to be as hands-on with Advait as he would have liked to. He tried his best to at least spend Sundays with his family, but with each promotion, the pressures at work had increased. Jyoti di had turned out to be a big support. She now worked part-time at the stockbroker's office where she had remained all these years. She brought Advait home from his playschool and looked after him until evening when Animey picked her up on his way back from work. This arrangement worked well. Spending time with Advait must give Jyoti di emotional fulfilment, Pankaj thought, since she had no children of her own. When he mentioned this to Ujla, she had looked at him in the strange way she had and said, 'Jyoti di chose not to have children. She wanted to ensure I remained first.'

Jyoti di herself made out as if she was doing this just so Ujla could complete her thesis. 'You've lost time already,' she said to Ujla. 'Your work is important. I don't want you to give it up again.'

Pankaj brushed off the hidden accusation in her words. He didn't have time to deal with Jyoti di's frustrations and negativity. The important thing was that Advait looked healthy and settled, and Ujla happier than she had been in Singapore. It had taken a couple of years and effort by her influential research guide for her to get back the permanent position she had resigned to go to Singapore, and her research was progressing well. She had written a couple of papers that had been appreciated in the small scientist-community. She had been invited to present her papers in international conferences. They had discussed her participation.

'I don't think this is the right time for you to travel, Ujla.' He had been candid with her. 'Advait and my father need you. If both of us travel, things won't work out. And anyway, you need to focus on your thesis too.'

Lately her research was eating into their evenings. Pankaj had not said anything yet. He had been tied up with the work on the new business proposal, but soon he would need to talk to Ujla about it. It was, of course, Jyoti di's influence. She often regretted Ujla's loss of seniority and missed opportunities.

'You gained an international perspective in Singapore. Why bother about seniority? You know you do this because you like to; we don't need your salary,' Pankaj reassured her. 'You are in a different league from your colleagues.' He meant it. He had met some of Ujla's colleagues and had found them boring. They seemed like an insecure bunch, incessantly talking about research, new books, class schedules, their conversation peppered with 'in' jokes. They had all seemed uncomfortable around him. He suspected they were conscious of his success and achievements. 'You can amuse yourself with your weird colleagues when I am travelling. I can't stand their pretence of intellectual superiority,' he had said to Ujla.

Pankaj considered his life a success. His career was on a trajectory that would lead him to even bigger roles, perhaps even the biggest. Ujla was everything he wanted in a wife. He appreciated her dedication to the family, the way she was bringing up Advait, her cooking skills, the efficiency with which she managed lab-schedules and open days at school. He was also proud of her achievements. The only point of complain he had was Ujla's reticence at social events. She would stand around, silent, stiff and awkward. He had spoken to her about it several times. 'You must at least make an effort, Ujla. You can't be such an intellectual snob. My position at the bank means we have a certain amount of socializing to do. It goes with the territory.'

'It's not a question of intellectual snobbery. They talk about things I know nothing about,' she answered mildly.

'Oh, come on. You are a bright girl. If you try, you can find common points.'

'They talk about the money they've made or will make, and things they've bought or want to buy. I really don't know what to say.' Ujla stepped out of their room to check on Advait. This was another thing Pankaj had to insist upon – that Advait sleep in a separate room so Ujla and he could have privacy. It wasn't healthy to have a little child in their bedroom all the time. Ujla had to get up several times during the night to go and check on Advait who was an uneasy sleeper. In Pankaj's view, that was her own fault, for when he was travelling, she allowed Advait to sleep in their bed. 'He'll never learn to sleep by himself this way,' he had warned.

Pankaj accompanied the directors to the limousine hired to take them to the airport and shook hands all round. He returned to his office and asked his secretary to order lunch from the famous Parsi restaurant in Fort for the entire team to celebrate their first success. Then he dialled Jyoti di's number. 'Hello, Jyoti di, sorry I was in a very important meeting and could not answer. What's up?' he asked in the breezy tone which he always adopted when he wanted to put people at ease.

'Pankaj, come to Breach Candy hospital. Ujla is hurt.' Jyoti di's voice was nasal.

'Hurt?'

'There was an accident. You better hurry, she may not be here for long.' Her voice became thick, and Pankaj realized she was crying.

'I am leaving now.' He hung up and stood frozen for a moment. He confessed to himself that he was shaken. Surely it can't be that bad. Jyoti di exaggerated everything: if the food was on the table for a few minutes, it was stone-cold; if Ujla looked a bit tired, she was not looking after herself – those kinds of things. Ujla must have tripped and fallen. She was a tad clumsy, which he used to find cute early in their marriage. He put on his jacket and asked his secretary to call for the car.

On the way to the hospital, he tried to recall Ujla from this morning. Did they have breakfast together or was she busy getting Advait ready for school? Had he hugged her and brushed her forehead with his mouth as he left for the day? Then he recalled that he had left home very early for a dry run of the board presentation. He had left her sleeping on her left side as usual, in a pair of orange pyjamas – her taste for bright colours in nightwear was something he had not been able to wean her away from. With a rare stubbornness, she continued to buy the most unsuitably coloured night clothes – fuchsia, turquoise, orange. She had brought Advait into their room at some point in the night. He was fast asleep clutching the comforter, also on his left side, just like Ujla, his head resting in the slight depression between her shoulders.

He called Jyoti di. Her phone rang a few times and was not answered. He slipped the phone back into his pocket and thought about the years he had spent with Ujla, a number which could be called almost a decade. He knew her simple, calm ways, her careful attention to detail when it came to her research work or Advait's schedule or cooking an elaborate meal, and her complete blindness to certain other things like cobwebs in corners, dust on the doors, old dry snacks at the back of the cabinet. Usually very cautious, she could at times be strangely reckless. He remembered her leaning out of the window almost to her waist to catch a glimpse of the moon or allowing Advait to pat and caress a huge dog which was without a leash while they were taking a walk on Marine Drive. But overall, Ujla was a simple woman, predictable and stable, and he could not believe that something as unpredictable as an accident had happened to her.

Pankaj entered the crowded reception area at Breach Candy Hospital and headed to the information desk. Disregarding the people milling around, he gave Ujla's name and asked where she was. The receptionist tapped into her computer. 'Do you know the name of the doctor who is treating her?'

'She ... she has been in an accident ... this morning...' Pankaj was surprised at how difficult it was to say these few, simple words.

'Go to Emergency please. Ground floor, straight ahead, first left.'

He walked down the corridor and called Jyoti di again. She answered, 'Pankaj, come up to the fifth floor. They have just brought her back from the operation theatre.' She hung up without giving him time to respond.

There was a nurses' station in front of the elevators on the fifth floor. The nurse on duty, a young woman with a pronounced south Indian accent, directed Pankaj to the Emergency Medical Services ward in the ICU area. He came up to the wooden doors marked EMS in large red letters and looked around. Jyoti di was crumpled in a plastic chair farther down the corridor, her head in her hands, her plump shoulders heaving.

'Jyoti di,' he said, 'where is Ujla?'

Jyoti di raised her head. 'Your important meeting is over? Ujla's life is almost over too. She is in there.' She pointed to the wooden doors.

Pankaj felt blood throb in his temples. 'I want to know what happened. Where is Advait? Was he with Ujla?'

'No, Advait is still at the playschool. I have sent Krishna ji to pick him up.'

Pankaj was confused. 'Krishna was not driving Ujla?'

'No, Ujla never takes the car when she goes to Colaba for her music class in the morning. She sends Krishna ji to drop Advait.'

'Music class? Ujla was taking music lessons?'

'Every Wednesday and Thursday. Surely you know.' Jyoti di blew her nose on a bit of soggy tissue. 'She was always good at singing. Around this time of the year, she tries to practise her vocals more for her performance at the musical evening of her department.'

Ujla learned music and performed before her peers and students? Pankaj did not believe he had ever heard her sing except in the very early days of their marriage. She would sing ghazals about two lovers in a jasmine grove or the incurable malady of love early in the morning. He found it a strange choice of song at daybreak. He considered it appropriate that mornings should begin with the name of God, not unsuitable songs about lovemaking. He remembered mentioning this to Ujla once or twice. He never suspected she was fond of music; she never seemed to enjoy the Western classical, folk and seventies' music which he played on the excellent stereo system he had bought, or the Hindi-film music that Advait had lately acquired a taste for perhaps from his playgroup.

'I didn't know Ujla sang...' he said.

Jyoti di looked at him. 'She was always mad about music. She'd sing all the time. Her colleagues joke that kajri and thumri are the undocumented ingredients in her experiments.' Jyoti di's eyes brimmed with tears. The door to the ICU swung open. Two doctors in surgical scrubs, with a nurse in tow, stepped out. Jyoti di stood up. 'Doctor...' her voice quivered, her throat filled up.

The elder of the two doctors, a man in his late fifties, Pankaj guessed, placed his hand on her shoulder. 'The operation went better than we thought it would, Mrs Dey. The biggest risk now is infection and septicaemia. You should pray to Him.' He pointed to the ceiling. 'We have done everything we can. It is now up to Him. The blood that bunch of youngsters gave this morning should help. It is young and vigorous blood.'

'Doctor,' Pankaj said, 'Ujla's my wife. What happened? How is she?'

'She met with a nasty accident. I think it was a speeding truck. Anyway, you can see the details in the report filed with the police. This is a medico-legal case. Her lungs, liver and intestines are all ruptured due to the impact; her spine, ribs, right arm and leg have fractures. She's lost a lot of blood too. On the plus side, she miraculously escaped any serious head injury which, together with her other injuries, would likely have been fatal. There was a concern that she may not survive the operation. I think Mrs Dey tried to call you. Anyway, she has made it this far, but you need to know that your wife is very ill, dangerously ill, and nothing can be said with any certainty. You need to be prepared for everything.'

Jyoti di stuffed the free end of her saree in her mouth and yet her sobs escaped.

The doctor patted Jyoti di's shoulder again. 'Have faith in Him. He can work wonders.' He walked away briskly.

Pankaj was annoyed. He had more questions to ask. 'How could they operate on Ujla without my consent? How could they take such a risk?'

'I gave consent when you didn't answer the phone. Without the operation we would have lost her...' Jyoti di's voice dissolved into tears.

Pankaj wanted to ask who would have been responsible if Ujla hadn't survived the operation, but he bit back his words. 'How did she reach here?'

'Some passers-by saw her lying bleeding on the road. They found her phone and called me, my number is on speed dial on her phone.' Jyoti di was breathing through her mouth, her nose congested by excessive crying. 'It was just as well, you wouldn't have answered your phone. I called some of her students who attend the music class too. They were closer to where the accident happened and brought her here...'

'Have you seen her?'

'Yes. She was bleeding all over. I ... I was afraid to touch her ... but she was conscious. She looked at me. She tried to speak but her teeth were chattering, I couldn't understand what she was trying ... Oh Ujla...' Jyoti di gasped, crying noisily, small wails escaping her every now and then. Pankaj stood by awkwardly.

The nurse who had accompanied the doctors came up to Jyoti di and put an arm around her holding her steady. 'Mrs Dey, you must control yourself. You will be of no use if you go to pieces like this. The doctor won't let you see your sister when she regains consciousness. He has prescribed an injection for you to make you fall asleep. If you cry like this, I will have to give it to you, but if you drink a cup of tea and calm yourself, I will quietly put it away. Do you understand?' Jyoti di nodded. The nurse turned to Pankaj. 'Please get her some tea and something to eat from the canteen. It is on the ground floor. She has been crying for hours.' Pankaj nodded. He felt uncomfortable confronted with Jyoti di's grief, noisy and jarring, and to him, indecorous. After all, the doctor did not sound despondent. Ujla could heal, recover, come home and tell him why she had Jyoti di's number on speed dial and not his. He passed the nurses' station on his way to the elevators. From the tail of his eyes, he saw the nurse who was consoling Jyoti di enter, look at her colleague seated behind the wooden counter, raise her eyebrows, purse her mouth and shake her head in the universal gesture of pity.

The elevator opened with a jerk, and five or six young people in jeans and T-shirts swept past him and made straight to where Jyoti di sat. Pankaj glanced at them. They must be Ujla's students, perhaps even the ones who had brought her to the hospital and, afterwards, given her their blood. Later, he must thank them and make sure they were not out of pocket. Images of Ujla lying on the roadside, her body broken, bleeding, flitted before his eyes. Had she cried for help, called out his name? Why did she not tell him about the music lessons? It dawned on him that the reason why Ujla had to spend her evenings at the lab was perhaps because she was missing the morning lab for music, that she was not putting extra hours, but making up for missed time. The elevator hummed and he could feel its movement in his body, through the soles of his feet, reaching the tightness in his belly. He took out his mobile and called his office. 'Vasu, cancel all my engagements for today. And connect me to Graham.' The elevator stopped and he stepped out. 'Hello, Graham. Sorry to call up during your lunch. I have a family emergency, my wife has met with an accident.' He paused to let Graham express his sympathy. 'Doctors say she is critical...' He had to clear his throat. 'I am at the hospital. I don't think I will be able to lead the project meeting tomorrow, but Rajeev and team are up to speed. In any case this is a preliminary one to brief the second level on plans which you and I have agreed on and the Board's approved today.'

He listened as Graham said he should focus on his wife and family and not worry about work, that he would babysit the project until Pankaj returned to lead it. Pankaj knew the criticality of time and presence in his industry, he had used it to his advantage on plenty of occasions. 'Thanks, Graham. I will keep you posted on the situation. I am hoping that she will regain consciousness and there will be answers ... I mean, answers to our prayers.' He was chagrined by his private thoughts seeping into what he said and wound up the conversation quickly.

The canteen was a large space dotted with tables and plastic chairs similar to the ones in the waiting area outside the ICU. There was a family group in one corner; they had dragged a few tables and claimed the corner for themselves. Closer to the counter, there was a lone boy bent over the table, his head buried in his arms. Pankaj walked up to the counter and asked for two cups of tea and some sandwiches. One of the youngsters he had seen on the fifth floor entered the canteen and hurried across to the boy. 'Bamboo, bro, come up. Suppose you are here and there is some news? What if we are allowed to see Ujla Ma'am or something? Besides you are worrying the fuck out of us.'

The boy addressed as Bamboo raised his head. His eyes were red and his nose was dripping. 'Man, I can't bear it. She is so badly hurt, and the doctors say they don't know. I swear I will do something if she...' He broke down and sobbed.

'Mate, we are all praying for her. You pull yourself together. I know how you feel about her, but this is not the time. Let's go up and help her sister, she is all alone.'

'I can't, man, I...'

'Come on, she might need more blood or something.' The boy took Bamboo's arm. He got up slowly, slung his bag across his body and followed his friend to the elevator. The server had to touch Pankaj on the shoulder. 'Your order is ready, sir.' Pankaj took the two paper cups filled with tea, finely balanced in a cardboard holder with holes to hold the cups and a convenient handle, and the box of sandwiches. As he waited for the elevator, he thought about Bamboo. He was no more than eighteen or nineteen, clearly one of Ujla's younger students, and as clearly, with an almighty crush on her. Pankaj was surprised that Ujla, quiet and decorous and distant, could evoke such sentiments in someone.

On the fifth floor, Jyoti di still sat slumped in the chair he had left her in. The gaggle of youngsters stood around her. They were quiet, most of them tapping into their smartphones. Bamboo sat on the floor near Jyoti di's feet and stared at the ICU door. Pankaj handed a cup to Jyoti di and asked the nearest student, a girl with some of her hair dyed blue and thick kohl all around her eyes, whether she and her friends would like to have tea. The girl looked around at her friends, undecided. Pankaj took a few notes out of his wallet. 'You guys go on and have tea and something to eat at the canteen. We can't thank you enough for what you did this morning. You must keep up your strength in case Ujla needs help.'

The group shuffled away, but Bamboo stayed put. He wouldn't look at Pankaj. He wasn't hungry, he said, he had had breakfast and was fasting now, besides, his stomach was upset. He remained seated on the floor staring in the direction of the ICU. Pankaj felt a bit sorry for him and also annoyed at his laying a claim over Ujla in this way. He pulled a chair next to Jyoti di.

'Jyoti di, when did this happen? Who operated on Ujla?'

'This morning, around eight. I called you as soon as I got the call. Dr Desai did the operation. He is the senior surgeon.'

'Is he the best here?'.

'Pankaj, do you realize that Ujla was bleeding to death? It was no time to check the doctor's testimonials.' Jyoti di's voice trembled.

Pankaj got up. He handed the plate of sandwiches to Bamboo. 'Make sure Jyoti di eats something. It is important. We can't have her falling ill at this time.'

The nurse who had spoken to Jyoti di was at the nurses' station. 'I want to see the doctor who is treating my wife,' Pankaj told her.

'That would be Dr Desai, but he is on his round.'

'I need to see my wife, sister. I am sure you can check with the doctor. I need to see her.' Pankaj controlled his rising voice with an effort.

The nurse picked up the internal phone and paged for Dr Desai. Pankaj walked up and down the brief corridor as he waited. Bamboo sat motionless, still intensely focused on the ICU door, as if trying to see beyond it. The plate of sandwiches lay on the floor beside him.

The nurse came up to Pankaj. 'You can see your wife if you are sure you'd be calm,' she said quietly. Pankaj nodded and followed her, avoiding Jyoti di's swollen eyes.

Behind the double doors marked EMS, there was another pair of doors with glass portholes in the upper panels. The nurse handed Pankaj surgical scrubs and opened the door softly. The large ward was divided into four bays with blue plastic curtains drawn around each of the four beds.

Ujla was in the far corner on a high metal bed, tethered to the machines surrounding her. Pankaj was shocked to see her – her face colourless, eyes half-open and unseeing, body covered in a cast, red and white IVs carrying blood and liquids into her body. The nurse turned to Pankaj and held his arm. 'Can she hear me?' Pankaj said, his throat dry and his voice sounding strange in his own ears.

'She is sedated,' she said, 'and it is best she is not disturbed. But if you wish to speak to her, speak softly.' The nurse moved away a bit.

Pankaj stood at the foot of Ujla's bed. He found it painful to look at her face and focused on one of her bare, thin wrists lying on her side. 'Ujla, hold on. My project went live today. Advait's fifth birthday is next month, we will go to Singapore as planned and you will submit your thesis this summer. We will all...' His throat closed, his eyes teared up. He stood quietly until the nurse indicated that he should leave. At the door, he turned to look at Ujla, but the nurse had drawn the curtains around her bed.

In the corridor, Jyoti di was nowhere to be seen, but the youngsters were back. The girl with the blue hair came towards Pankaj and offered him the remaining money. 'Keep it for now. We don't know how long...' The girl looked away.

'Where is Jyoti di?' Pankaj asked.

'She has gone home to your son, sir. He is back, and she said she will feed him and return in one hour.'

Pankaj walked to the other end of the corridor, away from the nurses' station, Ujla's students and the EMS door. There was a small window that opened on to a yard filled with parked cars and beyond it, the sea edged with black, sharp-looking rocks. Seagulls and kites swooped above the water, making wavering white and brown arcs in the sky. Looking out at the bright day, Pankaj admitted to himself that Ujla was in danger of her life, that Advait and he might lose her. 'We might lose her,' he said aloud and was surprised to hear his own voice. He was to lose her just as he was learning new things about her, her talent for music, the loyalty and infatuation of her students. What would he do if Ujla was gone? What about Advait? Ujla ran Advait's life with precision and care, was always around giving him hugs, reading him stories, and stringing together silly ditties to make him laugh, the only time she displayed any sense of humour. He didn't want Jyoti di to take Advait, but what was the alternative? How would he manage? With nannies and house-help? He could send him to his brother, but he lived in Dehradun, and if Advait went to them, he would perhaps see his son only during holidays or brief visits. With Jyoti di, he might be able to see him every weekend. He felt angry that Ujla had plunged their shared life into this sudden chaos and, at the same time, guilty about his anger. He would have to carry on, without the placid presence of Ujla, never having known the unknown parts of her, hidden from him all these years of their marriage. He turned around and walked down the length of the corridor.

As he neared the nurses' station, the elevator came up and a police officer stepped out followed by a constable. The nurse in charge spoke quietly to them. He felt the officer's appraising look taking in the dark suit, the branded silk tie, the expensive watch.

'We are sorry to bother you at this time,' the officer began in a careful voice, 'but some formalities need to be completed. We have taken everyone else's statement and need to take yours in order to file the FIR. You need not come to the police station, we can do it here.'

The nurse opened the wooden half-door of the nurses' station allowing them to enter.

Behind the Formica-topped counter of the nurses' station was a small, curtained area with chairs and a narrow bed. They sat on the chairs while the nurse switched on the electric kettle and took out cups, tea and sugar from a small overhead cabinet. Pankaj answered formulaic questions about his date of birth, age, address, relationship with Ujla, and then more substantive ones about his whereabouts that morning, whether Ujla and him had had any arguments recently, whether Ujla had any enemies, rivalries, relationships. At the last question, Pankaj's mouth curved into a faint smile. He couldn't think of Ujla, mild and somewhat distant, having enemies or rivalries. 'None, officer. Do you suspect someone deliberately caused the collision with Ujla's taxi?'

'At present we have no reason to believe that, sir,' the officer said cautiously. 'Your wife seems to be very popular with her students, they are devoted to her. She is a good teacher and well-liked by the faculty. Mrs Dey mentioned that all senior faculty supported her becoming a permanent lecturer from a research fellow earlier this year. You say the two of you never had arguments and she is even-tempered. To me it seems that a truck driver, drunk or sleepy or both, misjudged the curve or did not see the taxi in time as he took the corner and hit it on the side. We will know more as and when the taxi driver recovers consciousness; he has severe head injuries, though, and is in a medically induced coma.'

In the confusion, it had not occurred to Pankaj to ask about the taxi driver. 'Could we help him in any way, officer?'

'Mrs Dey paid his initial deposit, and the other expenses should be covered by the government schemes. The students gave him blood as well,' the nurse said as she handed out teacups.

'These are your wife's belongings. I think her jewellery, etc., have been handed over to her sister,' the officer said handing over Ujla's handbag, notebook and diary to Pankaj after he had written and signed his statement. Ujla was not fond of jewellery and hardly ever wore anything other than the diamond studs she had bought herself the first year of their marriage or the simple gold band with three diamonds that Jyoti di had given her on Advait's birth. She had recently acquired an intricate silver bracelet, with a finely-worked pattern, and wore it everywhere. Pankaj thought the bracelet was beautiful but not appropriate for someone in Ujla's position. He had told her that it was more suitable for his students than for her. Ujla had not said anything but continued to wear the bracelet to the university, removing it once home. He knew that because he would often find it in their bathroom in the little basket that contained Ujla's manicure set.

The police officer got up. 'We will let you know if there is any development.' Pankaj nodded. A young doctor walked in.

'The accident case is not showing much improvement in parameters. Please page the senior surgeon.'

The teacup shook in Pankaj's hand, and he rose hurriedly. A sudden dizziness made his head spin. The nurse caught his arm and gently pushed him back into the chair. The young doctor blushed and stammered. 'Sorry ... I did not realize ... Anyway, the patient is not worse. I am in the EMS if sir asks for me, sister.'

The police officer cast a look at Pankaj and cleared his throat. 'We will be in touch. At present this is a negligent and rash driving case.' Turning to the nurse, he added, 'Let us know if there is any change in the patient's condition. We might need to add other sections from the penal code to the chargesheet.'

They were all giving up on Ujla. Pankaj's eyes pricked; his forehead and temples throbbed. None of them believed she would recover and come home to Advait and him. The telephone in the nurses' station rang. He got up holding Ujla's things. 'If you want you can rest here for some time,' the nurse offered. Pankaj nodded, his eyes averted, and walked out.

Jyoti di was back in her chair, with Bamboo, now slumped sideways, by her side, his head resting against the wall. Pankaj veered in the opposite direction and found a solitary chair round the corner. He sat down and tried to ease the constriction in his chest that was making his breath catch. He placed Ujla's handbag on the floor and opened the notebook. It was filled with music – ragas, compositions and unintelligible markings titled taal, matras. He closed it and picked up the diary. Ujla always had that diary on hand. He had seen her make notes in it, lists, important reminders. It was filled with cryptic memoranda: '11.30 dentst, Ad', 'Rs 5000 to Krishna ji'. Reminders of birthdays, changes in class schedules and, surprisingly, food: 'Yum chaat at 3rd stall in frt of the uni', 'Del daal by Dr Bahari, follow-up for recipe'. He did not know she cared much for any particular kind of food.

As he turned the pages, Pankaj came across other observations jotted among the mundane 'Turnd awy to avd looking at fat man on motorcycle scratching his fat belly, utterly gross...' 'Sunset in all shades of pink, coral to salmon to shell-pink! Fab!' 'A little child clinging to his mother riding a scooter, no helmet, no safety-belt, some folk shd not be allwd to procreate.' 'Dr Kunjum askd what I thght of her new curtains, told her they rminded me of my childhood. They did, the drty brwn ones in the first flat Di rented!'

And to his deep astonishment, there were poems, rather explicit ones.

> I will cover your body with my kisses
> As the earth is covered with blades of grass
> Like blades of grass will my lips quiver over you

And gladden your body with dewy touch
We will be like two blades of grass
Insignificant but blissful

My breath will be in your ears
In your mouth, my mouth
Your arms in mine
Your loins crossed with my loins
My soul within yours

Pankaj closed the diary, rested his elbows on it and stared at the wall. He picked up Ujla's handbag and opened it mechanically. Unlike her lab, which was carefully organized, everything neatly labelled and arranged on the long laboratory bench, her bag was a jumble. He dipped his hand in and came up with a fistful of coins, old bills, a lipstick, and Advait's baby-picture in a plastic case. He placed the assortment on the diary on his lap, arranging the coins in a small, neat tower, laying the lipstick in a horizontal line at the base of the tower, Advait's photo next to it. One by one, he smoothed out the bills – an old toll slip, a Post-it with a mobile number and no name, a receipt from Starbucks, a doctor's prescription. Pankaj looked at the prescription. It was from a month ago and had Ujla's name and age on it. He did not recognize the name of the gynaecologist on the letterhead. Ujla hadn't mentioned seeing a doctor recently. He knew she occasionally consulted Dr Patel and invariably disregarded the medicines he prescribed. The prescription had 'MTP' written in a bold hand on the top followed by something indecipherable. He could only make out the words 'sonography' and 'medically terminating pregnancy'. There was a list of medicines. Pankaj stared at the piece of paper in his hand, confused. Drugs for inducing abortion? Ujla was pregnant only a month ago and had not told him? This was the right time to have another child, with Advait now almost five, and he had stopped practising the withdrawal method since a few months now. He was prepared for Ujla to tell him any day that she had fallen pregnant. The pregnancy would be different this time – Ujla had more help and Jyoti di too; she won't lie silent in the bed for days, unwilling to get up and shower, prepare a meal; they'd go to Koh Samui for a babymoon ... He looked at the paper again. Who was this Ujla who had an abortion and attended music classes and wrote poetry? He did not recognize her.

Soft footsteps approached. It was the nurse.

'Some good news for you,' she said, smiling. 'Your wife just responded to her name and has asked for you, Mr Advait.'

Pankaj got up slowly. The diary, coins, lipstick, all the things hiding in the recesses of Ujla's bag, pitched forward and fell on the floor with a clatter.

'Advait is our son's name,' he said dryly.

MAUNA

Mauna stepped out of the bathroom. Water dripped from her hair. She had beautiful hair, long and soft. When light fell on them, they turned from brown to copper. Besides her eyes, deep-set and with a liquid brightness, they were her only claim to beauty.

Vishwa had once said, 'Your eyes, they have a personality of their own...' Mauna smiled. She rubbed her wet hair with the towel and sang, '*Main boond bani satrang, tumhaare sang piya ho! Main raakh se ban gai aag, tumhaare saath piya ho...*'

Ranju entered the bedroom. Mauna looked at him with hazy eyes, her mouth curled in a smile, she was free, fluid, falling at her own will. 'Mauna—' Ranju looked at her with careful eyes. The skin on his forehead and temples was taut. 'There's been an emergency ... Papa ... he had to be rushed to the hospital.'

Mauna's humming stopped. Her song stuck in her throat. She was no longer a rainbow-tinted drop. 'What happened? Which hospital?' Her eyes skittered around the room trying to locate something. 'We ... I must go to him.'

'Mauna—' Ranju came closer. He stood right in front of her, blocking the door. 'Mauna, he is no more,' he said quietly.

Mauna's eyes narrowed against a blinding glare. The damp towel slipped from her fingers. She felt her body unfurl and jerk like a rope, she fell to the ground. Ranju's words sounded again and again in the hollows of her ears, again and again, holding no meaning. He is no more. No more. More. More. More. Papa's voice cut through their hollowness, through their leaden weight. 'There's nothing wrong with me, I am fine, Bachchi. If there's anything wrong, it's with your mother. She is scared at every cough, every sneeze. I am writing a poem for her these days. I call it "Ek Dari Hui Stri ka Geet!" It goes like this – "Agar mein khaansa, tum karahi, agar mein chheenka, tum kampakampaii!" It is long, I have to keep adding to it every day!' Papa is laughing. The phone's speaker flattens all inflections, but Papa's laughter, wavering between exasperation and mirth, rolls like waves. Mauna lay still, trying to focus. If she held herself absolutely still, absolutely silent, she'd be able to hear his voice again: 'Bachchi...' But the air around her is buzzing with sounds, words are falling like hail around her, she is trembling, trodden like grass. There are footmarks on the grass. 'Do you see, Bachchi, grass retains your marks momentarily, and then – nothing.' Her ears hurt. She covers them with the hollows of her hands. She doesn't want to hear anything any more. No more. 'He is no more.' She is falling through. Not like a drop, not like a stone, the air is cutting through her. There is nothing around her, under her. Who is crying? Why are their groans in her throat? Who is touching her, holding her shoulders? She shakes the hands away. Her whole body is a blister, pain-swelled. Do not touch. Do not. The pain collects in a throbbing, choking mass in her chest. She cannot breathe, she cannot be still. Gasping for air, Mauna raised herself on her knees, hating her body for holding her up, hating the breath that caught in her aching lungs but did not stop. She breathed deeply, one long breath after another, hating herself for needing to, wanting to breathe. A sickness just beyond the reach of conscious thought rose to her throat. She struck her head against the bedside table, stuffed her fists in her mouth, bit her knuckles. 'No,' she said. 'No, no.' Ranju held her locked in his arms. She breathed through the pain that rose inside her, sinking her teeth into her lower lip. Her mouth filled with a taste she could not identify. Ranju gently lifted her to her feet and helped her to the bed. Mauna sat shaking, holding back nausea. Holding back.

'Please, I need to go to him,' she said eventually.

'Yes, Mauna, I have checked for flights to Jaipur. The earliest is in the morning, at 5.30 a.m.'

'Morning? I can't wait until the morning. Please. I have to go to him...' Ranju put his arm around her and held her; her shoulders went rigid. 'Let me see. I will try, Mauna.'

'What happened, Ma?' Anshumali walked into the room. He had been playing with his friends. His clothes were soaked in sweat, his eyes in confusion. He had her eyes. Her own eyes looked back at her, scared, flickering, anxious. He came closer. 'What happened?' She could not bear it. 'I will go down to the garden. For a walk.' She rose. Ranju got up too. 'No, please, I want to go alone. You look after Anshu.' She hastened away, flinching from their touch.

The garden was dark and full of murmurings, rustlings, susurrations. The path, laid out in red bricks, was cold under Mauna's bare feet. Papa walked with slow steps, his hands behind his back, his eyes on the trees. 'Look at that peepul. See how it is clapping its leaves, wavering with laughter. How can one not write a poem about it?'

The peepul wasn't clapping now. It would never clap again, nor would it tinkle with raindrops, or thrum in a gale. It was just an ordinary tree now, dark and lonely like a ghost, outlined against the moonless sky. Mauna was crying. Tears spilled from her eyes, down her cheeks, soaking her shirt; strands of her hair stuck to her cold cheeks. Every time the tears surged, her body twisted and rocked. She sat under the kewra tree. The scent from the unseen flowers assailed her nose.

'Some things belong to the nights. Like the fragrance of kewra flowers. Your mother says kewra trees are infested with serpents at night. Snakes flock to them, attracted by their fragrance. I tell her such discerning snakes are my brothers, I tell her to come and join me in enjoying the perfumed air too. In fact, there are no snakes, Bachchi, just the fragrance, undulating like a snake, overwhelming, mesmerizing.'

Mauna rested her head against the dry bark. There was a sharp yelp. A ghostly white cat was fighting something invisible among the dark shrubs. Ranju came up the garden steps. 'It is impossible tonight. I have tried charter planes, too, but their flight plans need to be filed hours in advance.

There's no option but to wait until morning.' He took Mauna's arm. They walked back towards their home.

'Has Anshu had his dinner? And you? I want Anshu to come too.'

'If you wish. Though, usually, at such times, children don't accompany...'

'Papa would like to see him. He must go to him one last time.' Mauna cleared her throat. 'I'll have to go to the office for a little while. I need to make sure everything is taken care of, all open matters handed over. I don't know when I will be back...' Ranju put his arm around her.

'Mauna, you know you don't need to do this. I can call Steve and inform him. I am sure he will understand.'

Mauna removed Ranju's arm gently and opened the door. Her eyes, nose and mouth were red and swollen. There was a large bruise on her forehead, above her left eyebrow. 'I need to do this myself. Steve can't handle it all from Singapore. I have to ensure there are no loose ends. It isn't as if I will be gone for a day or two...' She breathed slowly. There wasn't enough air in her lungs.

Anshu was sitting on the bed, his thin legs dangling, a book open on his knees. His eyes, hers, were moist, and his mouth had a downward curve.

'Anshu, give Ma a hug.'

Anshu put his thin, bony arms around Mauna. She gritted her teeth and swallowed hard. She caressed his hair, his trembling shoulders, his shaking back. 'Beta, could you reach down the suitcases from the loft? We need to pack.' Anshu buried his head into her shoulder.

'The car is here, Mauna.' Ranju entered. Mauna gently removed Anshu's arms from around her.

The bright colours in her closet hurt her eyes. She rummaged at the back.

'You'd need white clothes. If you don't have suitable clothes, I can...'

'Nothing's suitable any longer when Papa...' Mauna's throat constricted painfully. She busied herself with packing.

'I'll be back. You stay here with Anshu,' she said.

The suitcases were packed. She had changed and combed her hair. Anshu was staring at his book. Ranju closed his laptop and rose. 'I am coming with you.' He touched Anshu's shoulder. 'Anshu, go to bed, please. I will bring your mummy back soon.'

Mauna lowered the window on her side as they sped through the empty streets. The cold November air dried her tears as they fell.

In her office, Mauna switched on the computer. While she worked, she was in a quiet place. The knell of the words resounding in her ears receded. At one end of her table was a photograph of Papa. He is holding a book in his hand, a finger marking the page he was reading from a moment ago. His eyebrows are slightly raised, his glasses have slipped down the bridge of his nose. The smile hidden in his beard shines clear in his eyes. He is reading a poem aloud to Mummy, who is sitting in her chair just outside the camera's frame. The mild, tree-filtered winter sunlight is streaming through the window with the fragrance of his favourite harsingar. Soon Mummy will remind him that it is noon, and he still hasn't bathed. 'You married a poet, dharmpatni,' he would say. 'You ought to know that a good poem cleanses the soul, but all you keep harping upon is cleaning this mortal body!'

Mauna turned her computer off, locked her office and left the key in an envelope on her assistant's desk.

Ranju was speaking into his mobile in the lobby of the building. 'Mauna is okay, she is holding up. We will reach by eight in the morning, Jijo sa. We'll be well in time for all the ceremonies. In any case, you and Kako sa are there, we depend on you completely, you'll have to guide us...'

On the way back, Ranju asked, 'You'd like to speak to Mummy, Mauna?'

Mauna turned her now dry eyes towards Ranju. What was there to talk to about? All conversations were always about him:

'He doesn't follow the doctor's advice, won't take his medicine on time and refuses to go for a walk. All he wants is to eat mithai and stay up half the night reading old books or scribbling ... You speak to him, Mauna, I am at the end of my patience.'

'What is left for her to say, dharmpatni? You have already said all there is to say, in fact, several times! Bachchi, now she is upset with me for laughing. In this house, I am not only not allowed to eat or sleep as I wish but also not allowed to laugh!'

Anshu was still awake, sitting hunched over his book in his bed. Mauna took the book from his hands and gently straightened his tense limbs. She sat beside him, stroking his forehead and temples, until his eyes drooped.

The kitchen was dark. The door of the servant's room was shut. Rekha had gone to bed. Mauna switched on the light. A pot of yoghurt set for the next day cooled under the open window and washed utensils stood on the draining board. Mauna emptied the yoghurt into the sink and rinsed the pot. She counted the money in the papier-mâché cash box; there was enough to pay the bills for milk and newspaper falling due next week. The box was smooth, its rounded sides fitted in the curve of her cupped palms. Papa had brought it back from his trip to Kashmir.

'It seems fitting, Bachchi: paper money in a paper box, in the paper-world of paper dolls.'

She opened the fridge and checked the perishables – fruits, vegetables, milk. All would need to be given away. Perhaps Rekha could take them for her family.

'Bhai Bachchi, your mother treats me like a child now that both you and your sister are not here. All day she is after me – bathe, eat vegetables, drink milk, go to bed. Who could say, from tomorrow she might force me to go to a school instead of to the university! To outsiders, I am a learned professor; to her, I am a recalcitrant child. You must come back home and put an end to all this, or I will have to go on a long pilgrimage.'

She was going back tomorrow morning, once this night was over. Mauna turned the lights off and touched her own tear-soaked face with trembling fingers.

Ranju was sleeping flat on his back, snoring softly. Quietly, Mauna lay on her side of the bed and waited.

The flight landed on time. Outside, the crisp cold air had the familiar dry woodsmoke-and-dust smell. It woke Mauna's numb body up. Winter had arrived. It will continue to arrive year after year in Papa's absence.

'It is the promises winter makes that keep the heart warm, Bachchi, not your sweaters and shawls. The promise that everything will last longer, that flowers will hold their colours and fragrances longer, and days their freshness. Everything is experienced more sharply, more clearly in winters.'

Mauna zipped Anshu's jacket up to his chin. 'Ma, Nanu…' Anshu held on to Mauna's cold hand in the car.

The house-door stood open. There was a jumble of slippers and shoes on the front step and bunches of incense sticks stuck in the flowerpots. Smoke rose in slow spirals. There were young men and women in the porch. Papa's students.

'Dharmpatni, until this cold wave lasts, I am reviving the gurukul tradition. No one can enjoy poetry in the stone-cold rooms in the department. Get some tea made. The class will be held right here, under the sun on the lawn!' Mauna held on to the door. Her hands slipped on its icy surface and she staggered. Everything seemed cloudy, out of focus. Papa was lying on the floor. Under a single thin quilt. In this cold weather. Why isn't there a mattress? And a pillow? Is there a pillow under his head? Who is moaning? Quiet. You will wake him up. Papa … 'Mauna, don't do this, Mauna … Pull yourself together, laado. Get up now, look at your mother. You have to take care of her, beta…' Mauna freed herself from the encircling arms.

'Let me go, Mami sa, I am all right.' She sat up straight. 'Let me see him.'

Papa lay silent under the quilt, unmoving. She lifted the quilt off his face. He looked as he always did while sleeping – the creases on his forehead soft, his eyes and mouth closed firmly. 'I am always serious when I am dreaming, Bachchi. One should dream seriously and take the rest of one's life playfully.' Mauna caressed his soft salt-and-pepper hair, his beard, the thin papery skin of his face, his shoulders. He is not here, not in this house, not under this quilt, even while her hands touch him. He is nowhere. The footsteps on grass, peepul leaves, winter. He is nowhere. Mauna bit her lip until her body stopped shaking. *He is gone.* Slowly, carefully, she covered his face again.

'Mauna is here, Bai sa. Look, she is here, and Anshu and Kunwar sa.' Mami sa gently shook Mummy. Mummy slumped further in her chair, her eyes tightly shut. Her moans made Mauna's body prickle. Naina jiji sat surrounded by women, her hair in tangles, her face swollen, crying soundlessly. Anshu crouched beside her, his head dipping between his shoulders. Mauna rose. 'Go to your Nani sa, Anshu.'

Ranju stood amid the knot of relatives discussing funeral arrangements. 'At least eleven pundits, plus a party of bhajan singers. I have called our Guru ji. He will guide us about all the rituals that need to be performed over the next twelve days.'

'Jijo sa, Papa was against all these rituals. What he didn't believe in all his life, I won't let anyone do in his name.'

'Mauna...' Ranju frowned.

'Kako sa, please call Vedpathi ji from Arya Samaj. He will ensure everything is done simply and according to the Vedic ways. That is what Papa would like. Shanti vaachan, ved mantra...' Her throat filled up.

'You are right, beti, Bhai sa used to call the pundits bund-bhoosund. He used to say feeding idle priests is the surest way to purgatory. We should do what he would have wished, though he is beyond all this now...' Kako sa's eyes brimmed.

'Don't delay it, please. We need to take him before midday. He didn't like the afternoon sun, even during winters...'

'Don't force me to go anywhere while the sun is straddling the sky, Bachchi. The noonday sun can darken the very deer in the forest. Come, sit here with me and watch the shade slowly paint the garden and the house-walls blue. If you are very still, you can hear the sunlight drawing back gradually, like a crisp sheet being pulled off.'

Mauna went inside the house.

In the kitchen, Shantibai ji and Kamala were squatting on the floor, sniffling and crying. 'Baby sa, Mauna baby sa...' Shantibai ji embraced her and wept. 'Baby sa, we lost our roof and pillar, our tree fell. We are orphans ... who will look after us now...' The stale-smelling kitchen resounded with her wails.

Shantibai ji had looked after Naina jiji and Mauna since they were babies. She had cried bitterly when, one after the other, they both got married and left the city. She religiously prepared parcels of ghevar and lac bangles for Teej-gangaur and pots and toys made of sugar for Karva-chauth for couriering to them. At Anshu's birth, she insisted on performing the ritual to ward off bad eye with handfuls of salt, chillies and mustard seeds. Her complaints about their being married off so far were bitter and always directed at Papa. 'How little you loved them to marry them off across the seas and blind distance away ... They can't even come home during the months of rain when all daughters return.'

'Bachchi, if you ever decide to contest elections, don't forget to take Shantibai ji along for campaigning. You won't find a stauncher supporter than her and you will also do me a big favour – every day she remembers something or other about you and looks daggers at me for sending you so far away. You should come back just to protect me from her barbs!'

'Shantibai ji, you have grey hair. What are you doing, sitting here crying instead of taking care of Mummy? Do you want me to wipe your tears and rock you like a baby? Come, make some tea. Everyone has been awake the whole night. Kamala, fill a hot-water bottle for Naina bai sa. Her back must be stiff like a board from sitting on the bare floor.'

Shantibai ji rose groaning, her hands on her knees. She wept as she heated the water in the electric kettle.

'Wipe your tears.' Mauna's voice was dry, her swollen mouth twisted in unfamiliar ways to form familiar words. 'We will have to wipe our own tears every day, as long as we live.'

Kamala spread mattresses in the living room and Mauna fetched pillows and bolsters. She slipped the hot-water bottle behind Naina jiji's back. 'Jiji, please ... Drink some tea. There's a lot to do today.'

'Mauna...' Naina jiji whispered hoarsely, 'Mauna...' She collapsed on Mauna's lap.

'Jiji, pyaari jiji, please have some tea,' Mauna said coaxingly, stroking her back and shoulders.

'You understand the laws of waxing and waning, Bachchi, of light and shadows. Naina doesn't. Things have to hold constant for her, always revealed, always bright. You are actually the older one, you just happened to come after her...'

Finally, Naina jiji sat up and began to sip tea. Mauna took a cup to Mummy. Shantibai ji was pressing her feet, stopping every few seconds to wipe her eyes and blow her nose on her odhna. Mauna sent her away and sat on the floor near Mummy's feet, leaning her head against her knees. Slowly, Mummy's hand moved. She caressed Mauna's hair, her cheek, with fluttering fingers.

'Take Mummy inside, Jiji. She has sat up the whole night, she must get some rest. Only you can make her.' Mummy had merely touched the cup of tea to her lips and had retched, her body rejecting everything but grief. Naina jiji rose slowly, stiffly. 'I will see to things here.' In fact, there was nothing to see to any more. No tea to be made and carried to the garden, no books to be brought out, no poetry to be recited. Papa wasn't there. He had left without a word to her, without taking leave. How could he?

'Travellers don't say goodbye, Bachchi. Who can tell whether the nomad is arriving or departing?'

Mauna fetched a fresh set of clothes from his almirah, crisply starched. Socks too. He has sensitive feet. And a comb for his soft, thick hair. 'Your mother constantly accuses me of vanity. Can I help it if my hair is beautiful, Bachchi? The only one who has more beautiful hair is you!'

Vedpathi ji and others had arrived. 'We have everything we need, beti. You go in. This last service is for us to render...' Vedpathi ji and Kako sa both wept as they took the bucket of warm water from Kamala's hands for the ritual bath.

'Please wait a moment. Let me get Papa's cologne. His bath won't be complete without...' She went into the house.

Papa was laid on a bier, tied with the red-and-yellow mauli thread. His students had piled the bier high with roses and marigolds.

'Harsingar and mogra, only two fragrant flowers are meant for me. The rest cause me to sneeze and your mother to panic. It is a mercy that I am not allergic to colours, else she would paint the whole world black and white!'

Mauna bent before him and laid a handful of harsingar blossoms on his feet. He didn't like anyone touching his feet. 'What's this? You are checking if I have washed my feet properly?! Bachchi, bending and bowing are mere movements of the gross body, the sookshm deh doesn't need this ostentation of regard.'

There was a crowd around the flower-decked bier. So many wanted to lift it on their shoulders in symbolic farewell. A bamboo pole rested for a moment on Anshu's thin shoulder. His legs shook and buckled, Naina jiji's sons stepped forward and gathered him in their arms. Mauna followed Papa out the gate.

'Na, na, Mauna bai sa' – Mangal bhai sa stopped her – 'you can't go to the shmashan. Women are not allowed there.'

'Papa used to take me everywhere he went, Bhai sa.' Mauna opened the door of the car directly behind the van carrying the bier. 'I will go with him.'

'Mauna, you must respect the rituals. You can't have your way in everything,' Ranju said in a brittle voice.

Mauna glanced at him. Her way? Nothing was her way. Papa left, was leaving, will be gone. She got into the car and stared ahead in silence. The coral and pearl placed in Papa's mouth, as fee for the God of Death to make his passage easy, gleamed softly in the winter sunlight.

At the cremation ground, Papa was laid on the pyre. Pale, golden mango and sandalwood were placed on him. His body was lost among the shining wood. Naina jiji's elder son lit the pyre with a bundle of dry twigs, and dropping them, fell to his knees, hiding his face in his hands. The wood crackled and threw up showers of orange sparks, long ribbons of flame. Mauna took a long-stemmed wooden ladle and poured ghee in the flames which were returning Papa to the five elements, releasing his soul, sealing her away from him forever. Tears fell in the ghee consecrated with mantras. Amidst the chanting and weeping, while the world around wavered and trembled through the smoke, Papa disappeared. Only later, while bathing after returning from the cremation ground, did Mauna realize that the heat from the pyre had raised blisters on her arm. Water felt like fire on them.

In the evening, Mauna unpacked her suitcase in her old bedroom. Ranju was to stay at Kako sa's place with other male relatives. He had insisted Anshu sleep there as well after the ritual first meal. 'You insisted he should come. He must learn to follow the traditions.'

Mauna took her phone out. There were condolence messages from co-workers, neighbours, acquaintances. A message from Vishwa too: 'In your city ☺ Looking for you at every turn.'

Vishwa and Mauna used to work for the same company, though not in the same department; they would occasionally come across each other in meetings or in the cafeteria. There was a feeling of connectedness, a nameless warmth that made Mauna smile involuntarily. She remained on her guard and avoided him. When she learned that Vishwa had resigned and joined another company, she told herself it was a relief.

They had met accidentally at an industry event and had spent the evening chatting. 'I don't want to lose sight of you again,' Vishwa had said, 'we aren't colleagues any more...' But what they were, remained unsaid. Their connection left Mauna conflicted. She pretended not to see the obvious. They continued to meet, for coffee or a meal, or for a run along the Worli sea-face, an occasional show.

She put away her phone and went into the hall to lay pattal for the Kadva Gras. Everyone must eat this first meal off peepul leaves, bitter with grief, on the day of the funeral, learn to eat it every day without Papa, to nourish the body, to go on living without him.

The women slept on mattresses spread on the floor in the hall. Mauna massaged Mummy's forehead and temples gently with almond oil. She felt the veins throb and beat like birds under her fingers. Mummy fell into an uneasy sleep by Naina jiji's side. Papa was in this room in the morning. Some earth was sprinkled where he had lain last and a diya burned, its thin flame trembling. Mauna rose. Carefully threading her way through the sleeping forms, she went inside the house.

The phone rang on the other side a few times before Vishwa answered. 'Mauna? At this time? All well?' He sounded sleepy.

'Papa passed away, Vishwa.'

'Oh god ... when? What happened?'

'Yesterday evening. Heart attack.'

'God ... Were you able to see him? Are you in Jaipur?'

'Yes.'

'I had no idea when I messaged you today...'

'Yes.'

'I am in Jaipur for the research conference. Tell me, is there anything I can do? Anything at all?'

'I don't know. Nothing seems to need doing now. I sent him off this morning.'

'I don't know how to say what I really want to say ... You must have been awake all of last night, get some rest please. Could I call you tomorrow?'

'I will call.'

'We can talk now, too, if you like.'

'No, you should sleep.'

'You won't forget to call tomorrow? I will wait.'

'Yes.'

'Mauna...'

'Bye, Vishwa.'

Mauna wrapped a shawl around her and quietly stepped out. In the last few years, Papa had planted a variety of trees in the small front-garden – custard apple, pomegranate, guava, a couple of slender gooseberry ones.

'Grass is a wasteful luxury in the desert, Bachchi. It drinks litres and litres of water and all it yields is a feeling of smugness from feeding a barren hobby. Now, these trees feed and shelter all sorts of birds. Look at those sparrows and barbets, they sing and fight all day long, like you and Naina used to, and the mynahs and bulbuls are busier than your mother. I am that old crow. See how he roosts comfortably in the neem tree and watches the world go by – *Ram jharokhe baith ke sabka mujra lait!*'

Papa's harsingar was perfuming the night-air. Its rough-leafed branches were full of tiny, star-like flowers. Mauna sat on the garden step until the shadows turned grey and began fading, morning-light bled from the sore in the sky. Her shawl and hair were wet with dew when she finally went into the house to rouse Shantibai ji.

The men got ready to return to the cremation ground in the morning, Ranju and Anshu among them. They must gather what remained from yesterday's all-consuming fire and take it for immersion into the Ganga. Mauna quietly arranged offerings of sweet rice, curds and sweetmeats in leaf bowls and platters. They were for the Gods ruling the ten directions, so they help the soul departing on its last, arduous journey. She also packed cotton mats, utensils, blankets, clothes and shoes to give to the Mahabrahmans who lived off the offerings made for the dead.

'Just see the irony, Bachchi! Mahabrahmans are otherwise shunned, they aren't invited for feasts or to perform rituals on holy days; but when someone dies, they are treated like kings. Nothing's too much for them, as if the debt of an entire lifetime of neglect is to be repaid upon death so they agree to take the sins of the dead upon themselves. Truly blind are we, in our blind selfishness!'

In the evening, Papa's ashes were brought home briefly, before the men left with them for Haridwar. The clay pitcher containing them, its mouth sealed tight with a red cloth, was placed on the marble bench in the garden where Papa liked to sit every evening. When the ashes are immersed in the holiest of all rivers, at the place made sacred by its first contact with this mortal earth, it will be the final farewell; the spirit will be set free in the timeless forever, never to return. Mauna will never, as long as she lived, hear Papa's voice again or see him stroke his shell-white feet, or touch his beard with her fingertips. Bowing in obeisance before the asthi-kalash, Mummy collapsed. Naina jiji struck her forehead against the marble armrest. Piercing cries scared away the bulbuls and barbets returning to their nests in the neem tree.

Mami sa brought the large, hardbound Ramcharitmanas out and placed it before Mummy on a wooden bookrest. Mauna sat close to her and began reading the 'Sundarkand'. Mummy's lips moved soundlessly at the familiar verses describing Hanuman's encounter with a frail, desperate Sita, her eyes drooped with fatigue. Mauna coaxed her to drink a glassful of hot milk boiled with turmeric and dates. At last, Mummy and Naina jiji, along with Kaki sa and others, lay on the mattresses in the hall, exhausted, heavy with grief. Mauna helped Shantibai ji and Kamala roll up the durries and mats, and stow them away in the storeroom at the back of the house along with the leaf-platters and ghee, the unused groceries and spices. The diya from last night was burning low; she replenished it with ghee, trimmed its wick, and turned the lights off.

The night seemed denser than yesterday. The filigreed shadows of gooseberry and pomegranate trees were indistinguishable in the dark. Harsingar flowers gleamed and dropped, shaken loose by cold, stray breezes. On the marble bench where the asthi-kalash had stood earlier in the evening, there was a faint mark, a ring of ashes. Mauna took her phone out of the kurta-pocket.

'Mauna, at last ... I have thought about you the whole day. How are you? Don't answer that if you don't want to.'

'I am standing under the harsingar tree, Vishwa. Perhaps its fragrance will take away the smell of smoke from my hair, my clothes, my body.'

'Mauna...'

'Harsingar blossoms are falling on me. I can smell them despite the smell of burning on my skin, in my nostrils. I want to feel them on my skin and crush them against my breasts. Do you remember when we met at that conference after months?'

'Mauna, honey, this is hardly the right time, but you know what I feel ... about you...'

'These blossoms only bloom for a night. You had asked if you could do anything for me.'

'Of course.'

'Could you come over?'

'Come over? Now?'

'Yes, right now.'

'Mauna, are you sure?'

'Come. Everyone's asleep. Just the harsingar and I...' Mauna's throat filled. The flowers, their saffron stems loosely attached to the branches, continued to fall. 'I will message you the address.'

Mauna opened the door of the storeroom and turned the light-switch on. In the feeble light of a single bulb, the room was full of dull shadows. She climbed on top of the big trunk and pushed open the latticed ventilators. The fragrance of harsingar floated in. She pulled out a colourful durrie from the mound of mats and, pushing the vat of ghee and sacks of grocery closer to the wall, spread it on the floor. She went back to the main gate and waited. At the soft thud of a car door closing, she opened the gate.

'Mauna...' They couldn't see each other in the dark. Mauna took his hand and led him to the back of the house.

She closed the door of the storeroom and turned towards him. In the dim, yellow light, Vishwa finally saw her – her hair was pulled back in a bun, her swollen eyes washed clean of kohl, the bruise on her forehead tender. Her lilac kurta was crumpled and stained with dew. Her frail arms hung by her side. He welled up. Pulling her close, he folded her in his arms. Mauna winced slightly when he pressed her to him. He pulled out the long pin holding her hair and kissed her deeply, his palm trailing down her neck and back. 'Mauna...' His breath fell on her, stirring the soft hair on her temples. 'Mauna...' His fingers fluttered on the buttons of her tunic. Mauna shut her eyes tightly as he lowered her on to the bright carpet. The bright reds and oranges flamed around her slender body. He knelt beside her, kissing her breasts, caressing her stomach, navel, thighs. 'Mauna, honey...' sounded like a chant in her ears. Her eyes closed, she felt around and dipped her fingers in the large vat standing against the wall. Vishwa smelt it before he felt the drops trickling down his back. She had anointed their now intertwined bodies with the ritual ghee.

SHAWARMA

T̲ʜᴇ ᴍᴇᴛᴀʟ sᴘɪᴛ rotates slowly. Layered meats ooze their juices into the circular tray underneath. A young man in a tall, white chef's hat cuts shavings from the thick roll of meat and stuffs them into freshly baked bread.

'Shawarma!' my companion says. Her eyes shine. 'Just the dish I have been craving! If you have no objection, shall we eat here?' This last bit with a questioning glance.

'Sure,' I answer. What objection could I possibly have today? Shawarma is fine, everything is fine with me today. Today, she is here with me. The hazy sky of Hong Kong is bright with the promise of early winter and the lunchtime bustle of Central seems festive.

We are colleagues, Jaya and I. We work half the world away from each other for an information technology company – a giant, with offices in all major countries – she in Chennai, I in London. We meet occasionally at work-related events. You might have come across colleagues who seem constrained in groups, avoid each other's eyes, make only the most superficial remarks to each other, but if you observe closely, you find an undefinable sympathy between them. They seem to be in tandem, in parallel orbits, apart and yet connected, as if the same wave touches and moves them, never bringing them closer but never allowing them to drift too far either. We are that kind of colleagues. We both know this; we are both aware of our danger, and are therefore very, very careful. Only once had we forgotten our masks and props, only once had we revealed ourselves to ourselves, and the need that lay coiled between us had stretched out and enveloped us. Only once. To both our credit. After all, we are two very pragmatic, cautious individuals. There are important, practical factors to consider, like families and shared homes and children and pets.

Jaya and I are in Hong Kong to attend an off-site, a work-meet where colleagues who work together, or at least are supposed to work together, gather to discuss new ideas, newer ways to collaborate. We have all left behind our homes, offices, routines for a few days to plunge into work politics. Old rivalries are being revived, new alliances are being built. Presentations, budgets, bickering, gossip. Days are spent in conference-room manoeuvrings, evenings drinking at pubs in Soho. Jaya and I have slipped out for lunch. By ourselves. Mid-Levels is crowded with office-goers. The narrow streets are lined with eateries on both sides. Whole glazed ducks and pigs hang in the display windows of Cantonese restaurants and fish and lobsters squirm in large glass tanks. Red-and-white chequered tablecloths gleam in Italian restaurants and men sporting large sombreros hand out menu cards outside Mexican ones. Out of this plenty, Jaya chooses the small

Lebanese restaurant tucked under the Mid-Levels escalator. And shawarma.

We enter the low-ceilinged irregular room dominated by the high counter with its magnificent shawarma meats and are shown to a small alcove. There are leather seats around a low, circular table. We sit side by side, our knees bent awkwardly, almost touching.

'What would you like to drink?'

'Virgin toddy. Lots of honey.'

I signal to the waiter. 'Two virgin toddies; bring some honey separately.' I turn to Jaya. 'You'll share a Mezze platter?'

'Yes, please. Don't forget the shawarma.'

The waiter walks away briskly. Jaya shifts in the back-and-armrest-less seat trying to find a comfortable spot. 'You won't believe how I have been craving shawarma...' – she rests her knee against the edge of the table – '... just an irresistible craving...'

'Which you clearly managed to resist until now.'

She smiles. I look at her kohl-lined eyes. The light falls on the planes and angles of her face as she moves on the comfortless leather stool. I, too, have irresistible cravings. The waiter brings our drinks. Jaya adds a spoonful of honey to hers.

'Don't you want to taste it first?'

'It is never sweet enough.'

I watch her as she carefully fishes out the star anise and cinnamon sticks, the cloves and lime leaves from her drink and arranges them neatly on the rim of her plate. I can smell the fresh, clean fragrance of her hair. The memory of that night comes back to me – the night when we had clung together like two desperate, drowning souls. I feel her heavy hair come undone on my shoulders again, my fingers tear at the buttons of her dress, her whisper sounds in my ear, there's wine on her breath, my mouth silences her nascent words. I shake my head. That one night always waits in the wings when we meet, and tacitly, mutually, we ignore it. She raises her eyes and reads mine. Something opens softly between us, throbbing and urgent. We look away.

'How is your time-travel working out?' I ask. Jaya still works with the California-based product development team she was a part of before moving to Chennai from the US a couple of years ago. The product-lead did not wish to lose her and convinced her to stay on the team. She works US hours on cutting-edge robotics technology. I am senior in the corporate hierarchy, but she is the real rocket scientist and we both know it.

'It's all right. I am working on quant-robotics these days. My objective is to cheat young math-whizzes out of opportunities. I am building an intelligent robot to take over not just solving financial math problems but figure out the sequence in which a series of problems should be solved for optimality, which variables to apply, which to disregard. I am going a bit slow, though; little sleep has that effect on me. Eventually I plan to make a robot that replaces me; it will work while I sleep.'

I look at her smiling eyes. The fine skin under them is stretched, bruised-looking. 'This time-zone commute is not such a great idea, Jaya.'

'Yes, it isn't,' she agrees, 'but I can't leave Chennai right now and I am too selfish to give up working, so I have given up sleeping.' She takes a sip of her warm drink. 'Actually, I am lying. I haven't given up sleeping altogether, just changed the style and rhythm of sleep. I have become an expert napper. Give me ten minutes, and I can sleep anywhere, anytime. I can compete with your cats. Which reminds me, how are the cats doing?'

Cats are part of my life; rather, I am part of theirs. My role might be limited but it is not insignificant. 'They are as usual.' I take out my phone and show their latest pictures to Jaya. 'I have no complaints. They still allow us to share the house with them and sometimes condescend to being patted. They still dislike my travelling, though. No pet kennel seems to be up to their taste. When I fetch them back home, they behave like teenagers – grumpy for days, won't eat, stalk out and stay out all night.'

The cats are my responsibility. My wife refuses to care for them in my absence. She dislikes the insinuation that the cats are a placebo for the children we don't have. This is one of the many things which I have never said to Jaya. There is no need to. She knows.

'I am on their side. At least they don't argue and bang doors.' Jaya laughs. She has twin daughters, fifteen years old. 'You are incredibly lucky that no one in your home is allergic to cat hair or considers them bad omen.'

Our food arrives. There is something special about shawarma. The succulent meats and greens encased in freshly baked bread go right to the core of your hunger. We share the food and eat with our fingers, dipping fluffy triangles of pita in flavourful dips, tearing pieces off the shawarma rolls. We avoid each other's eyes when our fingers touch occasionally.

'This baba ganoush is delicious.'

'The humus too. Creamy.'

'I saw the sales figures for your sector recently. The new products are doing very well, aren't they?' Jaya turns the Lazy Susan around so I can reach the dips more easily. 'I hear you are being tipped to head the whole of Europe soon.'

I laugh. 'Do you really want to talk about all this?'

She laughs too. It sounds like an echo of mine set to a sitar tune. 'No, I don't. I actually want to talk about concerts and musicals. Did you watch anything interesting at the West End?'

Jaya is devoted to music. Classical, instrumental and vocal. She often regrets not being able to sing or play. There's never been time to learn: first an engineering degree, then an advanced degree in math and computing in the US, a PhD, job, children. 'At least I have my ears,' she says.

'One or two shows. The season has been a bit underwhelming this year. But I have been reading incessantly.'

'Don't talk to me about books, please, I won't be able to eat out of envy. All I have been reading these past few months are course books to help my girls through their boards.' Her daughters are in high school. I know they are brilliant. Like her. 'Music's good; music is too pure to evoke anything but joy. Besides, this summer I managed to attend some concerts during the annual classical music fest. Not as many as I would have liked to but a few good ones.'

'Now I am envious. No one seems to be interested in classical or chamber music, and it is a chore to go alone.'

'Going alone is fine. In fact, it's the best way to hear music. Being alone with music is like being alone with memories, you can add flourishes, tune out the bits you don't like, enjoy more fully. The music heard alone is music deeply felt.'

I look at her animated face. I want to say, 'Experiences are complete when shared, Jaya.' I ache to take her in my arms. No one has ever stirred me as she does, this colleague of mine whom I meet perhaps twice every year. I change the topic. 'Tell me about the driving lessons. How are they coming along?'

'Oh, they are not coming along at all. In fact, I have stopped taking lessons. I have given up learning to drive.'

'Why?' This is unlike her. She had been enthusiastic about driving when she had begun, and I know she doesn't give up. Even when it hurts to hold on. 'I thought you were fed up with drivers and wanted to take matters into your own hands, literally and metaphorically. You'd said it is a life-skill, like swimming.'

'I...' she begins and then hesitates. Jaya never hesitates, so I know something is the matter and wait. She wipes her fingers carefully on the napkin. Her hands are small and pale – narrow palms and short fingers. She had once mentioned that her husband finds them ugly but cute. I had wondered to myself what it would be like to be able to hold those hands anytime one wanted. 'Yes, that was the idea.' She does not look at me. I remain silent. She sighs. 'Really, it's nothing dramatic. In fact, you can almost say I have learned driving and have given it up.' She looks at me through her lashes. 'It's just something with not much point to it.' I continue to remain silent. 'I have no issues in telling you if you really want to hear…'

'I really want to hear, Jaya.'

She breathes through her nose and attempts a smile. 'Sure. You know that I took lessons for some time. I picked up driving without difficulty. In fact, I wondered why I faced the inconvenience of taxis and inefficient bus services in Cali. As it turned out, I have a good sense for direction and I am a natural with traffic rules. I have a slight problem with judging distances. I have never been good at determining what is close, what is far. But my instructor was confident. He said I will learn with practice. So I practised. I did pretty well. I'd begun to drive short distances by myself, you know, fetching the girls from classes or getting mom-in-law's medicines, simple things like that.'

I raise my eyebrows, 'Without a licence?'

'I have a licence. I have had it for years from when I was ridiculously young. At that time, you'd just go to the Road Transport Office with an uncle or a neighbour, they'd have tea and chat about politics, and you'd return home with a bit of paper allowing you to drive until the pucca licence was made. You know how it worked.'

'I most definitely didn't know. Doesn't sound like the correct standard operating procedure, a bit like cart and horse in the wrong order. Did they at least ask you whether you could drive at all or even wanted to drive?'

She looks at me now and blushes. 'I was too young to know anything, and I did drive a bit in the courtyard of the Transport Office while the officer watched from a balcony above. But if you are going to interrogate me like this, I will turn defensive, I am warning you.'

'Isn't that warning a little late? Sorry, just ignore that question. You have a licence, it is valid, you picked up driving, all's fine. Then what isn't?'

'Ouch, such sarcasm. Folks who belong to Chennai have broad shoulders and kind hearts. We can bear your barbs without flinching and can also let people who are learning to drive do so without making them feel guilty about insignificant details like licences.'

'That is not the answer to my question. Besides, you do not belong to Chennai, you only live there.'

'I don't belong anywhere, and now it seems that I do not live anywhere either. In Chennai I pretend I am in California and in California, somewhere else.'

'Have you ever pretended to be in London?'

'No, never.'

'Good. I would have been offended if you had pretended to be in London without letting me know. Now, how about telling me what happened without hedging?'

'Hedging? I wasn't hedging at all. Since you are determined—' she picks a dark olive from the platter. 'This is from a few months ago. Late summer, right after the concert season ended. I think it was one of the US holidays. I remember because only I had an off, everyone else had a working-day. The girls came home from school a bit early.

I think a theatre practice got cancelled, and as usual I was still in the middle of preparing lunch. You'd think practice would make me perfect, but I can never have lunch ready on time.'

'You make lunch every day?' Jaya finds everyday-cooking boring. It isn't creative to do the same thing over and over again, she would say; that is for system-implementors, not for solution-developers.

'Yes. Everyone prefers my cooking, and since I am home and don't work during the day, why not? I do a decent Indian meal. Besides, mom-in-law is not comfortable with the house-help cooking, and one of the main reasons we moved is because of her.'

'But you work US hours. You need your rest. This isn't sustainable, Jaya.'

'It isn't such a big deal. Really. The help does all the hard work of chopping and cleaning. I just prepare simple vegetarian food. No non-veg at home; mom-in-law is a bit particular that way. Again, no big deal, we are none of us big meat-eaters in any case.'

I smile.

She shakes her head. 'You don't need to doubt everything I say just because I happen to have an out-of-turn driving licence!'

'Continue, Jaya.'

'Well. As usual, I gave lunch to the girls and mom-in-law and sent a tiffin to the Institute.' Jaya's husband is a famous professor at a premier science institution in Chennai. He is an authority in oceanography and underwater excavations.

His articles appear in academic journals, and he regularly features as an expert on international fora. 'I wasn't hungry, so I decided to skip lunch. Besides, the girls had a Chemistry tuition class. They were getting late for it.'

'Tuition for a science subject?'

'Just because you know no science, you overestimate my knowledge of it. Chemistry's never been my strong point. The teachers at their tuition class are very sure. They know which elements are stable and which aren't, which can be kept together safely and which will explode, which ones react with each other and how. I have never really understood all this.'

There is a brief silence. I sit looking at Jaya. Given a chance, I can do this for a long time, a very long time.

'Anyway,' Jaya continues, 'the driver had not returned from the Institute, and the class was not far from home. So I thought I'd drive the girls to their class. Traffic's slow in the afternoon, and I needed to do some grocery shopping as well, so it kind of worked from all angles.'

'Too many explanations, Jaya. It was a holiday, you wanted to go out, isn't that fine by itself?'

Her eyes flicker like candles. 'I dropped the girls and then browsed a bit in the shops. Bought some household things, some detergent, a sewing kit, a box of cereal that no one ends up eating, you know, the usual things a woman buys.'

'The usual things a very unusual woman buys.'

'My moral integrity is being relentlessly attacked today. First you undermine it over my driving licence, and now you are trying flattery.'

'I never try,' I try to match her facetiousness. 'Someone said that, I can't remember who now. But what has all this got to do with your driving?'

'I am coming to that. I took my time over my shopping. As I walked out of the supermarket, I noticed a new restaurant tucked in a corner. At least it was new to me. You know the kind of place that is all plate glass and blonde wood furniture?' I nodded. I knew the kind of restaurant she was describing. Modern, new, wildly popular for a while and then suddenly shut down. 'And would you believe it? There, on the open-plan counter was a shawarma spit, just like this one. I was suddenly famished for shawarma. It was like everything inside of me yearned for shawarma, a kind of shawarma-hunger flowed in my blood. I felt it was ages since I had tasted the succulent slices of meat layered in fresh Taboon bread. I just had to have some shawarma right then. But there was no time to eat. I had to go pick up the girls from their class shortly. I mean I couldn't just sit in that pretty, air-conditioned place and enjoy shawarma while the girls waited for me. So I got a few rolls packed. If I weren't a lady,' she looked at me intently, 'I'd describe to you how I felt carrying those rolls to the car.'

There was no need, I could picture her – a certain look in her eyes, her mouth moist, her fingers holding the food with an urgent pressure.

'I got into the car quickly, strapped up and drove off. You've not seen late summer in Chennai. From inside an air-conditioned car, the blue sky and brilliant sun seem so beautiful you wonder why the roads are empty, why aren't more people out enjoying the afternoon. And then you glance at the temperature dial and you notice it is 102 degrees Fahrenheit outside – it was that kind of a day. I reached one of the big junctions. The traffic light was on the blink but it hardly mattered. The traffic was thin. I drove across the junction, and just as I was approaching the mid-point, I saw this green bus coming in my direction. It was a typical city bus, rickety, clinking, and full beyond capacity. There was plenty of room on the road for me to give way or turn aside or even just stop where I was. I mean, there was hardly another vehicle on the road. But I just kept driving straight towards the bus. On and on. Just directly towards it ... At the very last moment the bus swerved and passed inches away from me...'

I released my clenched hands. 'Jaya...'

'I wasn't afraid or panicked at all. You understand that, don't you? I knew what I should do, I knew my options, but still I just drove on towards the bus. And do you know what passed through my head as the bus rushed towards me like a great dust-covered metal wall? That now I won't be able to eat that shawarma...' Tears pooled in the corners of her eyes, hung from her lashes. 'That was the only thought in my head ... the lone thought ... I haven't driven since...'

SONA

I

I RECLINE ON MY beanbag, a cadmium orange, the colour of my toenails today, and look at the lovely cobalt-and-silver day outside. I think of you. You called such days gold-leaf-showered, pointing out the small gulmohar leaves falling at every gust. The smell of grass wafts through the open picture window. It is green, like a compound of copper. Shade is sprinkled under the trees like soft, powdery carbon. I can see the bricked walking path from where I lie. I can't go for a walk, of course, but I don't need to close my eyes to imagine you walking thoughtfully along the path, gently parting pink and magenta leaves of Red Iceton crotons to reveal a mole's nest or tapping the bark of the jackfruit tree to bring a perfectly camouflaged stick insect to life.

Today I want to talk to you, not about this beautiful day, but another one, a summer day, the day you had come home for the first time. It was that awkward time of the weekend when people wake up from naps and do things that can be done in a half-awake state. I had removed the chipped colour off my nails and was painting them. Mummy had mentioned you were coming but I had not paid much attention. Mummy's friends were either pot-bellied and boring or shrill and poetry-spouting, or both. The doorbell had rung, but I had stayed put in the love seat, busy with my nails.

'Sona, this is Bhaumik. He has recently accepted the professorial chair at the university in world literature,' Mummy had said. I had looked up, fully expecting a bald man with a goatee and vague eyes. Instead, there you stood in the late afternoon light, in a white linen shirt and a pair of worn khakis. Your hair was wavy, the crests frosted. You looked levelly at me through rimless glasses, eyebrows slightly raised. A drop of golden-yellow polish fell on my T-shirt leaving a comet-like tail down the front. You smiled and held out your hand. I became conscious of my scruffy clothes and hair sticking out in all directions; I had fallen asleep without drying them.

'Glad to make your acquaintance,' you said, and glancing at my nails, added, 'This is the first time I have had the privilege of shaking such golden hands!' In my confusion I quickly put my hands behind my back. You laughed, and I watched with fascination the sternomastoid muscles move smoothly under the clear skin of your throat. Mummy laughed too.

'Sona will entertain you while I get us tea. She is very clever, aren't you, Sona? She has a gift for science. Her teachers have recommended she apply for the undergraduate science programmes abroad this year. She is only fifteen and has at least a couple of years or so to go before college, but her teachers think she is ready.'

I resented her saying I was only fifteen. I could see what she was doing. She was pointing out that I was just a precocious child, not to be taken seriously by someone like you.

'I am going to be sixteen in three months,' I said.

'You see how it stands, Bhaumik? My own daughter would not allow me to underplay my age by a few months!' Mummy shrugged her shoulders in mock resignation.

'Age can't wither your beauty, and though we have not given custom much chance yet, I am sure it cannot stale your variety.' You spoke to her in the same laughing voice in which you spoke to me. Mummy blushed. She is, of course, beautiful; Papa used to say so even during their fights. 'This accursed beauty,' he'd say between gritted teeth. I was only six when Papa left, but I remember everything. Arguments, things being thrown around, Mummy screaming in her shrill voice. Although she said he beat her, I never saw Papa raise his hand at her. I know she bruises easily. She'd show off bruises on her arm, on her waist, in sleeveless blouses and sarees tied low, to get people to look at her, to say – what a monster you've married. She's always liked attention, you know that, you've seen how she'd always butt in when you talked to me. Granted Papa used to get angry sometimes, but I know he loved me. He always bought me sweets and things. Even after he left us, without a word as Mummy always adds – up sticks and left, didn't have the courage to tell his daughter and his wife that he was abandoning them. But he never abandoned me; he couldn't stand Mummy, but he missed me. That's why he sent gifts for me every birthday until Mummy insisted we move cities. She'd say to her fat, boring friends that we had to leave the city because Papa threatened to kidnap me. I couldn't let him hurt my child, she'd say in that irritating, sniffling voice of hers; I have to think of her. As if Papa would have hurt me. It was only Mummy he hated. He loved me, I know he loved me. He didn't have any mental issue like Mummy claims. She simply could not accept that he hated her. You don't know all this. I didn't tell you when there was opportunity. Now it is too late.

Anyway, that afternoon Mummy's beauty was on full display. The saree she wore, the colour of red Manganese crystals, set off her creamy complexion, and she had lined her eyes with kohl. She had put on weight over the years, a fact that bothered her, but the soft material of the saree fell around her in flattering folds. You took one of the occasional chairs and stretched your long legs in front of you, looking directly at me. Light from the picture window, this same window by which I sit today thinking of you, fell on you. I noticed the deep brown alternating with a sort of golden in your corneas, making your eyes shine unlike any others I had seen.

'So, you are a science prodigy. Very interesting. Instead of the riches of literature which are all around you,' you waved your hand at the bookshelves crowding the room, 'you chose science. What is it that you like about science?'

I thought of the attraction science, particularly chemistry, held for me. Of course, Mummy had tried to interest me in literature ever since I was a kid. She made up funny rhymes and limericks and story cycles, bought pretty notebooks for me to write in, but I found all the make-believe wordiness silly. I liked playing with the Chemistry Lab set that Papa had sent me one birthday far more than the stories and poems Mummy droned on. When we moved to this city, Mummy had more work; she began taking evening classes at a nearby college besides teaching at the university during the day. My schoolwork also increased, and there was less and less time for reading together, which was just fine with me. You were waiting for me to answer your question.

'I like science because it does not lead you one way and lets you imagine you are going the other. Actually, with science there is no need to imagine anything; you can do experiments and discover things and prove what's true, what's false. Imagination is so imprecise. Science is full of certainties. That is very cool—' I had stopped to draw a breath. You had clasped your hands behind your head and were looking earnestly at me with your golden eyes. I got flustered. 'And I like the formulas and shit and the possibility of things turning into other things in a controlled sort of way,' I ended lamely.

'That is profound, Sona. A fairly succinct analysis of what science does. However, do not underestimate imagination. It can show you things which could exist before you discover them through science. Do you see what I mean?' I wanted to ask you to explain to me, tell me why imagination was important, but just then, Mummy entered with the tea. 'I am impressed, Sumi,' you said to her. 'There are flashes of philosophy there among the dross of science.' You smiled at me, your eyes rested on me. You had wanted to say more, but Mummy began to fuss around.

'You are getting late for your class, Sona. Drink your milk quickly and run.' I should have known then that she would never let me be with you. You waved to me as I left. 'Till we meet again, Sona, the golden girl. And I hope it shall be soon.' I felt the hot blood in my cheeks and ears, and Mummy laughed.

II

After that first visit, you came often. You would drive Mummy back from her evening classes or come over on Saturdays, staying until late in the night. Soon I identified a pattern: when Mummy took a cab to the university, it meant you would come home for dinner, and when she brought tall, fragrant fronds of rajnigandha home on Fridays and arranged them carefully in vases around the house, it was a sign you would spend the Saturday with us. Mummy, of course, monopolized you, but I knew you liked me to be around. You spoke soothingly to Mummy when she was annoyed with me about chewing my nails or not carrying my plate to the kitchen after dinner or being tardy with my assignments. She was irritable with me a lot those days, and she and I were always having arguments. Only you brought laughter and light into the house. You called me 'Golden Girl' and asked me which chemical compound I had painted my nails with this time and whether I had managed to blow up the school yet. 'Not even a small explosion?' you'd ask pulling a disappointed face. You made the tired joke sound funny. Even Mummy forgot her annoyance and laughed.

When you came over on the weekends, you liked to stretch out on the acid-green futon with its sulphur-yellow cushions. It used to be placed right here where my beanbag is. It was your favourite seat in the house, and I am very sorry that it got ruined. Mummy brought out the large floor-cushions from her room and reclined on them beside you, reading or chatting. Often, I, too, ensconced myself, with my books and laptop, in the love seat not far from the futon. I knew you looked at me from time to time, I could feel your glance on me. You usually stayed for dinner, and I liked how you were quite at home with us. You would go for a run up the hill, come back and shower, help Mummy lay the table, and occasionally try your hand at cooking. Mummy laughed when you mistook powdered sugar for salt or couldn't tell cumin seeds from carrom seeds and you appealed to me for support. 'Golden Girl, you hear the mocking laughter? I ask you, is it charitable to laugh at an honest mistake? Can I be blamed for not being able to tell one brown seed apart from another? Now if I made a mistake between Marlowe and Shakespeare, then she'd have just cause to mock!' Mummy laughed until tears moistened her eyes. She looked so beautiful that even I couldn't take my eyes off her.

After dinner, Mummy and you drank coffee. Mummy sometimes sat on the arm of your sofa or on the floor beside you. I felt heat surge inside me when I saw her sitting that way, reciting her new poem to you or reading an excerpt from a book, softly, casually leaning against you. She'd shoo me out of the living room. 'You have sports tomorrow morning. You must get your sleep. She is such an early riser,' she'd say to you. 'No matter when she sleeps, she is always up by seven. Sometimes I wonder if they switched babies on me!'

I retreated to my room, but I knew you would have liked me to stay by the way you looked at me and quoted with mock-seriousness, 'Thus we part for the night, dear heart. Sleep well, Golden Girl.'

A few months later, everything changed. It was the peak of summer, humidity intense, and monsoon still a couple of weeks away. Heat-haze hung late into the evening, and Mummy was restless. She read less, forgot what she was saying mid-sentence, overwatered the house plants. In that restive month, you took Mummy and I out for dinner on a Friday night. I wore a new white, sleeveless, eyelet cotton dress, reaching just above my knees. Mummy had a number of white outfits; white was her favourite colour, and she wore it often in the heavy heat of the city. But she didn't think it suited my dark complexion. 'There are plenty of colours, Sona, white's just not yours.' I believed her too until I learned that you thought differently.

Earlier that week, Mummy had had a heat rash. Instead of making her look ugly, the deep pink on her cheeks only made her buttery complexion more attractive. I returned from my athletics class and found you standing by the window, waiting for her. 'Out playing in this heat, Golden Girl?' you commented, turning. 'You are lucky not to have Sumi's sensitive skin. Otherwise, you'd not be able to step out into the sun without dabbing the evil-smelling lotion.'

I wasn't able to hold myself back. I had grown up hearing how I had not inherited Mummy's classical beauty. 'I would suffer anything for Mummy's complexion.'

You looked at me for a moment. 'Come here, Sona,' you said gravely. I joined you at the window. 'You see the lovely, deep shade of the mango tree?' You pointed towards the garden. 'Don't you think it is beautiful? Your complexion is like that shade – dark, velvety, soothing. Why do you compare it with Sumi's?' You placed your arm around my shoulders. I could smell the citrusy scent of your cologne. 'You will never see your own self clearly if you constantly look towards Sumi. You are not her reflection and you most definitely don't need to be her copy. You are perfect the way you are, full of promise and hope. You have your own unique beauty, like that of a young, slender shade-tree. Don't let anyone tell you otherwise.' I felt my eyes prick with tears and stole a sideways glance at you. You were looking at me. Your eyes had the liquid brilliance of the day we had first met. I felt your gaze like a spotlight, something exclusively on me, for me, making me sparkle. You bent down and kissed me on the forehead. The next day I bought the white cotton dress.

I enjoyed our evening together. The restaurant had a live band, and you made them play old English songs I had never heard. You joked with me, gave me your portion of ice cream, and asked Mummy didn't I look like a cool Champa tree in my white dress. Mummy, dewily beautiful in a peach salwar-kameez, put her arm around my shoulders. I knew she was only pretending, showing off her plump, fair arm against my bony shoulders. Only a short while ago she had complained about my untidy ways – leaving towels strewn on the floor, the jar of hair mousse unscrewed and daubs of toothpaste in the washbasin. But I was not afraid of comparisons any longer. You brought us back home after dinner and sat chatting late into the night. I could hear the soft drone of voices as I fell asleep.

The next morning, I emerged from my room for the milk and toast I always ate first thing in the morning, even before brushing my teeth. I found you sitting at the dining table in a white kurta-pyjama, a cup of tea by your elbow, reading the morning papers. I stood stock-still, in shock, trying to understand the meaning of your presence in the house, of your rumpled hair, of the faint red mark on your kurta. You looked over your reading glasses at me and smiled. I felt a jolt in my stomach and wanted to run to the toilet to throw up the bile I could feel rising in my throat.

'Slept well, Golden Girl? Sumi told me you feel peckish in the morning, so I made your toast with my tea. Sit' – you pointed to the chair next to yours – 'and keep me company.' There was a glass of milk and two pieces of toast on my favourite blue and white plate on the placemat. 'I hope the milk is the right temperature and toast the right crispness! I will, of course, improve with practice! I think you and I will have these early mornings to ourselves a lot. Your mother is not an early riser.' You were smiling, your eyes fixed on me, intent, penetrating. I sat down, and pushing the nausea away, nibbled at the toast. You returned to the newspaper. As I sipped the warm, sweet milk, you folded the paper, removed your reading glasses and looked at me. 'Sona, your mother and I are planning to get married. I wanted to tell you myself. I think we can be very happy together. You know how fond I am of you. And I think you and I understand each other. You are very important to Sumi and to me. I hope you understand that, Sona.'

I understood. The panic in my abdomen slowly ebbed. You wanted to tell me yourself, you said we'd be happy together. It was me you really wanted, not Mummy. That was just a sham, an excuse. I was determined we would be, you and I, despite Mummy. I nodded and smiled. You caressed my hair and kissed me on the cheek.

III

Mummy and you married in a civil ceremony. There was a reception in the evening for your and Mummy's friends and colleagues. There was not much family on either side – a frail, elder sister from your side and Mummy's elder brother who rarely visited – but both you and Mummy had many friends, and the banquet hall was crowded. I wore a deep magenta lehenga, a colour not found in the visible spectrum of light, with a small, snug brocade choli and a tissue dupatta. You had said I looked like a bougainvillaea flower in it. It was a special occasion for me; you and I were to finally live under the same roof. You stood with Mummy at the main gate welcoming the guests – Mummy in a cream-and-gold tissue saree and you in the dark bandhgala, taller, more elegant and more handsome than anyone else in the room. I stood awkwardly at the entrance of the dining area, trying not to shift from foot to foot or chew my fingers, inviting the guests to eat. I had turned sixteen a fortnight ago, and you had said I was just right for the dinner-hostess duty. Putting your arm around my shoulders and cutting through Mummy's misgivings, you had said, 'It is a special occasion, and you are a special girl, Sona. I want you to look after our guests, please.' Blood had hammered at my temples. I was special, and you wanted to show that to everyone. During the evening, you left Mummy's side at the main entrance and walked over to me. 'How is it going, Golden Girl? You are being gracious as ever and guests are feeding well?'

'All well, Doc.' I smiled.

The question of how to address you had come up. You preferred being called by your name and Mummy suggested adding your honorific 'Doctor' to it. I decided upon 'Doc'.

'That's great! It makes me sound like a character out of the more disreputable of the nineteenth-century spy novels!'

I watched you all evening as you walked among the guests, talking, laughing. You are one of the very few people who have perfectly symmetrical bones – spine straight, shoulders perfectly aligned, neck carried at the right angle. It was a joy to see you move. From time to time, you came over to me or flashed me a look or a smile. I knew that you loved me.

Mummy and you went to a seaside resort for a few days for your wedding trip. You had said you were not keen on the short trip. I knew the real reason: it was because I could not come along. But in the end, you had given in to Mummy whose idea it was. Those days were unbearable for me. I thought of you with Mummy, and nausea overpowered me. I could barely eat and threw up every time images of her with you floated before me. The doctor came and prescribed medicines which only made me drowsy and sluggish. By the time you returned, I had lost five kilos and was unable to get up from the bed. Mummy immediately stopped all medicines, cooked soups and dal for me, and read my study material to me as I lay in bed. I could see you were impressed; in fact, you had said that very few mothers would be so devoted. You could not see through her. It did not occur to you that the reason she wanted me to be healthy and well-prepared for my exams was because she wanted so badly for me to get admission into an undergrad programme abroad and go away. She couldn't wait for me to leave so she could have you to herself.

After the marriage, you had moved into our home. Mummy had said she did not wish to disrupt my life – my school, my tuition classes were all close to our home. I would have liked to live in your home where everything was yours, where I could have felt you everywhere. Life settled into a new pattern. Mummy and you left for work together and, most evenings, returned together. The two of you often went out in the evening for concerts or plays or dinner at the homes of mutual friends. I was not included in any of the outings, ostensibly because I needed to focus on my studies and preparations for the college entrance exams, but in reality, it was because she could see you liked me. In fact, those days I hardly got a chance to speak to you. By the time I returned from my classes, you would be out with Mummy, and when you returned, I would be asleep. I know this wasn't what you wanted, but you were trapped. By marrying Mummy to be close to me, you had given her all the power.

One evening, I returned early from my classes. You were in the sitting room. 'Golden Girl! At last! You've been overdoing the whole committed student thing, I hear. You have grown even more elf-like while I am becoming portly and old.'

Just seeing you there, relaxed and smiling, was overwhelming for me. You looked smilingly at me. 'You are not old,' I replied. You laughed. Mummy entered, dressed in a white chikankari outfit, mogra flowers in her hair. She always came at the wrong moment.

'Do you hear, Sumi? Golden Girl here says I am not old. Next time you comment on my white hair, please to remember!'

'I wish she'd remember to eat and rest. She has been worrying me this last month. Just look how thin she is. Just skin and bones.'

I hated her for saying that, pointing out my thin arms, my jutting shoulder blades. 'I was just remarking on her growing slenderer.' You looked at me. 'It is becoming, in fact you remind me of a rather lovely girl I mooned over in my lost youth, but you must listen to Sumi and take care of yourself. You need stamina for writing those monsters of exams.' You would have continued, but Mummy rushed you.

'We are getting late. I am reciting today, and it won't do for us to arrive after others.'

Mummy's complaints about my thinness increased, although she herself was desperately trying to lose weight. She said she was worried about my immunity, my growth, but I knew that in reality she resented that you admired my slenderness. She laced my food with ghee, knowing very well that I disliked it. All that slimy stuff made me feel queasy and I had to make myself throw up secretly. There was absolutely nothing wrong with me. If Mummy would have just left me alone, just let me have you occasionally to myself, all would have been well. But she wouldn't. She took me to see a doctor. The doctor was a pale-faced, tight-lipped man. I could see he took a dislike to me the first time he met me, and all that he has said to you about me is because like Mummy, he hates me. He examined me and asked silly questions, like was I being bullied at school, did I have a crush on some boy. In the end, he said there was nothing wrong with me, physically. Then he spoke to Mummy separately. I heard a bit of it as the door was not pulled shut. He mumbled about my vomiting being a response to something I did not like, that I perhaps resented your presence and could not accept you in place of my father.

Mummy must have told you what the doctor had said because after that consultation, I often caught you looking at me with anxious eyes. I wanted to tell you that the doctor was a fool. Why would I resent your presence in my life? You *are* my life. It is Mummy who is in the wrong place, always in the way. She became quite sticky, would not leave me alone with you, would take me to my favourite places without you, make every effort to keep us apart. You, of course, saw through it all. Your birthday was approaching. Mummy had planned a puja at home for the occasion and had invited friends. I wanted to get you something nice, but you said, instead of receiving gifts, you wanted to give gifts to mark your birthday.

'How about buying you both sarees to wear for this puja that you have rigged up, Sumi?'

Mummy looked very pleased. 'That's a good tradition to begin, but I doubt if Sona would want a saree. She has always refused to wear one.'

That was true, but this was different – this was you offering to gift me a saree. I said I would love to have a saree of my own. You took us to the most famous saree emporium in the city. The salesman unfurled saree after saree, the colours and smells of the new sarees, their embellishments and texture, made my head swim. Finally, I picked a deep red silk one with gold paisleys that you had been fingering. Mummy looked doubtful. 'This really isn't the right style for a young girl...' she said. The salesman sided with her. 'I think the blue chiffon or the pink crêpe de Chine with silver work and crystals would suit her better. This red and gold is just right for madam herself. It would suit her fair—' You had cut him off. 'What nonsense. It would look very well on Sona. This peacock-blue one is the right one for you, Sumi. Here, drape it on and see.' You had glanced at me over Mummy's shoulder and smiled conspiratorially.

I wore the crimson saree and make-up for the first time on your birthday. Mummy was arranging flowers and offerings in large platters for the puja when I emerged from my room. She raised her head and looked at me. 'That foundation is a shade too light for your skin, Sona, and the lipstick is too bright. Come here, the saree needs to be tucked right to give you some volume.' She dabbed at my face with a bit of tissue and began rearranging my saree. Tears pricked my eyes. You came over.

'What's the matter Crimson Glory? Why the unhappy look? Doesn't she look like a young pomegranate tree today, Sumi?'

Mummy gave my saree a final tug and smiled. 'The colour does look better on her than I thought.'

It did not matter what she said. You thought I looked beautiful. That was the only thing that mattered. After the puja and lunch, some of your friends lounged about and recited poems. Mummy read some of her own compositions. I could see you enjoyed them very much. You recited several too. One of them was about a pomegranate tree, its fragile flaming flowers and secretive ruby fruits, and the intensity that lives in its slender trunk and branches. You smiled at me as you intoned the lines. I made two resolves that day – one, to write poetry. If it gave you so much pleasure, I was determined to learn to write it. And two, that Mummy must go for us to be together.

IV

My preparatory holidays had begun, and I was at home except for the coaching classes I attended. I stayed up nights, drawing up and discarding plans for getting Mummy out of the way. I fell asleep during the day and missed my classes a few times. Mummy was very angry when she found out about it. 'I am fed up, Sona. You are not taking the medicines the doctor has prescribed, you are missing your coaching classes, your temper is growing worse by the day. Rekha said you threw the glass of milk at her when she tried to wake you up this morning. You are turning out to be more and more like your father. He could not see me happy and neither can you. If this goes on, I will wash my hands off you. I will send you to a boarding...'

The next evening, I prepared some soap-solution and poured it on the floor near the bathtub in the bathroom en-suite to your room. I just wanted to hurt her. How was I to know that Mummy had a seminar that day and you would return alone, that you would decide to take a shower immediately after coming back instead of going for your evening run like usual? I heard you fall, and sickness swept over me. I rushed to the bathroom and found you on the floor, your ankle bent at an unnatural angle. You were gasping with pain. I snatched a towel from the towel rail, wiped the slippery floor and helped you to the bed.

When I returned with an ice pack from the refrigerator, you were trying to sit up on the bed. 'Seems like you'd need to help take your Doc to the doctor, Sona' – you tried to smile – 'Sumi is on her way, but it will take her some time to reach in this traffic and the doctor wants to see me immediately.' I couldn't speak. I had caused this pain to you. I wanted to bang my head against the wall, hurt myself for hurting you, but there was no time. You needed my help. I sent Rekha to fetch a taxi and helped you get up from the bed. You placed your arm around my shoulders and tried hard not to lean fully on me, but your injured leg could not take any weight. The intensity of the pain made you break out in a sweat, a groan escaped you and you gritted your teeth. I begged you to let me help you, to not put any weight on the injured foot. My voice sounded raspy, breathless in my own ears. As always, you saw my distress. 'Don't cry, Sona. There, I will place the weight of my hoary years on your tender shoulders.' You even managed a smile to reassure me.

At the hospital, I did not wait for nurses or attendants and got a wheelchair for you, wheeling you to the emergency ward myself. I held your hand as the doctor examined you and, shaking his head, said he suspected a fracture. I wiped the sweat from your forehead as you were moved to a stretcher and taken to the radiology room. Through all the pain and suffering, I still felt a sweet relief – I was with you, I had you all to myself. But it was short-lived. While your foot was being X-rayed, Mummy arrived.

You had a fracture of the fibula, a lateral malleolus, the doctor said. A firm cast was put on your foot, from ankle to calf, and six weeks of complete rest prescribed. I threw up violently in the hospital washroom; the cleaning-woman made me sit on a plastic stool and fetched some water for me to rinse my mouth. We returned home. Mummy cried and thanked God alternatively all through the car ride home. 'It could have been so much worse. You could have hit your head on the bathtub ... How could Rekha leave the bathroom floor slippery like that? Oh God, Bhaumik, Bhaumik...'

I am sure you had guessed that it was I who had poured the soap-solution in the bathroom, that it was meant for her not you. You spoke in your soothing way: 'Don't cry, please, Sumi, just be still. It is all right. I am all right.' You held Mummy, and I gritted my teeth.

At home, Mummy helped you to your room and closed the door behind her. I went to my room. You don't know how I suffered that evening. I imagined your pain. I wanted to kill myself. After a while, Mummy came to my room. 'Come, Sona, Bhaumik wants to see you.' You were lying in bed dressed in fresh clothes and smelling of cologne. I stood near you, unable to say a word. You reached out and touched my cheek gently. 'Poor Sona, you've had a rough time of it. I never suspected you could cry enough to fill a moderate-sized pool while fetching and carrying quite so energetically!' I was unable to control myself and buried my head in your chest. 'Don't cry, Sona, don't cry, honey...' you said as you stroked my head and shoulders. It was bliss.

The next few weeks were our best time together. After a couple of days at home, Mummy had to return to work, and then it was just you and I. You spent the day in the living room on the futon, surrounded by books and papers and your laptop. I brought my books and sat beside you where Mummy used to. I watched over you. It was I who placed a small cushion under your ankle for elevation, got you juice, water, more books, your phone's charger, anything you needed. We ate lunch together, and I helped you to your room to rest before leaving for my coaching class. Neither you nor I spoke much. There was no need. The understanding between us was perfect. You and I both knew. When you were allowed to walk a little, I accompanied you to the garden. We enjoyed peaceful walks. You told me the names of birds and trees. We gazed in silence at the melting western sky. But those short weeks passed quickly, and all too soon, you were permitted to go back to work. My exams began, and Mummy regained her ascendancy over you, helping you to and from the car, taking you for physiotherapy sessions. She virtually banished me from your presence on the pretext that I needed every bit of time for studying. I wasn't fooled. She had seen how happy we were without her and wanted to separate us.

But I wasn't worried. I had already formulated a plan. I brought home some sodium azide crystals from the chemistry lab. We used it as a preservative, and I knew it was highly toxic. I also brought a bottle of buffered isotonic saline. I prepared a solution of saline and sodium azide and stored it in an old jam jar in the back of the medicine cabinet in my bathroom.

V

The night my final exams got over, I filled a carefully cleaned small bottle of eye drops with the sodium azide solution I had made. I felt an intense energy in my body as I put the bottle in the pocket of my shorts and went to fetch my milk from the kitchen. As usual, both your and Mummy's coffee mugs were on the tray, small plumes of steam rising from them.

I had bought the mugs for Mummy and you right after your marriage and had got them personalized. Yours had a pair of glasses on a glazed yellow background with the words 'Dr.' on each lens, and Mummy's a couple of mogra flowers. You liked your coffee without sugar and Mummy liked hers sweet, and the cups came in very handy. I took out the eye-drop bottle. I wasn't sure how much solution I should administer and emptied half the bottle into Mummy's cup. I carried the tray to the dining room just as Mummy entered, wearing a white muslin tunic, her hair loose. She smiled as she took the tray from my hands. 'You should do something fun for a few days, Sona, before writing your SAT. Go to a salon tomorrow and get that unruly hair cut.' She touched my hair with the tips of her fingers and kissed my cheek.

The next morning, the first day of my holidays, I woke up a little later than usual. The house felt empty. No one seemed to be around. I went to the kitchen to get my toast and milk and saw the note on the fridge, stuck, interestingly, with one of the coffee-mug-shaped magnets Mummy had brought back from the seaside trip. In a harried scrawl you had written that Mummy was very unwell, that you had rushed her to the hospital, and I was to call you when I woke up. It seemed to have worked. I warmed my milk and switched on the toaster. I thought carefully as I ate. Before giving you a call, I retrieved the jam jar from my bathroom and poured the contents down the toilet. Next, I wrapped the bottle in layers of newspaper and smashed it with one blow of my shampoo bottle. I then placed the bunched-up newspaper in a plastic bag, threw it in the communal trash bin outside and washed my hands carefully. Then I called you. Your voice sounded tired over the phone. 'Sona, Sumi is not well at all. Doctors have stabilized her in the ICU, but you should come quickly.'

Mummy's blood pressure had dropped dangerously, and she had difficulty breathing. Doctors said it was a near-fatal cardiac episode. If you had only waited a half hour before taking her to the hospital, all would have ended. But you did not know, I hadn't told you about the plan. Though no one seemed to suspect anything, I was scared. You gently circled me with your arms and held me to your chest. My heart hammered in exhilaration and tears fell. 'Don't be afraid, Sona. Everything will be all right. I am here for you, do you understand?' I did. There was still hope, but there were doctors and nurses all around and we must be careful.

As you know, things did not end as planned. After a few anxious days, Mummy was out of danger, and in a very few more days, back home. Doctors had concluded that perhaps her crash-diets, the supplements she was taking, and stress were responsible for the episode. She was very weak, though, her pretty complexion sallow and lustreless, her hair dry and lifeless. She took your place on the futon during the day now, reading and writing or simply gazing out the window. You called during the day, and I could not hide my loathing at the smile that played around her mouth, the way her eyes shone exultantly as she spoke to you. She noticed it and I caught her looking at me from time to time, her eyes troubled, brooding. I had to do something before she made her move, for I was sure she was plotting something. I still had the small eye-drop bottle, half-full with the sodium azide solution.

Though I had been very careful about the jam jar, I had forgotten all about this bottle and it had remained in the pocket of my shorts. Rekha had found it, and I had snatched it from her. I had hidden it carefully in my cupboard. But I did not want to use the azide salt so soon. Another unexplained cardiac episode might raise suspicion. So I thought up another plan. I began mixing a strong laxative in her coconut water, cooled soy milk, lassi. I thought if she was weak and the hypotension recurred, doctors would put it down to her dehydrated condition. She declined rapidly and soon needed help to and from her room, but I could see she was uneasy. She insisted upon getting a nurse. 'I don't want Sona to spend her entire holiday cooped up at home, looking after me. She will go to the US soon, she should go out, resume her athletics class, spend time with her friends.'

I had, of course, not told her that I hadn't written my SAT, that I had no intention of letting her separate me from you. The nurse supervised the preparation of Mummy's meals, and I had no opportunity to slip in the laxative. Soon she began to regain her strength.

You remember the evening I came back from my athletics class to find you and her sitting at the dining table like old times? She had my notebook, the one in which I had begun composing poetry, open on the table, and was laughing helplessly. Seeing me, she wiped her eyes and held out her arms to me. 'Sona, sweetheart!' In an auto-reflex, I went to her. Holding me close she said, 'Please, stick to your science, beta. Poetry is really not for you unless you want to attempt the comic! To call someone a perfect skeleton, balanced and integrated, and extol the length of the femur and the firmness of the humerus might be good science but is very bad poetry!'

I felt a hot wave of anger rise inside me. I stood stiffly in the circle of her arms as she mocked me. And you, even you, smiled. That night, I retrieved the eye-drop bottle. I had to use it again; she was turning you against me, making me look ridiculous before you. I went to the kitchen, the bottle held in my fist. The mugs were on the tray, but they were not the usual mugs. These were a pair, exactly alike, deep blue in colour with pink elongated rhombuses on them. As I stood hesitating, Mummy entered. 'What's the matter, Sona?'

'I ... I came for my milk,' I stuttered.

She looked at me strangely. 'You've had your milk. You had it immediately after dinner. What's that in your hand?'

'It's ... it's just some eye drop ... I have dry eyes...' I turned quickly and went back to my room. My heart was pounding. I was certain she suspected me. I had to do something quickly.

The next day, when Rekha went out on an errand, I made two cups of tea. I poured the remaining sodium azide solution into hers and placed the two cups and a plate of her favourite biscuits on the tray. She looked almost her usual self as she lay against the cushions on your futon. She smiled upon seeing me. 'Spoiling your old mother before you go away to college, Sona?' She reached for the cup, the wrong cup.

'That's mine. It has no sugar,' I said quickly and handed her the right one.

'Since when have you stopped taking sugar in your tea?' She looked surprised.

I took a hasty gulp. I was worried that she might ask to taste my tea and find out it was sweet. She placed her cup on the floor beside her and went back to the book she was reading. I wanted her to drink the tea quickly. Rekha would return soon. I wanted it to be over by the time she came back. So I told her to drink the tea before it got cold. She looked at me, the strange look from last night in her eyes again, her brows drawn together. 'Why are you in such a hurry for me to drink the tea, Sona?' she asked.

And then it dawned on me. She knew. She knew all along, perhaps even before I brought her the tea. She had taken the cup so she could send it for a chemical analysis, so that she could accuse me of trying to kill her, hand me to the police, take me away from you forever like she had always wanted to. A red curtain fluttered before my eyes and my body throbbed. I placed my cup on the floor carefully and picked up the heavy stone candlestick that stood against the wall. I swung it with all my might towards her head as she lay there reading. She must have sensed the movement and flinched away. The candlestick missed her head and connected with her shoulder instead. The impact tore the seams of her tunic. The skin on her shoulder broke.

'Sona!' she shrieked and raised her arms to protect her head as I brought the candlestick down again and again on her body, swinging it each time with all my weight. I could barely see through the rippling red curtain, but I heard each impact distinctly. She rolled off the futon and frantically jabbed at her phone, still trying to duck from my blows. I did not realize she had managed to dial your number. I learned later from you that you had heard her shrieks, her calling my name again and again as you raced to your car. I did not hear Rekha enter the house, but suddenly she was in the living room, letting out piercing screams. I am not certain what happened after that. All I remember is there were red splotches on the green silk of the futon, and I was crying that your favourite seat had been ruined.

That evening you came to my room and stood at the door. You were not smiling, you did not call me your 'Golden Girl'. She had managed to turn you against me. You said you knew everything – the tea, the stone candlestick. 'Sumi has begged and begged that the matter not go anywhere. Do you realize what you have done, Sona? Her right arm is smashed, she has a head injury and two of her ribs are broken. You need help, Sona, and I cannot bring Sumi back here until you are here. Tomorrow, I will take you to a hospital where they can help you.'

I, of course, understood that you were doing this to protect me from being handed over to the police. She must have insisted that I be sent to the mental asylum. After you left, I rooted around the cabinet in your room and found the X-ray of your fractured ankle. I studied it carefully, holding it in front of one of the lamps. Then I sat on the stained futon and carefully marked the exact spot on my ankle. I lifted the stone candlestick and brought it down on my ankle with all my strength. I passed out with the pain.

The next day, the doctor at the hospital identified it as a fracture of the fibula, almost in the same place as yours.

VI

I am back home now. You can't put me in the asylum until my ankle heals. You say she has told you not to, but I know better. I see you sometimes, but you never stay for long. She is out of the hospital, and you have moved her into your old apartment. It is almost four weeks now and soon it would be time for the cast to be removed. I have already picked the next bone. Another ankle fracture would look suspicious, so it will be the left wrist this time. I will break all the bones in my body before I allow us to be divided.

INSECTA

M CAME AWAKE WITH a jolt to a loud buzzing. He cracked open his eyes with difficulty. Damn. Had they taken to invading his room during daytime as well? The room was dim, but the curtains on the large window were edged with a dazzling brightness. It must be past noon. Had he slept through the knocks and thumps on his door or had they for once allowed him to sleep his fill in peace? The buzzing had stopped. Then he remembered – today is the day. He threw back the bedclothes hurriedly and sat up. Something prickly and hot churned in his gut. He felt dizzy and exhausted, his eyes burned, his feet were icy. Sleeping a little longer for a single day cannot make up for the lack of sleep night after night for years.

Ever since the nightly invasions had begun, he hadn't had a good night's sleep. Hell, there haven't been any good nights. They've invaded the room every night, night after night, through gaps and cracks and holes and crevices – countless, unstoppable, relentless. And I fighting them all alone ... a losing battle, one against the hordes overrunning the room. All I can do is clamber on the bed and try to knock them off as they trail up the bed frame. Like bloody Abhimanyu surrounded by enemies in the chakravyuh. But Abhimanyu had to fight only once, not night after bloody night. M ground his teeth. At least Abhimanyu's father taught him to fight. Or was it his mother? Anyway, whomever taught him, no one taught me anything – neither attack, nor defence. They don't even believe me. 'There's nothing. It is all in your head. You need to focus on your studies and stop imagining this nonsense. No one else has ever seen anything.' M clenched his fists until his nails left bloodless moons in his palms.

How would they see anything? As soon as night falls, they disappear into their bedroom and shut the door, the world outside could burn for all they care. Stay in my room one night, see how they climb up from the garden and slink back when the sun rises. But no. They won't. That would spoil their fun. They can't be expected to babysit a seventeen-year-old, they must have time to themselves. They don't realize what would happen if one morning the invaders don't retreat. Or if I open my door and let them loose in the house to leave their slimy trails all over the oh-so-precious teak furniture and the old silk-brocade sofas, the antique walnut china cabinet. And would the fucking door of their bedroom hold up? Not a hope in hell. The only reason this house is safe is me, because I fight a war night after night. But I can't go on much longer, I won't last. Already my head aches constantly and my heartbeat's like a hammer in my own ears. I have cold sweats, nausea. My eyes burn, sounds startle me ... My body is giving up, I can't hold out much longer, I can't...

INSECT INVASIONS WERE not new to M. He had coped with occasional invasions by bugs for years now. The old garden and the deep, low house might seem picturesque to outsiders, but M knew what an insect-ridden hell it was in reality. There was a chronic damp problem in the walls. The windows of his room opened on to the old, dank garden, their wooden frames were warped from years of rains and the shutters did not close properly. In any case, closing the shutters would be of no avail. They'd still find a way in. They always have. The room is filled with their stench night and day.

'It is only a bit of damp. People are ready to pay millions in this city for tiny, open spaces. You have a whole garden, and all you do is complain about it. We got the waterproofing done because of your complaints. Now what do you want us to do? Cut down all the old trees and pour concrete over the grass?'

Yes. Cut the damn garden down. Destroy it. What good is waterproofing? As if they don't know that the third night after the treatment, termites had entered my room. Armies of them, and moving at such speed. Within minutes they destroyed all my notes, practice sheets, quick revision sheets, all the hard work of the whole term. Fucking creatures chewed up everything just right before the exams. And what did they say when they saw the shredded books and papers?

'Waste all your time with worthless boys, don't study for exams, tear up all your books yourself and then blame imaginary insects. You should be ashamed of yourself, you should hang your head in shame for doing badly in exams and then lying to us...'

They don't care whether I live or die so long as I get good grades ... I can rot among the horrible creatures night after night so long as they can boast to everyone that I got a 100 per cent in Physics. 'He is just like me, going to ace science and math!' No, I am not fucking like you. I am better than you. With no sleep I still manage to pass, remain among the top ten in class, but that's not good enough for you. Nothing I do is good enough for you.

THERE WAS A time when M did not have a problem with insects. In fact, they had interested him in the beginning. He used to observe what they ate, when they mated, how they nested, who preyed upon whom. He read books and learned about their orders and families, genus and species. He collected them, the shelves in his room were lined with cardboard boxes containing caterpillars, painstakingly segregated by species and labelled, ladybirds classified by the number of spots, earthworms, dung beetles, crickets, bees, wasps, and at one point of time, a fine selection of centipedes. He knew what to feed them, when to raise the lids and let them get some sunlight, how moist the earth and dry the leaves in the boxes should be for eggs to hatch.

They were proud of my hobby then, telling stories about how I would bring unusual creatures, a bright burgundy millipede or an ashen strangling beetle, in a matchbox or in my knicker-pocket to puja ceremonies and family get-togethers. 'He even tried to give a rather large and handsomely coloured jewel beetle to his grandmother as a gift once!' they'd recount at dinner parties, laughing, looking at me proudly. 'It was her birthday, and all the family was gathered. Everyone recoiled, but to her credit, Ma merely smiled and declined politely!' It was a long time ago. There was no insect problem then. They stayed safely in collection boxes and jars. I used to be top of my class then; they were always talking about me. Now they don't talk about me with anyone. Because I am bringing shame upon them with my bad marks. I am no longer their golden boy, and I don't give a flying fuck about it.

THINGS CHANGED AFTER M won a place in his father's old school. They had insisted he write the entrance exam and were very proud when he passed. 'It is a hundred-and-fifty-year-old school, everyone from our family has studied there, every single one has been on the honour roll and at the top of their class, and if someone stood second, it was because a sibling or cousin was in the same class! Now the third generation is taking the family tradition forward.'

Third bloody generation, hundred bloody fifty years. No one cared about what I wanted. Did anyone ask me whether I wanted to leave my old school for a weird school halfway across the city? I knew no one there; all the cool boys already had their groups. And all those snooty, snide, sniggering girls, swarming like bees, but unlike bees, stinging for fun. I missed my friends, the teachers who liked me, my sports coaches.

Everyone laughed at me there – at my old school, at my insect collection, even at my hair. Once Headmistress Ma'am got a barber to cut my hair because they reached my collar. She made me stand in the quad in front of everyone and, with a straight razor, the barber cut my hair, a circular cut, like someone had placed a bowl on my head and cut all around it. How they laughed at me...

Then there was the incident of the stag beetles. M had taken a pair of stag beetles to the school for a nature project. It had been difficult to find a pair; they live underground and only emerge for a few weeks in a year. The lights and noise had scared them, and they had huddled in a corner of their box, clambering over each other. The teacher had raised her eyebrows. 'This seems to be their mating season!' The whole class had laughed. Ignorant bloody fools. That's when they started calling me 'Mating Season'. Especially the girls. 'Oye, Mating Season...' they'd yell. Everywhere I went – in the playground, in the corridors, even in a mall if I ran into them – it was always 'Oye, Mating Season...'

I told them I was being bullied, but they wouldn't hear a word. 'Why take such insects to school at all? You know not everyone likes them. At the parent-teacher meeting, your teacher said you collect grasshoppers and praying mantises from the playground. If you do foolish things, you'll have to bear the consequences.'

Now I'll see how they bear the consequences, always defending the school, always blaming me.

The buzzing began again. It was the mobile ringing. M had bought this cheap handset a couple of days ago. He had to give his iPhone to Dedha. He had had no choice. Perhaps it was Dedha calling. His legs shook as he got off the bed and picked up the mobile. It was Mayur. 'What the fuck, man! Dedha has called you so many times. What the fuck are you doing, not answering his calls?'

Mayur was his only friend at the new school. They didn't approve of him of course. 'He is the wrong kind of company, wrong influence. He is involved with drugs...' They didn't know that it is Mayur who had kept him sane all this while. Without Mayur he wouldn't have survived.

'Saale, MC, say something. You are off your fucking head or what? You'll get into a bunch of trouble yourself and get me into trouble too.'

M disconnected the call and, with trembling hands, dialled Dedha.

'Motherfucker...' Dedha whispered.

'Dedha Bhai ... everything will be ready, just as you had said, everything will be according to the plan ... There won't be any trouble, Dedha Bhai...' There was a moment's silence followed by a metallic click. The phone disconnected. M glanced at his wrist and remembered that Dedha had his watch too. Anyway, it seemed late. A quick shower, something to eat, and he would be all set to carry out the plan. Today is the day. Everything will be solved today. He stepped into the bathroom.

His first report card at the new school had shocked them. Their golden boy, the one who was to carry on the family tradition of gold medal and honour rolls, fifth in the class? How was it possible? He had tried to tell them then: 'Daddy, Mummy, nothing's right ... Insects come into my room every night, swarms of them ... swirls of lacewings and dragonflies, cicadas and crickets crackling like dry twigs, slugs and snails oozing slime ... They make so much noise I feel my ears will burst ... They fill the room to the ceiling, I can't breathe, I can't see ... During the exams, every night, clouds of emerald moths flew in, they blotted out all light ... They entered my mouth, my ears, I couldn't shout for help ... I can't sleep, Mummy, there's always a rustling in my ears, Daddy ... They come every night ... Sell this house, Daddy. Let's live somewhere else, close to the sea where the salt breeze would kill them...' But did they listen? No fucking way. He had begged and begged them but all they did was scold him. 'You've gotten into wrong company, you don't focus on your studies and now you are making up these absurd stories.

'You've thrown out your collection, we get the garden fumigated every other week, there are insect-nets on all windows. How can there be insects in your room? You should be ashamed of yourself for making up these childish tales. The bungalow has been in the family for three generations. We were married here, your grandparents breathed their last here.'

Well, so would their only grandson, unless something is done and quickly. I am tired of their disbelief. And their lies.

They lie to everyone about my results. 'He has topped the class, as usual; he is on the honour roll...' And if someone asks, 'But isn't the Vashkars' girl in his standard too? She tops the class every year, no?', they get angry with me all over again. 'Not a single good university has accepted you yet. We spent lakhs on your tuitions and counselling, and this is the result. You are such a disappointment ... The family tradition...'

M turned off the shower and held his head in his hands. Everything will be resolved today. Dedha and Dedha's ghoda will solve his problems. He will finally be free of the insects he had once kept captive, and free of this house too, of its closed doors and rigid disbeliefs, of its suffocating expectations.

WHEN MAYUR HAD introduced him to Dedha the first time, M had been a little disappointed. Dedha looked like a shop assistant in a readymade garments store or a clerk in a trading concern. He was puny, short and bow-legged; his scrawny neck and skinny ribs peeped through the open buttons of his shirt. Only when you looked closely did you notice his alert, shooter's eyes and broad, strong hands.

'He is the person to solve all your problems, bro,' Mayur had said. 'Don't go by his physique. He looks like a sheep, but he is a lion, with or without his gun. Just like his name, he is more than one man.'

Dedha hadn't smiled. 'You want some work done?'

'My daddy, mummy ... I mean my, mmm ... parents ... my...' M had stuttered.

'You are not the only one to have parents in this world, everyone has them. You want me to off them?' M had frozen, unable to utter a single word. His voice had vanished, words stuck in his throat. 'You want their full-work done?' Dedha had asked negligently. 'I only do full-work; no hassle, no trouble. You are not the first one with a mummy-daddy problem.'

'No, no not to ... I mean I only want them out of the way for some time...' M had mumbled. 'You know, like out of action ... I will sell this house then and everything will be okay ... There are so many insects here ... termites and ... and centipedes...'

Dedha had glanced at Mayur. 'Is this one crazy? I've only ever done one half-work. The woman was paralysed, but her brother couldn't get his hands on the property. Half-work is devil's work, no good to anyone.' He turned to M. 'Your head is crammed with cow-shit if you think you can touch a brick of your house unless your parents are offed.'

No, I don't want that, he had wanted to say, but no words emerged from his mouth. Instead, he had stood silent as Mayur agreed with everything Dedha said. 'Solid, Dedha Bhai, solid. You are absolutely right. Look here,' he said to M, 'when you are sick and go to a doctor, you don't tell him which medicine you want to take. Dedha Bhai is the doctor, you have come to consult him. Now leave everything to Dr Dedha. Just follow his prescription.'

'You are a shithead,' Dedha had said quietly to Mayur. To M, he said, 'Listen up, pappu, you want the work done, yes or no? Don't waste my time with your puppet impressions.' M had stopped shaking his head and twisting his hands.

'I will take full payment now. Otherwise I would have to do your own full-work for free later on for not paying.' Dedha had smiled a brief smile.

'I don't have money ... I mean ... I just have pocket money right now...' M had stammered.

'Dedha Bhai, his parents are rich. Big jobs, this bungalow.' At Mayur's suggestion, they had all met at M's home one afternoon when his parents were at work. 'All this is his only. Take whatever he can give now. I am there, no, where will he run? He will pay the rest later.'

In the end, M had given Dedha his iPhone, his iPod, his watch, his new sneakers.

'I will come through the gate at the back and through the garden. Leave the house-door open. It will take no time. I will be in and out like that.' Dedha had snapped his fingers. 'Afternoon, between one and two.' M had memorized – back gate, leave the door open, in and out, Saturday afternoon ... Saturday, that is today.

AS HE STEPPED out of his room, M was struck by the unnatural quietude. By this time, usually, the whole house would be smelling of mutton curry. Old songs would be playing on the music system, and they would be in the living room, pointedly turning away from him as he entered. He crossed the living room and peered down the corridor. The door of their room stood wide open. The room was tidy except for a half-folded saree flung on the bed. Mystified, he returned to the dining room. The table was set with only one place. The maid emerged from the kitchen.

'Saab-Memsaab left for the races, Baba, they will come back after lunch.'

M froze. Fuck. Bloody race-Saturday. How could he have forgotten? He had never known them to miss the races, whether he had exams or was sick with typhoid. Without uttering a word he raced back to his room. There wasn't a minute to be lost. He must stop Dedha.

'Dedha Bhai, there is a small change ... Today's horse racing. They've gone to the club, but not to worry. They will be back after lunch. So if you come between four and five...' As if I am inviting him to bloody tea.

'Maadar...' Dedha growled abuses, filthy abuses from the gutter. M held the phone away from his ear. 'I don't give a shit if the fucking firang-fuckers are at the horse race or pigeon parade. We have our setting for today, the plan must be carried out today or you must pay regardless.'

'Dedha Bhai, it is just the time ... Everything else remains same ... back gate, front door ... Just between four and five...'

There was the trademark silence. Then, 'Don't fuck it up, or I will auction off your ass.' The rest of what he said was lost amid loud street noises. M hung up and breathed deeply.

The maid was still hovering in the dining room. 'Baba, dal-chawal is ready. Will you eat now?'

'Forget about dal-chawal. Actually, take the rest of the day off and take the dal-chawal with you. No need to come tonight.'

'But Memsaab said...'

'I spoke to Memsaab. She said I can order pizza. Go.'

The door closed behind the maid and M slumped down on the floor. His brain felt coated with something sticky and his ears still buzzed from the chirruping of the crickets that had trooped in last night.

When his breathing evened, he called the nearby restaurant and ordered two pizzas and a large bottle of their sweetest, fizziest drink. Then he dialled Mayur's number. 'Come over. There's a slight change in the plan.'

'Son of a b... Because of you I was abused and threatened. Dedha properly chewed me out, and here you are talking calmly about change of plan, you fucker...' Over his torrent of abuse, M hollered 'pizza' and hung up.

Mayur arrived at the same time as the pizza.

'Yaar, I was shit scared. You must be careful with Dedha. He has a fucking temper.'

M opened the pizza-box. 'I forgot today was race-Saturday...'

'Anything could have happened.' Mayur swallowed a mouthful. 'Do you think he'll think twice before shooting you or me if he thinks we are up to something funny? You need to be damn careful.'

'They don't talk to me these days except to say Mr Joshi's son scored this much, the Vashkar girl got an offer from that uni ... As if I am nothing if I don't get a good grade or a uni acceptance...'

'Don't worry, bro, it will all be okay soon.' Mayur rolled and lit a joint.

They returned a little after 3 p.m., laughing and chatting. M was in his room. He had heard the car come up the driveway.

'Mehul Bhai's horse never wins but he doesn't give up hope!'

'It is not hope, it is tax-chicanery that brings him to the racecourse!'

'Really? There's a strange smell...'

'Yes, there certainly is.'

They wrinkled their noses. M sat sweating. Could they still smell the pot? Mayur had left half an hour ago, and he had opened all the windows. He pretended to study. They changed their clothes and read the weekend editions of newspapers in the living room. A little before four, M rose and walked through the dining room to the front door. The doorbell rang just as he got to the foyer. He trembled violently; for an irrational moment he thought it was Dedha who had arrived early. Perhaps he wants to shoot me too ... The moment I open the door, he will whip out his ghoda ... Breathing hard, he managed to undo the latch. Their next-door neighbours stood at the doorstep, the only ones left from the time when the street was still full of bungalows.

'How are you, beta? See, who is here...' The old woman pushed forward the two little children who were hiding behind her. 'They just arrived yesterday. Arti and Aditya have gone to London for fifteen days.' They entered the living room.

'The little ones are visiting? How perfectly wonderful!' M's mother hugged the woman and then scooped the kids in quick embraces.

'They have grown quite a bit. I can't remember when our son was this age...' M's father smiled and shook hands all around.

M's throat felt dry. The rustling and buzzing in his ears rose. These people shouldn't be here. Any moment now Dedha will be here ... What should I do? Call Dedha ... The woman held him by the hand and gently pulled him towards her. 'How are you, beta? You've lost weight. Are you not eating properly?'

'He is working very hard,' M's mother supplied, 'studies all night. Preparing for university admissions.' She peeled an orange and offered the juicy wedges to the two children. They ducked their heads shyly and sat holding each other's hands.

'You will get into a good university, beta. You are so brilliant. But look after your health too,' the man said, smoothing the children's hair. 'I still remember how he used to collect all those bugs and things when he was small.'

The woman laughed. Light bounced off her spectacles as she turned towards M. 'Do you remember you used to prowl around in the garden at night, torch between your teeth, butterfly net in hand, to catch night-bugs? You were always so serious and studious.' M disengaged his hand from hers and craned his neck to check the clock on the dining room wall. It was half past four. Through the rising noise in his ears, he could hear the sound of the back gate dragging. Dedha ... he was entering the bungalow ... I must do something...

'We have only one son. All our hopes rest on him.' M's father looked at him. It was months since he had looked at him in this way, eyes soft and mouth relaxed in a smile. He remembered that he hadn't closed the front door. Dedha will see it standing ajar and think ... Over the hammering of his heart, he heard footsteps ... the crunching of dry leaves underfoot. He looked around wildly. 'Everyone must take cover inside the house,' he tried to scream. 'Lock the rooms, save the kids ... save them...' But no sound issued from his mouth. He lurched out of the living room. I must lock the door before Dedha reaches it ... I have to ... I must stop him from entering the house ... He tried to close the door, pushing it with both hands, with all his strength, but it was already too late. Through the opening, insects poured in, surging waves of Coleoptera – stag beetles, spittlebugs, dung beetles, click beetles, deathwatch beetles, blood beetles – every species once painstakingly identified with the help of the *Insecta Encyclopaedia* exploded into the house in a red-black-grey tide, rising, rising...

He was drowning ... the house was drowning...

THE DRAGON IN THE GARDEN

'There's a dragon in Roxy's garden,' Raghu declared. He thrust his bright blue spoon into the beige mush of milk-soaked Weetabix and stirred up a small, slow whirlpool. 'He is small, so he cannot breathe fire. But when he is big, he will open his mouth wide and a big fire will come out and Roxy will be toast.'

Roxy was Raghu's new best friend. He had acquired new vocabulary along with new friends in the past few months since we moved to Singapore. He had attended a cozy little kindergarten in Bombay with neighbourhood kids, and I had been worried when we moved. The school in Singapore was vast with over five hundred children and a three-acre compound. He had seemed so small, so quickly lost in the crowd of other light-blue-shirt-and-navy-blue-shorts-clad children, the first day I had dropped him off. I had felt anxiety unfurl in my stomach like the banners of dragon-dance. At work, I felt needle-pricks of tears every time I thought of Raghu walking towards the shadowed blue-grey building on the other side of the large quadrangle. Perhaps he was lonely among the strange children, missing the cheerful, sun-orange rooms of his old school, and Miss Menon, who let him eat a snack before break because he got hungry. But I needn't have worried. Roxy took him in hand from the very first day.

I had taken half a day off at work and reached Raghu's school well before pick-up time. Little boys and girls spilled out of the building and crossed the grassy quadrangle in a two-toned blue wave, but Raghu wasn't among them. I suddenly felt breathless. There were swimming pools in the compound and unending corridors and innumerable staircases. That concrete building had sucked him in, and he wasn't ever going to return to me. Panicked, I darted across the grassy quadrangle.

'Mummy! Where are you going, Mummy?' Raghu stood beside me. A golden star was painted on his left cheek and in his grubby fist he held the hand of a little girl with feathery, blonde hair and freckles on her wide cheeks. I bent down and hugged him. 'I couldn't see you, beta.'

'I finished all my puzzles first and I did all the colour-ins. Miss gave me a star,' he announced proudly.

'I helped him to colour in the lines,' the girl said, her light blue eyes fixed on Raghu, 'and I gave him my sweetie and he doesn't know how to wash his hands.'

I smiled. 'What's your name, sweetheart?'

'She is Roxy. I will marry her when I am big. Can she go home with us, Ma?'

'That's nice.' I laughed. 'Will you invite me to the wedding?' I took Raghu's bag and opened the taxi app on my phone.

'Yes, Ma. I like you too. I will marry you, too, after I marry Roxy.'

Roxy gave Raghu a stern look. 'You can't marry your mom. Jesus won't let you.'

Raghu threw his head back and clung to my arm. 'I will. She is my mom. She is not Jesus's mom.'

Roxy's fair brows gathered in a frown and her eyes clouded. I took Raghu's hand. 'You know there's lots of time to decide all this. How about we go home? Yaya has made some chocolate milkshake.'

'You come, too, Roxy.' Raghu extended his free hand to her.

Roxy smiled happily. 'I like chocolate milkshake with lots of chocolate.'

I looked around. Hadn't anyone come for her? 'We can't just take her with us, Raghu. Is anyone coming to pick you up, Roxy?'

'Ma'am, I am the one to bring Roxy home.' A Filipina woman in denim shorts and a T-shirt proclaiming love for Coca-Cola and good life, came forward. 'My Ma'am has said you go to your ballet class from here, Roxy.' Roxy reluctantly let go of Raghu's hand. The corners of her mouth turned down.

We walked out of the school porch. 'They've become such good friends on the first day. Perhaps Roxy can come to our place one of these days, and she and Raghu could play together. There is a lovely play area with jungle-gym and slides in our building.'

'I will ask Rosalie Ma'am,' the Filipina answered, looking away. 'Your boy can come to our house too. We have a big garden and two dogs.'

'They are very naughty,' Roxy offered. 'They ate all the nice birthday cake Mom got for me and Eva had to go out and buy another one. You'll come to see them, Raghu?' Roxy shook off Eva's hand and dipped hers into her pink satchel, encrusted with rhinestones, and took a fistful of colouring pencils out. 'You take them,' she said, handing them to Raghu, 'but don't chew them. That's yucky. I will draw a picture for you and you draw one for me.' Raghu took the colours.

Eva looked at me conspiratorially. 'Don't think that the dogs are bad, Ma'am. They are good dogs. My Ma'am forgets to buy a cake and make a story!' She rolled her eyes.

The sun was high and bright in the cloudless sky and orderly rows of rain trees threw sparse patterns of shade on the ground. Roxy stepped into a waiting car. She waved to Raghu as the chauffeur turned the car. Raghu didn't see her. He was busy opening the packet of caramelized nuts I had bought for him.

RAGHU HAD MADE other friends at school, other boys with whom he played football or raced in the grassy quadrangle, but Roxy remained his special friend. Soon after his first day at school, I had received a call on my mobile while at work. It wasn't a number I recognized.

'Hello, this is Roxanne's mother.' The voice was slightly nasal, each word carefully articulated. I hadn't been able to place her immediately. 'Our children are at school together.'

I had absently clicked on an email. 'At school? Oh, sorry, you are Roxy's mom? Roxy and Raghu are great friends.'

'I know.' Her nasal voice remained flat. 'That's the reason I am calling. Please send your son over for a play date tomorrow after school.'

'Tomorrow?' I straightened my desk calendar. The next day was Thursday. My husband was travelling, and I had planned to take Raghu to the zoo. But I knew he would love to go to Roxy's home. Besides, it would be good for him to make friends and feel more settled in the new city. I could always take him to the zoo another day.

'Yes. My helpers, Marie and Eva, will be there the whole time to supervise them. We have two Labradors. They are very well trained. Roxy has almond milk and organic chocolate-chip cookies for snack after school. If your son has any allergies or dietary restrictions, please send a note and Eva will take care. If he prefers to eat Indian food, please feel free to send that with him. We use a lot of turmeric and coconut oil ourselves, so the smell won't be a problem. I will text you the address.'

She hung up before I could reply. I felt blood rush to my face. My mobile rang again. It was Raghu. 'Ma! Roxy says I am to go to her home tomorrow!' His excited voice bounced in my ear. 'She'll show me the secret place in her garden and will teach me to skip!'

'That's nice, beta. Now wash your hands and drink your milk. I'll be home in the evening. Love you.'

Saleena turned towards me. 'All okay with the youngster? He is settling in well?'

I worked in the Bombay office of the firm before relocating to its regional headquarter in Singapore late last year. The forty-floor building I work in now is filled with my co-workers. Yet, I don't know anyone. I don't know the name of the man who is in the cubicle across from me and whose phone's ringtone sounds like the braying of a donkey, neither do I know the woman to my right who lines up three cups on her desk every morning, fills them with a bitter-smelling tea from her thermos and drinks them quickly one after another. At the coffee point, people stand in tight knots and chat with each other in Chinese or the heavily accented Singlish, filling their bottles with warm water, pouring wood-coloured coffee, with a film of oil on top, into their mugs. They look at me stonily and mutter a greeting when I say good morning, but mostly they just nod and continue talking amongst themselves. Saleena is the only friendly colleague I have here. She is in the cubicle to the left, and we sometimes step out together during lunch break to buy a sandwich. She shares her Singapore survival-tricks with me. It is from her that I have learned that the big supermarket in Bukit Timah is the best place to buy reasonably priced fruits and the best dry-cleaner for silk sarees is in Little India. She laughed when I told her how no one makes eye-contact or smiles. 'Welcome to Singapore, la! You've got to give everyone some time to get used to you. Anything or anyone new is an unknown quantity and a potential threat. In about five years' time, people might actually smile at you and offer you a slice of Durian!' She is joking, of course. There are posters all over the office with large red crosses on pictures of the spiky fruit. Its pale-coloured sweet-tasting flesh has a nasty smell and its consumption in the office is strictly prohibited.

'Yeah.' I slipped my mobile into my handbag.

'Better than his mother?'

I smiled. 'Funny. He has found the girl he wants to marry already and wants to go to her house tomorrow.'

'Aha! And you are green with jealousy! Typical Indian mom. That's the reason I haven't married yet because every Indian man I know has a super-possessive mom.' Saleena is British but makes much of her Indian origin.

'Not me. I am happy to resign my rights in Roxy's favour. She is a capable little lady and manages Raghu rather well. If you need further proof, I have cancelled our planned outing and will instead drop Raghu to her home for a play date.'

'Impressive. Does Raghu's heart-throb live somewhere near your condominium?'

'I don't really know.' I clicked my mobile phone and read out the address Rosalie had sent. Saleena whistled. 'His gf is a posh little lady. That is a very posh place.'

'Raghu has been invited for a play date tomorrow.'

My husband looked up from his laptop. 'That sounds vaguely sexual.'

'Everything sounds sexual to you. Roxy's mother called this morning. She demanded I send Raghu over and condescended to tell me she does not mind the smell of Indian food. She hung up before I could answer, otherwise I would have told her that I am not as tolerant as her. I totally mind whatever she's been eating.'

'Yaar, you are oversensitive!'

I pressed my lips together. Oversensitive is not an accusation, the counsellor at a recent women's networking event at work had explained; all it means is you are aware of what others say and do and respond to it at an emotional plane. For far too long this has been used as a pejorative, she had bunched her ruby-red mouth in disapproval; you should accept it, embrace it, wear it like the insignia of emotional connectedness. The roomful of women, mostly Asian, had looked on in silence. There had been no sign of anyone embracing anything anytime soon. I decided to try.

'Yeah, I guess I am. And she is obnoxious.'

'Who is she?'

'I don't know. She is on the class list.' I clicked open my phone.

'Don't send Raghu if you don't want to.'

'But he wants to go. Roxy and him are besties.'

'Yaar, you are impossible. Just do what you like.'

'I don't want to send him. She doesn't come across as someone I'd like to know or have around Raghu.' I had located the class list on my phone. 'It says here, mother's name Rosalie MacPherson, occupation modelling; father's name Patrick MacPherson, occupation shipping...'

'Pat MacPherson?' My husband raised his eyebrows. 'He is one of those guys who run Singapore. Heads the largest shipping company in Asia and is the chair of the chamber of commerce here. My company did some work for his at one time.'

'That explains the chauffeur-driven car and the posh address.'

'Send Raghu. Useful to know them. They are big shits.'

'MA!' RAGHU JUMPED out of the bus despite the restraining hands of the bus attendant. 'Ma, Ma, Roxy says I am to go early to her home. Can I go now?' He hopped around me.

'Don't you want to go to the zoo? We could see the monkeys and eat ice cream. There's a train in the zoo too.'

'But I want to go to Roxy's, Ma. You said I could, you said...' He jumped up and down.

'Okay, if you want to. I'll go to the zoo by myself then.'

Raghu clung to my legs. 'No, you won't, you won't, Ma, you won't go without me.'

I laughed. 'Of course, not, beta, I am joking. We'll go to the zoo another day.'

The sunlight was somehow softer in the avenues of Holland Village, which seemed to be populated entirely with women, children and pets. Women with shiny hair sat in the al fresco cafés, sipping at coffee and chatting, or stood about in small groups, yoga mats slung on their backs, drinking green smoothies. There were children and helpers and well-groomed dogs in the public-play areas. It felt like Sunday.

The taxi stopped outside a house with a white façade and high walls. I pressed the buzzer set in a niche in the gatepost. The gate opened immediately. Roxy stood in the driveway with Eva. She darted out and pulled Raghu's arm. 'You are late.

We baked the cookies already. They are all puffed up. Come and see.' They ran inside.

'I will look after him, Ma'am,' Eva said to me. 'Don't worry. I am the one to take care of Roxy from a baby. Is he allowed to eat eggs?'

'Eva, come and open the oven...' Roxy shouted from the house door.

'I am coming, Roxy.' Eva turned to go.

'I will pick Raghu up by six,' I said.

'Yes, Ma'am, don't worry, Ma'am,' Eva said over her shoulder.

I stepped aside as the gate slid shut.

IN THE TAXI on our way back home, I slipped off my high-heeled pumps. My ankles ached from walking in them, and my mouth tasted sour from the coffee I had drunk while waiting. Raghu bubbled with excitement.

'Roxy has so many colours, Ma! I built a house with blocks. I wanted it to be blue and red but there were only five blue blocks, so I made it a bit green. And I played with Handsome and Beauty. They licked me here and here.' He pointed at his neck and cheeks. 'And we played in the garden. Roxy hid and I couldn't find her and then her Yaya said you had come, so Roxy came out. She says I am to come next week, Ma. She'll show me her top-secret hiding place. Roxy's Yaya gave us cookies.' He slipped his hand into the pocket of his hoodie.

'I saved one for you.' He held out a crumbling cookie. The fuzz from his pocket stuck to it. I bent down and kissed him.

'How was the play date with the posh gf?' It was a 'healthy choice' day in the '30-day-nature diet' that Saleena was following. She stabbed half-heartedly at her salad with a plastic fork; it was the kind sold in plastic containers and had a lean salad-dressing that smelt suspiciously synthetic. 'Did they drink tea out of bone china cups and eat bread and butter?'

'Roxy is American. They had cookies and cold milk and played with dogs called Handsome and Beauty.'

'Such chink names for dogs,' Saleena said through a mouthful of baby spinach. 'What are her folks like?'

'I don't really know. The father is someone big in shipping and mother's listed as a model.'

'Ah, the marriage of an exploiter of earth-girding seas and arm candy. Typical. Tell me about them. This is the first time I have come within gossip-distance of folk living in "landed property".'

'I can't tell you much. I wasn't invited in. I just dropped my son like a mail-order friend and collected him after two hours of browsing nail-spas and organic food shops and drinking bitter coffee in the neighbourhood.'

Saleena placed the fork in the salad box and patted my knee. 'Don't take it personally, darling. What can one expect from white, fat-cat expats but utter low-bred rudeness? I am sure Raghu will soon outgrow their spoilt brat.'

I nodded.

'How was it at the MacPhersons'?' my husband asked on Saturday morning. He had returned from the week-long business trip the previous night and was stretched out on the floor in the living room, a tangle of newspapers around him. Sunlight fell in a bright, broad shaft through the picture window on to the floor and bounced back, filling the room with light-haze. The house was quiet. Raghu had gone to the supermarket with the helper. He was fascinated with the self-checkout counter and insisted on accompanying her when she went shopping, so he could stand on tiptoe to swipe the bottles and packets, and make the barcode-reader beep. 'You won't believe what happened in Taiwan!' he continued while turning over and propping an elbow on the floor cushion.

I closed the book I was reading, slipping in it the receipt from Kinokuniya I was using for a bookmark. It annoyed him if I kept the book open when we chatted. 'Yaar, what is so interesting in the book that you can't wait to get back to it?' he would say testily.

'What?' I looked at him.

'I'll tell you,' he said gleefully. 'First you tell me, how did it go?'

'Oh, Raghu had a really good time. Roxy is quite proprietary about him, and he loved the dogs. I didn't get to meet the parents because...'

'Of course, you didn't!' he cut in. 'They were in Taipei! I ran into them in the lobby of Shangri-La. I had met Pat MacPherson a couple of times when we were doing the automation project for his company. I don't think he remembered me, but now he will! Raghu made an excellent conversation-opener! I told him our kids were great friends.'

'What did he say?'

'He was very pleased! I think marriage and the kid are late-in-life ventures for him. His wife's much younger and a looker!' He closed one eye. 'Not that I have anything to complain about in that department myself!' He pulled me to himself. The book slid from my lap.

'MA, CAN I go to Roxy's home tomorrow?' Raghu asked.

I rubbed his damp hair vigorously with the towel and pulled the nightshirt over his head. 'You went to her home last week. Let's ask her over this time. We can make coconut squares and chocolate milkshake and do puzzles.'

'But she will show me her secret hiding place in her garden. She has promised to.' He clambered into his bed.

'That sounds exciting.' I straightened his pillow and caressed his forehead. 'But I am sure the secret place won't vanish in a week's time. This time show her the nice things you've made with coloured putty and you can play with Mr Big and Mr Bigger.'

'Yes, yes!' Raghu bounced in the bed. 'I'll take Mr Bigger and she will take Mr Big and we will have a race. Tell another story, Ma. What happened when Mr Big bumped into a big crow? Did Mr Bigger help him?'

Mr Big was a toy airplane and Mr Bigger a monster truck, and every night I spun tales about their friendship and rivalry to amuse Raghu.

'Why did you say no to his going to the MacPhersons'?' my husband asked after Raghu fell asleep. 'Because you didn't like the way the woman spoke to you over the phone? You are unreal, yaar!'

'It is not that, Abhay. I googled them. There are stories about Mr MacPherson being found with underage prostitutes in Thailand and the whole thing was hushed up with bribes.'

'Googled them? That's extreme. Why should we bother with rumours anyway? This is Singapore. There are rumours around all the time. If I paid attention to every rumour, I would have no clients and would do no business. I am pitching to MacPherson in two weeks for a big project and so is half of Singapore.'

'But this is not about clients and business. Their whole set-up is strange. His wife was a small-time model from Shanghai and their marriage was in the news because of a particularly nasty prenup he made her sign. The gossip papers quoted parts of it and called it a slavery contract. Basically, it says that she is not to have a penny if she is found to be indulging in immodesty or indecent conduct. It is positively medieval.'

'Why should that bother you? He has every right to protect himself against any hanky-panky. That wife of his is a bomb.'

'That doesn't mean he can enslave her.'

'Really, I don't see what you are getting excited about. The woman signed it and the man is loaded – end of story. Can we keep this in proportion, though? We are talking about a play date here, we are not letting them adopt Raghu. It is good for him to meet different kinds of people, it is part of the socializing process. He is learning to be more independent because of that girl.'

The night before, Raghu had pushed my hand aside and taken hold of his spoon firmly. 'I am a big boy, Ma, I can eat by myself. Roxy says only babies need their moms to feed them.'

My husband turned away. 'Let's just scale this down. I have meetings early morning tomorrow.'

My head buzzed with words. I switched the bedside lamp off.

'WHY DO YOU say Roxy will be toast? That is not a nice thing to say.'

Raghu looked up from his bowl, his mouth smeared with Weetabix, his eyes rounded with surprise. 'But she wants to be toast. She says she wants to be brown, like toast, and then we will be the same colour.'

'But to say someone will be toast does not mean being brown.'

'It does. Roxy's Yaya told us.'

'What did she tell you?'

'She said if she told Roxy's mom about Uncle Peter, he'll be toast.'

'She said that to you? Who is Uncle Peter?'

'No, she said to the other Yaya at Roxy's home. Uncle Peter drives Roxy's car. Roxy's Yaya said that her mom has many colours to put on the face and can make Uncle Peter brown like toast. Uncle Peter is yellow in colour. Roxy is white. I am brown.' He peered at me. 'You are brown too, but a different brown from me.'

I poured more honey into his bowl. 'Hurry up and finish this. We are getting late for swimming.'

Raghu lifted a dripping spoon to his mouth and tasted the added sweetness. 'Yum! Roxy says her sister likes sweeties, but she doesn't.'

'Roxy has a sister?' The Wikipedia page on Pat MacPherson had mentioned an only child.

'She is a secret sister. She lives in Roxy's cupboard.'

'And why does she live in the cupboard?' I took the spoon from Raghu and wiped it on the edge of the bowl. 'See, if you wipe it like this, the cereal won't drip.'

'She has to live in the cupboard because she is mean and her mummy-daddy put her in the cupboard one day and Roxy is not to be mean and must do as her Yaya says, otherwise they will put her in the cupboard too.'

'It isn't true, Raghu. Mummy-Daddy love their children. They don't put them in cupboards.'

'But it is true, Ma.' Raghu's spoon tilted and cereal dribbled down his chin. 'Roxy said her sister gets very angry sometimes and sneaks out of the cupboard and does naughty things. One time she bit Roxy's Yaya so bad she had blood coming out of her hand and she threw away her mummy's nice red dress. But she loves Roxy and is never mean to her. Roxy says she'll tell her not to be mean to me.'

I wiped Raghu's mouth and chin. 'So, Roxy has a secret sister and a dragon in the garden. It seems like she lives in a fairyland.'

'She says I can come to her home for a sleepover and meet her sister. I told her I have to sleep with you because you tell me a story at night. But she said it is all bull and it is gross to sleep with mummy-daddy because they do not wear any clothes at night. You wear clothes when you sleep, no Ma?'

'Of course, beta. And you used a very bad word just now. You mustn't say "bull".'

Raghu shook his head. 'I didn't say it. Roxy said it.'

'Then you must tell her not to say it either.'

'Okay, Ma. I will tell her tomorrow. She says when the baby dragon is big, she and her sister will ride on him and come to school. Then she won't have to come with her Yaya and Uncle Peter. They are always pinching and tickling each other. Uncle Peter tickles Roxy too. He says it is a game, but Roxy doesn't like the game.'

I felt a chill run up and down my body, a tingling, like my arms and legs were going numb. I cleared my throat. 'Roxy must tell her mummy and daddy about Peter, Raghu.'

'She can't. He says if she is naughty, he will come at night and lock her in the cupboard and she will never be able to come out.'

'That is just nonsense. Tell her not to be scared of anyone. Her mummy and daddy will take care of her and punish Peter.'

Raghu looked at me solemnly. 'But Peter is not actually Peter, Ma. He is a monster. He can get so big, he can touch the roof and his eyes are red like traffic lights, and Roxy says he can smash the house. He'll do swoosh and the whole house will fall.' Raghu swung his arm. I caught the toppling bowl.

'Haven't we talked enough about Roxy? Close your eyes.' I sprayed sunblock on his face and arms and legs. 'Don't you have other friends? How about Sam and Isaiah?'

Raghu wiped his mouth with the back of his hand and wiggled into his bathing suit. 'I play with them only at games-time because Roxy says I am to marry her and must play only with her, otherwise she'll not tell me when the baby dragon is big.' I stowed bottles of water and lemonade, and my sunglasses in a wicker bag and locked the apartment door. 'I want to see the dragon when he is big.' Raghu reached out and pressed the button for the elevator. 'Right now he is small. His head is blue, and he has one yellow wing and two brown wings, and he can become invisible.' The elevator traversed the twenty floors noiselessly, and we stepped out. The brass-coloured sunlight glinting off the periwinkle swimming pool dazzled our eyes.

'Your posh friends are in the news!'

The Monday morning bustle was around us. I was slightly late and was hurriedly logging into my computer. Raghu had missed the school bus and I had dropped him off before coming to work. At the school gate, Roxy had waylaid me.

'What did Raghu do yesterday?' she asked raising her earnest eyes to me.

'Hello!' I smiled. 'We went swimming yesterday, and afterwards, Raghu ate a super-cone of frozen yoghurt. You had fun on Sunday?'

'I can't eat ice cream. I get all itchy and red. Can Raghu come to my home today?'

'Sorry, honey, but his daddy is back today after many days, and they have a plan for this evening.'

'Then tomorrow?'

'Let's see. Why don't you come over, and we can all go swimming or to the Botanic Gardens?' I bent down and caressed her freckled cheek. She drew back.

'He promised he would. It is mean of you to not let him.' Her lips trembled and her voice rose.

I straightened. 'I see. If he promised, then he must keep the promise. Now run along. You are getting late for the singing-circle.'

I clicked open my inbox. 'I have no friends, posh or otherwise.'

'Funny,' Saleena mimicked me. 'That is because you are so serious that you would rather critique a joke than laugh at it. I mean the fair Rosalie.' She tapped the screen of her computer with emerald-green gel nails. 'Seems she has wicked hands and is too free with them.'

'I couldn't understand a word of what you just said, Saleena. Plus I have a ninety-page contract in my inbox to review today.'

'The contract can wait. This is juicy, and the fox who wrote it has style too.' She read from the website open on her screen: '"The Lady M went shopping at a boutique in Clark Quay. Don't ask which one, dahlings, for you won't be able to enter it anyway. It is a 'by-appointments-only' temple of your simple, everyday clothes to wear to a millionaire's morning reception. The Lady M, for one reason or another, felt she did not receive the homage due to someone of her divine looks and her husband's even more divine bank balance and took the matter into her own hands, literally. In other words, she got shirty and slapped the shop assistant."'

I turned around. 'Slapped?'

'With her own pretty, pampered hands delivered a blow to a common working girl. The contamination will linger. I am wasted here, I should write gossip columns!' Saleena shook her head.

'I don't understand...'

'For an otherwise bright woman you are exceptionally obtuse this morning. What's unclear? She slapped the shop girl because she is a rich, spoilt bitch. Her past is strewn with slappings it seems. Anonymous sources are quoted here as saying she slapped helpers, punched a nurse, an attendant at China Club ... the list goes on.'

'But how do you know Lady M is Rosalie MacPherson?'

'Oh, because there is a photo of her here, right next to the article. Apparently, this website has cracked the defamation laws. They don't name the celebrity or socialite involved, just place a photo alongside. Now, if people want to put two and two together, it is their business.'

I stepped across to her desk. The photograph showed a tall, pale woman in a jade-green cheongsam, hair pulled back in a formal style. Her long eyes looked straight ahead and her lips were folded together in an unsmiling rosebud. 'I can't believe she is Roxy's mother...'

'WHAT A TRIP it was.' My husband leaned back against the pillows and stretched his legs. 'Loads of BS and precious little achieved. But I got my entire resource-request through. I execute more projects than teams many times bigger than mine. I gave them an ultimatum and they buckled. Your husband knows how to play his cards. Leave all that, yaar, come here.'

I dropped Raghu's LEGO pieces and picture books in the large toy-basket, and came over and sat on the edge of the bed. 'Abhay, Raghu said some disturbing things about Roxy the other day. I was planning to call her mother today, but there are stories in gossip papers about her...'

'You mean the slap-gate? It is even in *The Straits Times*. There's no real news to report and this ridiculous stuff makes headlines. Anyway, shop assistants can be a bloody pain here.'

'Saleena showed me an article that said she has a vicious temper. I told you the first time she called me how cold she sounded. And now she doesn't even bother to call, her maids call about play dates. Who behaves like this?'

'The Page-3-worthy wife of a rich and powerful man. Why does it bother you so much, though? Raghu seems to enjoy the play dates. It is only your ego that's hurt.'

'It is not that, Abhay. It just doesn't seem right. Roxy told Raghu the driver gets physical with her and threatens her. And today she screamed when I said Raghu can't come to her home. She seems a bit unstable. She has an imaginary sister, dragons in the garden, hiding places that no one knows of.'

'She has too much imagination, yaar, just like you. Seems like a woman's thing.' He looked at me through half-closed eyes. 'How come you never channel that wild imagination elsewhere? Come on, I am back after a week, and you are bothered about the MacPhersons.' His hand slid down the front of my T-shirt.

I GLANCED AT my ringing mobile and eased the headset off one ear. It was Raghu's school. I muted the conference call I was on. 'Mrs Suresan?' The woman's voice sounded tense. 'I am Anita Denver. I am the Infant School administrator. Could you come over to the school please?'

'Come over? You mean right now?'

'Yes, please. There's been a rather unfortunate incident. The school's medical officer has examined Raghu and he thinks Raghu will be just fine, but if...'

I stood up. The headset's wire caught in the chair's armrest and jerked my desk-phone to the floor. Saleena turned her chair to look at me. 'I am coming right away.'

'Please Mrs Suresan, there's nothing to panic about...'

I tore the headset off and grabbed my bag.

'Are you okay?' Saleena stepped over to my desk. 'What happened?'

'I ... Raghu...' I realized I didn't know what had happened to Raghu. My breath stuck in my chest. 'He isn't well. I need to go to his school right away.'

'Go, I'll tell the folks here.' She picked up my desk-phone. 'Call me if you need help, okay?'

I nodded.

A woman came up to me as I entered the school building. 'Mrs Suresan?' she said nervously, 'I am Anita. We just spoke. I am sorry you...'

'Where's Raghu?'

'Please calm down, Mrs Suresan...'

'I want to see my son.'

'Mrs Suresan.' Another woman appeared next to me. 'I am Susan Hall. I am the head of Elementary School. Could you please step this way? We can talk in my office.' She placed a hand on my elbow.

'Where's Raghu? Why can't I see him?'

'He is...'

'Ma...'

I turned. Raghu shook off the hand of a woman in a nurse's uniform and ran towards me. I picked him up. His mouth was swollen, his lip cut. There were nail-marks on his cheek. 'Ma...' I held him. My arms trembled and I couldn't see clearly. 'What happened, beta?'

'Please, Mrs Suresan, let's go into my office.'

Recess was just over. Children were swarming in the lobby, heading to their classes. 'Hey, Raghu!' one of them called out. Raghu laid his head on my shoulder.

The office was large. Susan Hall walked me to a comfortable sofa. 'Mrs Suresan, I am terribly sorry that Raghu is hurt. Believe me, we do everything to keep our children safe, but sometimes these unfortunate incidents happen.'

Raghu lay against my chest. His body felt hot, and I could feel his heartbeat. I saw red bite marks on his arms, bluing bruises on his shins. 'This isn't an unfortunate incident. He has been bitten, scratched and beaten. How did this happen?' My voice sounded loud in my own ears.

'He wouldn't play with me. He said he wanted to play with Sam and Isaiah. I gave him all my colours and I drew him pictures, and he said he didn't want to play with me.' I hadn't noticed Roxy or the man and woman seated beside the large writing desk on the other side of the room. Raghu clung to me. Tremors passed through his small body. The man and woman rose from where they sat beside the desk and came towards me.

'I am Pat MacPherson, Mrs Suresan. We are extremely sorry for what happened.' He and his wife seated themselves in the chairs next to the sofa. Roxy followed and stood between them, touching neither, blinking hard. 'She hasn't any siblings and she has gotten very attached to your son. Things got a bit out of hand it seems. Kids, you know. We will, of course, pay for your boy's treatment. Before you know he'll be fighting fit again.' He gave a short laugh.

The woman next to him remained silent. She did not look at her husband or Roxy. Her eyebrows slightly raised, she studied a glass case filled with trophies and awards.

'I will pay for your daughter's counselling. You need to take her to a good child psychologist,' I said. The woman's pale cheeks flushed, but she remained silent and still.

'Look, let's keep our cool. I know your husband. We are looking forward to working with him on a project. I spoke to him before you came and made my apologies. I think you'll find he agrees with me, that we should be reasonable about this and not get carried away. I can understand you are emotional right now.'

'And I can't understand why you aren't. You see how your child has hurt my son? Does this level of anger and aggression seem like a children's quarrel to you? Aren't you concerned about it? Or these kinds of incidents happen all too often in your family and you are used to them?'

Rosalie MacPherson turned her long, gold-lidded eyes towards me. Her mouth remained firmly closed. I looked at Susan Hall. 'I want to lodge a formal complaint. I also want to know whether this is the first incident of this sort or there have been others.'

Susan Hall's face blanched under her make-up. 'Mrs Suresan, a child's school records are confidential.'

'Not if the child puts other children at risk.'

'I ... we'll take the complaint to the School Board if you insist...' She looked sideways at Pat MacPherson.

'Look, Mrs Suresan, let's wait till your husband's back from his work trip. Let's all get together and discuss calmly. If you think about it, you'll see it is not such a big deal after all.'

I rose from the sofa. Raghu kept his head buried in my shoulder and wound his legs around my waist. 'I need to take

Raghu home.' Susan Hall came to the door of the office with me. 'Believe me, Mrs Suresan, we will act in the best interest of both the children. Raghu is a lovely boy. Very well-adjusted and very clever. We'll make sure he is comfortable at school.'

I turned and looked at her. She tried a reassuring smile. A nerve in her temple throbbed. 'I am not sending Raghu to school until you inform me about the action taken on my complaint. I will write to the school's trustees. I can't believe you put children at risk in this way.'

THE SCHOOL LOBBY was deserted. I sat in a plastic moulded chair, Raghu on my lap, and waited for our taxi to arrive. Raghu rubbed his eyes. His tongue explored the cut on his lip. I wiped his face with a wet wipe and tried to smile. 'Is it hurting, beta?'

'Yes...' he said. 'Roxy bit me, Ma, here and here.' He pointed to his arm. 'And she said she won't let me see the dragon when he is big...'

I rummaged in my bag and took out a box of juice. 'It's all right, beta. Dragons are not real anyway.' He slowly sucked on the straw. The MacPhersons emerged from the school building accompanied by Susan Hall and walked over to the far end of the lobby. Susan Hall came up to me and took a chair. 'We will work things out, Mrs Suresan. Here, Raghu, your class teacher has sent this for you.' She placed a Spiderman figurine on Raghu's pliant palm.

There was a patter of running feet. 'Roxy, come here.' A slightly nasal voice, cold, thin and taut like a wire, called out.

Roxy skidded to a stop before us. She held out a bit of paper towards Raghu. 'I made this for you.' It was the drawing of a brown lizard with a startling blue head and yellow neck-cone, mottled brown wing-like membranes extending from its sides.

'That's a lovely drawing of a Sumatran Flying Dragon, Roxy. It is a difficult-to-spot lizard. Well done on spotting it.' Susan Hall smiled a tight smile.

Raghu took the creased paper and looked at Roxy. 'It was your mean sister who punched me, no, Roxy?'

JANAKI AND THE BAT

The Peepul tree faced east. Its sunbaked brown branches spread wide, patches of the lightest of greys glimmered where the bark had peeled off. Clusters of deep green leaves, broad at the base and tapering to a fine tip, hung from slender green-yellow stalks. Rays of sun fell directly on the tree every morning, embracing it like the old friend it was. For the Peepul was ancient. No one knew its age; perhaps it had first flourished under a younger sun, on a less tired earth.

Though the Peepul itself was older than man's memory, everyone in the apartment complex knew the story of the English architect's love for it. The story went like this: Some white sahibs, and some brown ones who considered themselves only slightly less white, wanted to alleviate the hardships of living in a country where, at the stroke of one fateful midnight, some of the privileges they felt justly entitled to, vanished. To console them and save them from the contamination of the city's swelling population, the foreign companies they worked for decided to build homes for them, homes that would create new privileges in place of the old, lost ones, new barriers where the old had fallen. A young English architect was imported from the old kingdom for this purpose. As fate would have it, the architect fell for the blue and gold and green beauty of tropical Bombay. However, though young, he was not lacking in tact. He carefully hid his affliction from his employers and nodded his sympathy when they complained of its heat and dust and humidity. It only showed when he gazed at the endless taut sky over the rolling Arabian Sea or at the waving rows of coconut palms.

To continue with the story of the Peepul, the architect surveyed the areas from Colaba to Nepean Sea Road, Peddar Road, Carmichael Road, Altamount Road ... suffice it to say, he looked at all the right locations. Of course, he never considered congested Dadar or far-flung Parel. The sahibs had their offices and clubs firmly planted in the southern part of the city, and anything beyond the Turf Club was like crossing a border. He liked many places but again demonstrated that prodigious tact, which was to eventually lead him to the top of his profession and a knighthood, by choosing the softly rising heights of Malabar Hill for the construction site. It was at an acceptable distance away and above the city and had the view of the Arabian Sea that he himself never tired of. There was a slight issue, though – the land was owned by a small-time prince, and he had no wish to sell it. However, that was not a big hindrance. The companies had not forgotten the tactics that had acquired them kingdoms. Soon the land was in the possession of a collective of the sahibs, and the architect began taking measurements and laying out his plans.

The first time he saw the Peepul, already a grand tree then, he was mesmerized. He regarded its great girth, its spreading branches, the sunlight falling green-gold in the blue shade pooled under it, with awe. At that very moment, he decided to incorporate it into the architectural plans for the apartment complex. 'It would be sacrilege to fell this magnificent tree, older than any other I have seen,' he wrote in his diary in a pardonable moment of incautiousness. 'This tree will always stand here, on the eastern horn of this hill, raising its green arms towards its blood-brother, the Sun.'

In accordance with the plans drawn by him, six apartment blocks were constructed in a semi-circle with the Peepul holding court at one end of the arc. Upon completion of the construction, the young architect returned to England but left behind sketches of the tree as his tribute to its majestic beauty. The sketches hang to this day in the lobbies and clubhouse of the building, and the Peepul continues to flourish, its tightly plaited trunk and broad canopy resembling a colossal green bouquet. It casts a cool shade even at the height of summer, and under it mosses and clover thrive.

The Peepul's boughs lean close to Janaki's window. Sunlight filtering through its leaves fills her room with a soft, green radiance. In the evening, the moving branches create fanciful shadow-play on the walls. Chacha spoke against the tree from the beginning. 'Those branches cover the entire window. Your room already feels dank. In a couple of months monsoon will arrive and whatever little sunlight we may be lucky enough to get, this greedy tree will drink it all. It needs to be pruned for sure.'

Janaki objected. She found the friendliness of the close-leaning branches comforting in this strange city. 'I like it. The leaves make such a lovely rustling sound against my window, and you are advocating violence against it. What kind of a botanist are you, Chacha?'

This further irritated Chacha. 'First of all, I am not a botanist, I am a physicist. In all these years, this one simple fact has not managed to lodge itself in your head. Secondly, this tree does not need your protection. It is a Ficus, the most stubborn of the fig family. It takes root with little encouragement, and then nothing short of an earthquake can shake it out.'

'You know so much about trees and you say you aren't a botanist! And if Peepul Raja is tenacious and strong, it only proves it has the right to live. You only taught me about the survival of the fittest.'

Chacha had taken time off work to coach Janaki in science for her high school exams. Despite her lack of interest and inattention, he had persisted in the hope that she would eventually see the pure light of science. It was only when Janaki opted for Accounting and Economics that he finally gave up.

'You leave science alone now. You only have brains for adding and subtracting like a baniya. When all of you fall sick because of this damp, pestilential tree, then you'll see. We are superior species, there's nothing wrong with sacrificing a few of this Peepul's branches for your health,' Chacha said decisively.

'How are we superior, Chacha? We've only been around for a hundred thousand years or so, the trees have been here for aeons.'

'This argument is unnecessary. Bhai,' he turned to Janaki's father, 'you must raise the issue of pruning the trees in the management committee meeting. This building has turned into a jungle. I told you, look for a flat in a newer development, but...'

Janaki's brows creased, her mouth rounded in a pout. 'Papa, don't do that. This tree and the old garden make this place so special.'

In the end, their argument proved unnecessary. The building's residents were proud of the fact that the rules for the building's management had also been written by the young English architect and, like the building itself, had never been altered. They believed it proved the pedigree of the building. A special mention was made of the Peepul in those rules. 'The Ficus religiosa at the eastern end of the building is a protected tree owing to its great age,' the rules stated. 'A record of the tree has been presented to the Natural Heritage Society, and the Municipal Commission of the city has exempted it from seasonal pruning.' Only loose or damaged branches were allowed to be cut. 'Any harm to the green and healthy branches will attract sanction against the offender, including but not limited to a fine.' Though the fine was the princely sum of five rupees – after all the rules were written in the fifties – the Peepul's inviolable status was established. When she heard of it, Janaki's laughter had chimed like the leaves of the Peepul.

JANAKI HAD MOVED to Mumbai this summer with her parents. Her father worked for a large company and had been transferred to its head office in Mumbai. A promotion was imminent, and he often returned late from work. Chacha had been working at a well-known research institute in Mumbai for the past several years. He hadn't married, and since their move to Mumbai, most evenings found him at Janaki's home. 'He is a great help,' Janaki's mother said. 'It is because of him that Mumbai feels like home.'

'Not to me,' Janaki answered. All her friends were back in Kolkata, and she felt lonely at the thought of going to a college where she knew no one. 'Who could be happy to exchange the four seasons of Kolkata for the two-and-a-quarter of Mumbai?' The phrase was Papa's: 'Mumbai only has two seasons,' he would say, 'summer and monsoon, and if you are very charitable, a barely-there-winter – two-and-a-quarter seasons.'

In reality, Chacha's presence did help. The evenings he visited, Mummy prepared something special – okra filled with roasted spices or fried bitter gourd, or rice cooked with almonds and raisins and saffron, or delicacies made from cottage-cheese and milk-cream. He brought along books he thought Janaki should read, and the gram flour and lentil savouries she liked. Janaki complained to him about Mumbai's weather and crowds. 'I can never go out in this city. The heat's a killer, and there are already so many people everywhere, I don't feel like I want to add to the crowd.'

'Moving here has been good for you then. You used to waste time roaming about all day long in Kolkata. At least now you will stay at home and study for your college-entrance exams,' Chacha retorted, and though Janaki pouted, the bickering and arguing made the evenings pass.

The pre-monsoon heat of Mumbai was breathless and humid. Windows were closed and curtains drawn before ten in the morning, and air-conditioners hummed all day long. In the oppressive closeness, the Peepul's shade seemed cool and inviting to Janaki. Its tapered leaves chimed and trembled without any breeze, and the mosses and wild grasses growing under it formed a thick, soft carpet. She took to sitting under the Peepul with her books and a bottle of chilled water as soon as the sun began its westward decline. The house-help spied her under the Peepul. 'Janaki baba sits under that old Peepul in the evening,' she reported to Janaki's mother. 'All sorts of spirits and ghosts live in the Peepul. Janaki baba is unmarried...' She widened her eyes. 'Don't let her sit there in the evening. The Peepul's Dev looks for beautiful virgins to possess...'

Mummy brought it up at dinner time. 'Suneeta is afraid that Janaki will be possessed by the spirits who live in the Peepul,' she said serving hot kachoris in everyone's plates.

'It is too late for that particular fear. She has been possessed by that unruly tree since the first day.' Chacha broke open the crisp crust of the kachori to cool it and some of the crushed lentil-filling spilled on to his plate. Janaki reached over and picked the filling with her fingers. 'So spicy!' she said licking her fingertips. 'And Chacha, it's you who has been possessed by the Peepul. You always have something to say about it – get rid of it, it blocks the window, it is the home of diseases!' she mimicked curling her mouth. 'It is so cool in the Peepul's shade, and you should see its leaves dance even when there is no breeze.' She took a piece of crust from Chacha's plate.

'How will you get admission in any college with your poor manners and utter ignorance?' Chacha chided her but gave half of the cooled kachori from his plate to Janaki. 'The Peepul has what's known as drip-tip leaves. They are light and their stalks are flexible, and the slightest movement of air causes them to move.'

'This is not about the Peepul—' Mummy replaced the cooling roti with a fresh hot one on Papa's plate, '—this is about you sitting on the damp grass in the evening with half the population of mosquitoes and bugs in the neighbourhood around. You will fall sick.'

'What bugs? There are no bugs. You should come and sit there yourself in the evening, then you'll see,' Janaki said.

Both Chacha and Mummy protested in unison. Papa placed his spoon carefully in his bowl of dal and looked up. 'From tomorrow onwards, do not sit on the grass, Janaki. Take a folding chair.' Janaki laughed.

'You are allowing her to sit under that tree in the evenings?' Chacha challenged.

'Why not? Unless you believe in the Peepul's ghosts and spirits.'

Chacha was silenced.

IT WAS MAY and the humidity was intense. Under the Peepul, it smelt of rain.

'I see you are ensconced on your throne.'

Janaki looked up. Chacha had come directly from office. He had a leather satchel slung across his shoulder and was carrying his lunchbox in his hand. 'Chacha, you look like a college student! So cute! Really, how old are you?'

'As old as this Peepul. Why are you bent upon blinding yourself reading in this gloomy place?'

'I was just about to go home.' Janaki rose. 'It is so quiet here. If you listen closely, you can hear the sap rise in the roots.'

'It is just the sound of water seeping into this clayey soil.' Chacha pressed the moss under the tree with his foot. 'This moss retains moisture too. There must be mosquitoes here.' Chacha looked at Janaki's sleeveless kurta.

'Nope, none. The spirits of the Peepul have devoured them all! But look at these...' She pointed to the knob-like fruits studding the branches of the Peepul. 'I didn't know a Peepul bore fruits. These were green until a week ago and now they are red.'

Chacha plucked a maroon tinted fruit from a low-hanging branch. 'Ficus's figs. In fact, these are very clever creations of nature. These are not just fruits, they are also its flowers. Fruit, flower, seeds – all in one neat pack. Economy of structure.' He pressed the fig between his fingers and the fruit split, spilling its pale pink flesh and minute black seeds. 'These are still raw. When they ripen, birds will eat them.'

CHACHA WAS RIGHT. As the figs ripened, birds began arriving on the Peepul in an avian beauty parade – showy golden orioles with kohl-like black markings around their eyes, elegantly shaped bulbuls with crested heads, pale green leafbirds, small enough for two to fit with ease on one Peepul leaf, common mynahs with flashes of white hidden in their glossy brown wings, coppersmiths with red marks burning on their heads, and numerous others. The Peepul was noisy during the day with them, and every evening Janaki found the ground under it littered with half-eaten fruit which broke with a satisfying crunch underfoot.

It was around this time, with Peepul-figs ripening rapidly in the May heat, that the bats arrived. One evening, as the brief lilac-coloured dusk fell, Janaki saw a number of them winging their way darkly across the sky, their black, arched shapes drawn boldly against the delicate shell-pink sunset. She admired their deliberate, almost imperial flight. Unlike the birds which fluttered and darted nervously among the branches during the day, the bats knew they ruled the darkening skies. Janaki's heart beat faster as they began landing on the Peepul's branches. She quickly gathered her books and retreated to the shelter of the building.

'Oho, so you came up early today?' Chacha commented as Janaki entered the flat. He and Papa were sipping tea in the living room. Papa had returned from his business trip that evening and the house seemed lighter, livelier. 'It must be because of you, Bhai, otherwise Bhabhi has to send Suneeta at least twice to call her home. Our Janaki thinks it is a kindness to let the mosquitoes feed on her blood.'

Janaki took the cup from Papa's hand and took a sip of his tea. 'No sugar.' She made a face. 'Chacha, give me your tea, na.'

'You might not know the way to the kitchen since you never visit it, but it is right there. Go and get some for yourself.'

Janaki curled her mouth and picked up a slice of fig from the platter. 'Chacha, you are so ungenerous. Are you really my papa's brother?' She settled next to Papa. 'There are bats on the Peepul today, Papa. I never saw so many at once in Kolkata. Suneeta di says they bite off your ears and suck blood.'

'Excellent, absolutely fantastic,' Chacha grimaced. 'The source of all your knowledge is now Suneeta. Kindly try to read some of the books I've given you instead of imbibing this nonsense.'

'You mean bats don't bite?'

'Of course they bite, but only if you bother them. Even rats and squirrels bite if they are cornered. But the Chiroptera are generally harmless creatures. In fact, they are beneficial – they eat rats and other vermin. The ones generally seen around here are the Indian flying foxes. They are a Megachiroptera, which, as you doubtless know, or' – he added with a touch of asperity – 'you would have known had you paid any attention to your science lessons, are the larger fruit bats.'

'Chiroptera,' Papa repeated. 'Interesting name. It means hand-wing in old Greek.' Learning languages was Papa's thing. He had the beginners' books on a number of languages, ranging from Mandarin to German. 'It is very humbling to try to learn a language,' he would say. 'How can you feel arrogant when you can't pronounce "window" in Japanese or when you discover that there are more words for "colour" in Turkish than you can hope to learn?'

'Exactly. Bats are called hand-wings for obvious reasons. They are mammals like us and have digits on their hands. What people generally refer to as their wings are actually membranes stretched between these elongated digits. The flying foxes are fruit bats; they eat only fruit, like the Guru ji your mother had insisted on taking you to when you were little and who had blessed you with a bad case of whooping cough.' Janaki's mother, who had been frying mathris in the kitchen, merely smiled and set down a plate of the crisp and crumbly savouries on the table. 'In fact,' he continued, 'bats are amazing creatures in many ways. The flying fox has passable eyesight, but most bats have very poor vision. They use echolocation to find their way. What that means, Janaki, is that they make noises, and when the sound waves bounce against an object, an echo is produced. The bats judge where the object is, what's its size, and so on, from this echo. Really amazing stuff.' Chacha took a satisfied sip of the tea.

'But bats call only on moonless nights...'

'I told you, you should not source all your information from Suneeta. Just wait, you'll hear them call tonight.'

'But...'

Chacha sighed. 'If I give you my tea, would you stop inflicting your ignorance on me, at least for this evening?'

Laughing, Janaki took the teacup from his hand.

That night, Janaki stood at the window and watched the bats. They hung like paper lanterns from the topmost to the lowest branches of the tree and moved with the agility of acrobats, catching hold of twigs laden with fruit and bending them to feed on the Peepul's abundance. They were of all sizes – small and flimsy, like wisps of carbon paper, and large and rustling, like a ceiling fan. One particularly attracted her attention. It hung close to her window and was as large as a raptor. Moving along the length of the branch, balancing itself with feet and claw, it deftly picked a fig and bit into it. It proceeded to suck the juice and the soft flesh of the fruit and dropped the shell on the soft earth under the Peepul. Then it pirouetted and opened its wings, darkening the shadowy night gathered on the tree. Janaki saw its rat-like body, the male organ showing dark and protuberant on the pale belly. She raised her eyebrows and moved away from the window.

THOUGH IT WAS early morning, the summer sun, red like a pomegranate, was already high in the sky. Janaki opened the window to make the ritual offering of water and honey to the sun. She let the water trickle slowly from the small silver lota and repeated the twelve names of the Sun God. A shadow moved on a branch nearby as she finished. It was the bat from last night, hanging upside down on the Peepul's shade-filled branch. Janaki looked as it moved to the tip of the branch. The red-gold fur on its throat glowed and its leathery wings, tightly wrapped around its body like a shawl, gleamed. 'You are quite magnificent. Perhaps I should make an offering to you too?' She sprinkled a few drops in the bat's direction and chanted, 'O King among Bats, you carry the night on your wings and dawn in your throat. Please accept this offering of water sweetened with honey.'

'Hai Ram! Janaki baba, who are you talking to?' Suneeta entered the room.

'To this bat. He has been hanging here all night. All his friends have left but he is still here.'

Suneeta's eyes popped. She quickly closed the window. The bat hung there like a dark cloth-bundle.

THE SKY HAD begun to darken and Janaki was in her usual place under the Peepul when a fig dropped onto her lap – ripe, smooth and hard. She looked up. The bat was hanging from one of the lower branches. Janaki smiled and raised her hand in a mock salute. 'Thanks for the fig, O King! You've been here the whole day?' She gathered her books. 'There come your subjects. I shall take your leave.'

Bats were circling the Peepul, looking for perches to land. The large bat, rocking on its branch, slowly spread its spined wings and rose. It emitted long cries and wheeled between the tree and the group of bats coming to feed. Janaki was intrigued. The group hovered in air, but the bat flew diagonally between them and the tree, truncating their flight, not allowing them to land. After several unsuccessful attempts, the group began to turn back one by one. Left in solitary possession of the tree, the bat settled back on its roost, opening and folding its wings a few times.

'I HEARD YOU'VE been chatting with a bat,' Chacha said accepting the glass of iced raw-mango panna that Mummy offered. 'Your science teacher was just telling us.'

'Janaki baba was calling it "O King"! An ugly, stinking beast as that...' Suneeta ducked into the kitchen with the tray.

'He is not ugly or stinking. He is handsome and valiant. He just chased a group of bats away.' Janaki dropped her books on the table. 'Perhaps he is this Peepul's Dev, Chacha, the Guardian of the Peepul Tree!'

'Rubbish! You've surpassed even your teacher in nonsense. Indian flying foxes are not solitary. They are gregarious creatures and live in large colonies.' He moved Janaki's books to one side and placed his empty glass on the table. 'And it is a camp of bats by the way, not a group.'

'Well, this one is. He lives alone and comes to my window every night. I can swear he looks at me, Chacha. He even dropped a fig in my lap this evening.' Janaki held up the fig.

'Come. Papa is at the dining table already,' Mummy called.

'What imagination our Janaki has!' Chacha said settling into the chair next to Papa. 'Did you hear the latest, Bhai? There's a bat who is the god or whatever of the Peepul tree, and he just gave Janaki his blessing. In the form of an inedible fig!'

'You are just jealous because such a handsome bat likes me!' Janaki moved her eyes and neck from side to side like a dancer. 'Do you think he will eat a mango? I will leave a slice on the window tonight.'

'Don't be foolish, Janaki. Bats are not domestic animals. They are the biggest carriers of rabies. Keep your window closed at night,' Chacha said sternly.

'I once held baby bats in my hand.' Papa tore a hole in the roti puffed up like a balloon to let the steam out. 'Do you remember?' He glanced at Chacha. The gardener had opened the water-metre box and there was a bat's nest in it. We had picked up the baby bats and taken them to Maiya.'

'I don't remember,' Chacha said shortly. 'Anyway, Janaki must stay away from them. They are wild creatures, they aren't safe.'

'You confuse me, Chacha!' Janaki curled her mouth. 'The other day you said bats are harmless and now you say they aren't safe! What did the baby bats look like, Papa? Were they soft and furry?'

'They were ugly like rats, and dry and papery. That gardener was a fool. Maiya had scolded him for allowing us to hold those dirty creatures,' Chacha said irritably.

'Oho, suddenly you remember everything!' Janaki's laughter rolled like waves.

The Peepul's bat defied Chacha's scientific knowledge. The group of bats didn't return after their aborted landing, and it continued to live in the tree in solitary splendour. Only the bold mynahs or flocks of noisy parrots ventured to the Peepul during the day and dared eat its figs, but they stayed away from the bat and took flight if it moved amongst the branches. As soon as Janaki's chair was placed under the tree, it appeared and hung from a nearby branch, balancing its great mass on the slender stalks, making leaf-clusters tremble and rustle. Janaki gazed at it as she memorized her notes. With its pinions spread and claws jutting out and the glorious sunset-coloured fur around its neck, the bat looked like a caped superhero to her.

June had begun, and the humid heat was at its peak. The wind was heavy with unshed moisture. Everyone was irritable and everything seemed impossible. Mummy wanted to buy new curtains, and Janaki was doing the rounds of furnishing shops with her. It had been three days, and they had been to all the shops from Colaba to Warden Road, but Mummy hadn't been able to make up her mind.

'I am not coming with you this evening,' Janaki said picking up her books. 'My entrance exams are close. I need to study.'

'It is just a couple more shops. Mrs Pai told me there's one near Churchgate.'

'I can't stand one more stuffy shop or oily salesman. And whatever I like, you find too dull or something.'

'I don't know what you will do when you have a home of your own, you have so little patience.'

'Little patience? We have seen tons of curtains. You just can't make up your mind. And anyway, I won't take so long to choose anything.'

'We got very little opportunity to choose,' Mummy said, but she put away her handbag. 'Perhaps I will go with the deep blue silk we saw the first day. I have the swatches. I'll show them to your papa and chacha today to see what they think.'

'Yeah, also show them to the neighbours and the sabzi-wallah and the guy who walks his dog in the lane. You don't know what you like unless others like it too.' Janaki descended the stairs.

There was no breeze, and it was only slightly cooler under the Peepul. Janaki settled into her chair and opened her book. The branches rustled. She smiled. 'You are late today, Bat-King.' The rustling changed to a scraping sound. She raised her head. The bat was on the fluted trunk of the Peepul, its wings outspread, slipping down slowly. It came all the way down and, with one clawed wing hooked into the protruding roots, stretched on the ground near Janaki. Inching forward, it reached out a wing and moved it over her slippered foot. Janaki sat transfixed. Flourishing colours of sunset reflected in its glass-bead eyes, the glinting fur on its neck prickled. Uttering low cries, the bat dragged itself forward and rested its body on her feet. Janaki felt the bat's weight and the touch of its dry, rough wings. Bending, she reached out and touched the warm fur on its throat. The bat's body jerked, a long tongue emerged from its mouth, so long that Janaki wondered how it fitted in the neat little pouch of its mouth, pointed like a fox's. It began licking her right foot, tracing its slender shape. The lithe tongue curled around her ankle, her smooth heel, caressed the protruding ankle bone and the hollow under it.

Dusk deepened and lights came on in Janaki's home. 'Janaki baba...' Suneeta came out to call her. In the dimness under the Peepul, she saw the bat at Janaki's feet. Screaming she ran back towards the house. Janaki got up hastily. The bat slid off her feet to the ground. The bat's cries echoed in her ears as she climbed the stairs to her home.

'Bhabhi, come quickly ... That demon ... it is biting Janaki baba. I told you ... virgin girl ... the bat...' Suneeta was panting.

'Suneeta di, Mummy, it's okay. The bat wasn't biting me. It was ... it...'

'It was as big as a palm leaf, Bhabhi ... coal-black ... on Janaki baba's feet ... teeth like the kitchen knife...'

'Arre, Suneeta di, stop it. When did you see his teeth?'

'Go, get the first-aid box, Suneeta.' Mummy's face was ashen and tight. 'And warm water. Janaki, come, sit here.'

'Mummy, please yaar, I am okay. Look—' Janaki took off her slippers. The shiny, smooth skin of her feet had a pink flush and was unblemished.

'What's that about a bat? What happened?'

'Nothing, really, Mummy...'

'He was going to suck her blood, Bhabhi. It flew away because I screamed.' Suneeta was back with the first-aid box. Chacha emerged from the spare room with Papa's air gun. He liked taking it apart and cleaning it every once in a while. 'What happened?'

'What would happen, sa'ab? It is that Peepul. Black magic. Janaki baba couldn't move. I screamed so much...'

'You are still screaming. Janaki, what happened?'

'The bat came down from the tree today...'

'What do you mean – came down? To the ground? Flying foxes are arboreal. They aren't ground-dwellers.'

'He is just lonely, Chacha, all by himself like this. I think he just wants to be friends. He knows me now, so...'

'Don't talk nonsense, Janaki.' Chacha's brows creased. 'I have told you, bats are wild creatures. You can't be friends with a bat.' His voice rose.

Papa entered. 'The door's open, your voices can be heard on the landing.'

'Bhai, a bat attacked Janaki today. Came down the tree and tried to bite her.'

'I recited a mantar and scared it away, sa'ab.' Suneeta improved her narrative.

'You have to stop her from sitting under that tree all evening. As it is, it's damp and unhealthy, and now there's a mad bat. She just refuses to understand.' The veins on Chacha's forehead stood out.

'Papa, the bat did not attack me. He is ... just so lonely. And it's so hot all the time, steaming like a sauna. I feel caged indoors all day. That Peepul's shade is the only cool place.' Janaki's eyes became moist. 'I don't know why you all hate him so much. I like him. He is handsome.'

'Handsome? Have you seen its claws? And teeth? Sharp like a wild dog's. You need to stop this, Bhai.'

Papa raised his eyebrows. 'Is this a matter of such heated debate? Janaki can decide for herself. If the Peepul is indeed so unhealthy and infested with bloodthirsty beasts, surely, it can't be comfortable, but if she prefers its shade over everywhere else, it can't be all that bad.' He went into his room to change.

Janaki continued to spend her evenings in the dubious guardianship of the Peepul, the bat hanging by her side, swaying gently, preening, and occasionally showering her with figs and beautiful, new copper-pink leaves from the Peepul.

UNBELIEVABLY, THE HEAT continued to mount along with the humidity. Water vapour rose from the clayey earth and the sky turned the colour of smoke. The shade of the Peepul, too, felt oppressive, airless. Janaki was bathed in sweat even in her thinnest mulmul kurta and felt exhausted. Only the bat, hanging on a low branch, seemed untouched by the heat. 'This weather's intolerable, Bat-King.' She wiped her face and pushed back the soft tendrils of hair stuck to her cheeks and neck. 'I want to bury myself in ice. I think I will go home early today.' The bat rocked gently. The Peepul's leaves rustled. Suddenly, without any warning, it let go of its perch and dropped like a stone into Janaki's lap. Its wide-open wings spanned her thighs, embracing them. Its clawed hands dug gently into the thin cloth of her tunic. It moved in her lap, head raised, eyes fixed on her, tongue darting out. Janaki felt a rush in her blood. A pulse beat violently in the hollow of her neck. She bit her lip and forced herself to remain still. Then, as suddenly as it had descended on to her lap, the bat pushed against her, and with a violent heave, rose. Its arched wings grazed her face as it lurched towards her head. Ducking reflexively, she screamed and tumbled off the chair. The bat wrenched around in mid-flight. Its wings tore against the lower branches of the Peepul. Emitting piercing cries, it fell with a thud on the ground and thrashed around. It was then that Janaki saw the triangular head of the snake grasped in its clawed hand, the long body whipping viciously against the bat's own. She trembled violently. Her screams mingled with the bat's cries.

Windows were thrown open. Mummy leaned out. 'Janaki, Janaki...' she called, her voice wavering. Chacha raced down the stairs carrying the air gun, followed by Papa. He caught sight of the bat writhing on the ground near Janaki and turned the air gun clutched in his hands towards it. In an instant, the earth at her feet was pierced with the flat-headed, pinch-waisted metal pellets of the air gun. They lodged in the struggling bat's soft chest and belly. Blood oozed from the holes and darkened its shining fur. It shrieked and thrashed about for a few moments, still holding on to the wriggling snake.

'A snake!' Chacha exclaimed as he saw the snake in the dying bat's grip. He quickly raised the air gun and brought the butt down with force on the snake's head. 'It is a young vine snake, fairly venomous. Must have been in the tree; they live in trees.' He turned the bat over with the toe of his shoe. 'This one's quite a fine specimen. Full-grown. We can get it stuffed. Are you okay, Janaki?'

Janaki's father held her as she struggled to free herself. Tears streamed down her cheeks. She was calling out endearments and curses in a hoarse voice. Evening light fell on the bat's open, dead eyes. Its ears, like leaves of polished leather, and the auburn mantle around its neck, quivered as the first drops of rain finally fell.

THE BIG TOE

'It might seem strange to you,' said the man with the sad eyes, 'but someone's entire life can be marred by a disfigured finger or toe.'

I smiled at his exaggeration. 'Just one finger?'

The man averted his eyes. 'A big toe, to be precise. I am not making it up. This has happened with a friend of mine.'

I was intrigued. I am always on the lookout for stories. You could say I am a sort of collector of curious tales. It irritates my wife. She considers it one of my small-town vices. 'You and your plebian nosiness,' she says. But whatever she might say, I have a treasure trove of strange stories because of my habitual curiosity. They serve as great ice-breakers everywhere I go, from client meetings to dinner with friends. I looked at the man with the sad eyes. He had gone back to eating his dosa, breaking small bits of the paper-thin crêpe, dipping it in sambar and chewing carefully.

We were at a popular eatery in Matunga. 'Authentic South Indian Food', the old signboard, faded by years of monsoon rains and blazing sun, declared in severe, straight-edged lettering. And authentic it was. It was the spicy, aromatic oily food that had drawn me here from the other end of Bombay on a Sunday afternoon. I had entered the restaurant at the fag end of the lunchtime rush. Another fifteen minutes or so and the tables would have emptied for the next two hours when the evening-snack crowd would begin trickling in. But I was hungry and didn't wish to wait. So I pulled the first empty chair at a two-seater table and signalled to the waiter. There was no need to observe the formality of asking permission from the other occupant of the table. It wasn't that kind of a place, eating was not a drawn-out ceremony here; it was a quick but intensely experienced ritual – you sat wherever you found a seat, ordered without consulting the menu that had remained proudly unchanged since the time of the restaurant's founder, and left as soon as you finished your meal. Still, the man on the other side lifted his head and fixed me with his sad eyes in such a way and for so long that I felt obliged to offer my hunger as an excuse.

'I ran seven kilometres this morning, and my wife insists that fruits are the only healthy breakfast, so you can imagine how hungry I must be. I hope it is not inconvenient, my sitting here.'

'No, of course not. It is nice to have another person across the table. I eat alone all the time, always alone...' he repeated in a low tone.

'But that's impossible. No one can be always alone in Bombay, there isn't enough space in the city for that!' I tried to share with him some of the Sunday brightness that brimmed inside me.

The sadness in his eyes only deepened. His lips moved soundlessly as if he knew that what he had to say wasn't worth listening to. I tried again, 'Take me for example. My wife and kids don't like the smell of sambar-dosa or being served by waiters who wipe the tables down with a smelly rag and don't wear uniforms, so I decided to eat what I like by myself. But here I am sitting with you instead of eating alone.'

'Oh ... if you'd like to eat alone ... I ... I can move to another table.' Half-rising, he glanced around. 'One is sure to become empty soon...'

'I didn't mean it that way at all' – I tried to salvage the situation – 'I was just illustrating the point that one can't be alone in this city.' The man with the sad eyes sighed.

Our food arrived. We had both ordered the house-specialties – paper-thin dosa coated with a spicy paste, a serving of mashed potatoes fried in ghee and garnished with a handful of lentils on the side, rasam tangy with tamarind, and chutneys. Rounding his shoulders further, my companion slipped back his shirtsleeves and began eating. I noticed he held his elbows close to his sides and kept his head averted slightly, as if he had somehow guessed my expensive car, my fat salary, the newly-bought apartment in the old part of the city. I tried to put him at his ease. 'The food here reminds me of my student days when, every once in a while, I used to forget about my budget and splurge on south Indian thalis with friends. I remember the taste of that food to this day – appams and vegetables in a coconut stew and medu-vada fried in ghee. I would spend two hundred to three hundred rupees on it. In those days, that used to be a lot of money for me.'

The man looked at me through the corners of his sad eyes and wobbled his head. I was chagrined. Perhaps that sum was still a big deal for him. I am proud of my ability to talk to people from all classes, but today I seemed to be saying one wrong thing after another. I beckoned to one of the waiters and pointed to the empty chutney bowl. He hurried over and set small bowls filled with white, grainy coconut chutney and smooth, spicy tomato-and-lentil paste on our table. I noticed he had a tiny sixth digit hanging helplessly beside his right thumb. 'Six fingers! You are a lucky man!'

The waiter, a skinny boy with ribs peeking through his worn shirt and thin legs sticking out of a pair of dirty shorts, glanced at his hand with shy pride. 'I had wanted the vaid in my village to chop it off; the boys used to tease me so about it. But my folks said it is very lucky. So I kept it.' He touched the digit softly. It was a mere piece of cartilage with no bones. For a moment, the man with the sad eyes looked at the tiny finger, trembling and useless like a severed tail, and then quickly looked away.

'I see that you do not believe in such superstitions.' I felt an urge to engage my melancholy companion in a conversation. How could he be downcast in this place humming with sated voices, redolent with fried food, and reminiscent of a time when I was young and the world was just opening up for me? Life had turned out fine for me, I had done well, earned my place in the world, and I wanted the man with the sad eyes to cheer up a bit. It was right then that he made the dramatic statement about fingers and toes ruining lives.

My curiosity was tickled. I pushed my chair back and stretched my legs. The lunchtime rush had abated, and the restaurant was emptying swiftly. 'I must say I have never considered fingers or toes to be of such importance that they have the power to ruin a life! I have a misshapen digit myself.' I spread my right hand and displayed my squashed thumb. 'I caught this in a gate one summer vacation. You can say it was a just punishment. I was throwing stones at the ripening guavas in the neighbour's orchard. The guard came after me and I just sprinted out the iron gate, pushing it shut hurriedly behind me. That's when I caught my thumb in it. I still remember it hurt like hell.'

I have never felt disadvantaged by my squashed thumb. It has always been an object of interest. In the early days of marriage, my wife used to caress its rough, discoloured surface with her pretty fingers. 'Guava thief,' she would say, her eyes alight, and kiss it. It also makes for a connection with others like me who grew up in small towns and made good in the big world. The story of my guava-theft has broken the ice in many a meeting and invoked nostalgia in successful entrepreneurs and professionals with bright, shining, big-city lives, for the homes they had once been impatient to leave. You can say that my thumb has served as a bridge to memories of lost times and forgotten places.

The man with the sad eyes cast a furtive look at my thumb. 'It must have been painful – the injury, I mean ... But there's not much wrong with your thumb. It is slightly squashed and the nail is curved, but it is otherwise normal in shape and a healthy colour. My friend's case is completely different. Your thumb can't be compared with his big toe...'

The waiter brought over aromatic, chicory-flavoured filter coffee in steel tumblers. The man with the sad eyes spooned more sugar into the already sweetened coffee and poured some into a steel bowl to cool.

'A toe is bound to be different, but it has the added advantage of being hidden most of the times, unlike a thumb which is out there for all to see,' I said. 'Unless you are a surgeon or a thief and wear gloves!'

He took a sip of the coffee. The cloying sweetness reached some secret place inside him and, for a moment, the despondency in his eyes lightened. 'If you give it a thought, you'd be surprised to note on how many important occasions and places we have to be barefoot. Birth, death, temples, ritual banquets, in bed ... And for my friend, it wasn't even possible to completely hide his big toe. His situation was very bad ... and through no fault of his own, his whole life was ruined...'

'All because of a misshapen big toe? It has to be an acute case for that to happen.'

'Yes. I see you find it difficult to believe, but if you knew his story you'd understand.'

I smiled encouragingly. I could see he wanted to tell me the story. It happens to me a lot. People want to tell me their stories. God provides sugar for the one who feeds on sugar, as the saying goes. 'Then why not tell me? What could be a better way to relax on a Sunday afternoon after that big meal we ate than listening to the story of the life-destroying big toe? That is, if you have the time.'

The man with the sad eyes looked at the open door. Outside, the weekend hawkers' market was in full swing. Women in shiny sarees, chains of white and orange flowers adorning their hair, were thronging the shops that sold stainless steel utensils and other household articles. Children dressed in stiff, occasionally worn clothes, faces sticky with sweets, ran everywhere. Men with faux-leather belts encircling their pot bellies walked about complacently, casting satisfied looks around. The whole atmosphere was of a minor festival, and no one seemed to mind the harsh midday sun. He let out a sigh. His shoulders drooped even further. 'Time isn't an issue for me but ... my friend's life-story is not for a relaxing Sunday afternoon. His life ... In fact, he has no life, not in the real sense.'

'I can't agree with you here. However miserable you might think someone is, there is always something that keeps them going.'

'Most of the time it is the habit of living that keeps them going,' the man said slowly, 'and inertia and the utter unfamiliarity of death. Life's just more familiar than death ... If,' his voice rose slightly, his bunched-up body straightened, 'if death were not wrapped in such mystery, if we were not taught to fear it and knew exactly what would happen after death, if we were sure that consciousness, memory, the burden of a lifetime would be extinguished in one stroke, half the world would choose death over life.' White foam collected in the corners of his mouth. He placed his elbows on the table and leaned forward. 'If you think about it, the solution to all of life's problems is just one – death. Once everyone discovers that, why only half the world, the entire human race would choose death. That's why religion and law employ all kinds of tricks to make death seem fearsome when it is the only relief ... the only cure ... to living out of habit and fear...' His mouth curved in disdain.

I raised my eyebrows. 'You mean your friend's life is not worth living and he should commit suicide?'

He shrank away. His elbows slid off the table and his shoulders rounded again. 'My friend doesn't have the courage...' He gave me his sideways, defeated glance. 'Believe me when I say that from the day he was born, he has been hated because of his cursed toe. Even his own mother ... He was in breach position and the doctor had to cut open his mother's belly to birth him. The first thing the doctor saw was the large, misshapen toe; she thought it was some kind of worm or parasite that had attached itself to the baby's foot. It was only her years of training that prevented her from dropping the baby. When she thrust him into the nurse's arms, the young and inexperienced nurse let out shriek after shriek. Her screams were heard outside the operation theatre, and my friend's father, who was of a nervous temperament, suffered a heart attack and had to be hospitalized. The task of looking after the baby and the unconscious mother fell upon the relatives. They swaddled the baby, taking care not to look at the toe, for even a glimpse of it set everyone retching, and did not say a word to the mother...' He took out a large handkerchief from his pocket and wiped his face.

'But why didn't they tell his mother?'

'Because his mother had a special liking for feet...'

'A foot fetish?'

'No, no, nothing like that ... She was just very fond of tiny baby feet. She had knitted dozens of socks and booties for her baby and had bought silver anklets ... No one had the courage to tell her about my ... my friend's toe. They were revolted themselves, and pitied her...'

'I am still unable to understand what could be so wrong with his toe to cause such revulsion in everyone.'

'If you saw it, you'd understand. It was ... it was darker than the rest of his body, misshapen with coarse folds of skin hanging from it. It looked nothing like a toe...'

I tried to imagine a toe that looked nothing like a toe. 'Perhaps it was a disease,' I suggested. 'There was a girl on the TV the other night. Her skin was turning into the bark of a tree. With each passing day she looked more and more like a tree. Doctors said it was some rare disease, they couldn't seem to find a cure for it.'

'Turning into a tree is not a disease, it is a blessing. What we cannot understand we term as disease,' he muttered, 'or God. Anyway, my friend's big toe was examined by many specialists. They ran all sorts of tests on it, but in the end, they couldn't find anything medically wrong with it. His toe remained as ugly and inscrutable as his fate.'

'At least your friend did not suffer from any disease. Surely that was good?'

'You think that was good?' The sadness in his eyes deepened. 'My friend wouldn't agree with you. If the toe were diseased, at least there could be hope for some cure. As it is, his case is hopeless...'

'When did his mother finally find out about his toe?'

'When they returned home and she undressed the baby for the first time. She fell in a faint at the sight of the toe. The father, who had been discharged from the hospital by then and knew about the toe, revived her with the help of their neighbours. For days she refused to have anything to do with the baby except feeding him. She trembled with aversion every time she had to pick him up. When the naming day arrived, the relatives saw how puny he was, how thin and wrinkled. They scolded the mother and told her to take better care of him. He was after all a boy and the carrier of the father's lineage. Who bothers about the shape of laddus made from ghee and sweet jaggery, they said. Still there were murmurings about the big toe, speculation about whether it was some sort of a punishment or curse. The mother pulled herself together after that and knitted new boots, one for a normal foot and one to hide the foot with the misshapen toe. She looked after the baby, and he began to thrive. The only thing she was adamant about was not having another child. "Here's your son, he will bear your name," she would answer whenever my friend's father mentioned another child. "If you want another baby, you will need to find another wife." She would not let my friend's father come near her.' The man picked up the coffee tumbler and put it down again. The coffee had gone cold and a thin, brown skin had formed over it. 'So you see, my friend's big toe ruined his parents' marriage and caused him to grow up a lonely boy.'

'That indeed sounds serious. It must have impacted his childhood.'

'Yes, though in the beginning he wasn't aware of the havoc his big toe was causing in his life. He didn't even realize it was different from anyone else's. Children accept everything until they are taught differently. But he did notice that no one caught him up in their arms and smothered him with kisses or tickled him to make him shriek with laughter or called him by silly endearments. There were only furtive glances and whispers...'

'So, when did he find out?' I found it difficult to believe in the mythical big toe but was caught by his tired, slow, hypnotic monotone.

'When he started school. Because of his monstrous big toe, he needed special shoes which his mother got a cobbler to hand-stitch. At school, other children noticed the asymmetrical shoes, the right one broader and bulging, and his uncertain walk. They teased him, but it was a good school – English medium, expensive. Children had learned to pretend to behave and satisfied their instincts by copying his gait and calling him "shoe-boy". Things came to a head when the principal decided that all children must learn gymnastics. That was the year gymnastics was fashionable, and schools in big cities were teaching it. A young teacher was recruited, and children were issued shorts and T-shirts to wear to class. My friend was excited. He had watched gymnasts on television, and they had seemed liked wingless birds to him, light and untied to the earth. Like other students, he took off his shoes, carefully tucked his rolled-up socks into them and joined the queue of his classmates. For a moment, complete silence fell. The teacher, a young man, looked stricken. Then, a couple of girls screamed, then, a couple more. In no time, everyone was screaming. Some of the smaller children were crying. In a trembling voice the young teacher ordered my friend to put on his shoes and socks and go to the class. That day no one wanted to sit next to him or talk to him. He ate his lunch alone and watched other kids play. When he reached home, his mother washed his tear-stained face and gave him a sweet snack. She did not need to see the marks of tears on his cheeks to know what had happened at school, though. The principal had already called. The next day my friend's parents went to meet the principal. They showed him reports of all possible tests and certificates from doctors that said the disfiguration was not due to any disease. His mother urged the principal to take a look for himself and asked my friend to take off his shoe. The principal couldn't stand the sight of the toe and turned away. In the end, my friend's parents were told to withdraw him from the school.'

'Because of his toe? That was very unfair.'

'Yes' – he nodded slowly – 'yes, it was. But if we are to question the fairness of things, we would need to go to the root of the matter: Why did my friend have a big toe like that in the first place? There was no fault on his part...'

Clearly this wasn't a question I could answer. I motioned to the server to bring more coffee.

'My friend's parents found it difficult to get him admitted to any of the better schools in the city. My friend was a quiet, obedient child, and had good report cards, but word about his big toe had gotten around. In the end, his parents applied to the nearby government school where the principal took one look at the big toe, spat in the dustbin, and said that even if my friend had three heads, he would have to admit him, he was bound by rules to do so ... but he took the precaution of warning the teachers.' He dropped his gaze into the fresh cup of coffee. 'In that school, my friend fully realized the effects of his accursed toe. Kids deliberately stepped on his foot, threw muck and worms at him if he ventured into the playground ... My friend was careful and none of the children had seen his toe, but they knew all about it and called him slug, drain worm and worse. He figured that there was no point hiding his toe; he must hide himself, for, to others, he was his big toe. As long as he was visible, his misshapen toe, though hidden in his shoe, was visible as well. So, he decided to make himself invisible.'

'Invisible? What do you mean?'

'I mean he found places to hide from his classmates. The darkest corners of classrooms, the windowless library, a shed ambitiously called the laboratory. He became so good at hiding that eventually his classmates forgot about him. When they talked about him, it was as if they had been told a story about someone with a misshapen toe who had been a student at the school, someone they themselves had never met...'

I clicked my tongue. 'It must have been difficult for your friend. He must have found it tough to study under such circumstances.'

'Oh, no. In fact, he did well in his studies. While he was hiding from other children, there was nothing else for him to do except read and reread his textbooks. He was of average intelligence but had a good memory and got good grades. He was awarded a scholarship and got admission in a premier engineering college.'

'I am glad something good came out of his ordeal.'

'You think so?'

'Why, you don't?'

The man with the sad eyes looked at me. 'What you and I think makes no difference. My friend definitely did not think so. After the solitary invisibility at school, he found himself in the glare of communal life in a college hostel. It was impossible to hide his toe there, living four to a room. Soon word got around to his seniors. He was made to show it during ragging sessions. Some girls vomited when they saw it for the first time. They began calling him a crude word, one that meant penis in the local language. That's when my friend began to get the nightmare that continued to disturb his sleep for years. He dreamt that his whole body had turned into his big toe, dark folds of skin hung all over him, and in the deep wrinkles on his body grew rows upon rows of misshapen big toes. Every night he woke up gagging with repulsion at his own self...'

'Tch, tch. Didn't he make any friends? No one with whom he could share what he was going through?'

The man with the sad eyes shook his head slowly. 'He wasn't the only loner in the college. There were others. But loneliness is a strange quantity. When one loneliness touches another, it increases exponentially...' he fell silent. The restaurant had emptied completely. The clatter of utensils in the kitchen had ceased and the man in a smart shirt at the cash counter was enjoying a cup of coffee. The boy who had served us was cleaning the large grandfather clock with a rag. 'The end of college was liberation for him,' the man resumed. 'He got a job with the municipality in a big city. This was the best time of his life...' He crumbled sugar in his fingers and sprinkled it on the table where its fine crystals caught the receding sunlight and shone like crushed glass. 'The best time ... In the city, no one had the time to bother about his big toe, and he was a government officer. People gave him respect, bowed before him. He liked his work and threw himself completely into it. Sewage, garbage dumps, landfills – he wanted to cure all the deformities of the city. His hard work bore fruit. Citizens' associations felicitated him, and some large contractors and mafia-types began to regard him as an enemy. When he visited the parts of the city he was responsible for, people recognized him. His parents began to search for a bride for him. He would read their letters eagerly and examine the photographs they sent. In preparation for marriage and a wife, he applied for a government quarter and collected cuttings of scenic places to visit from magazines and newspapers. Around this time, somehow word got around about his big toe. Perhaps it was an old batchmate from college or the garrulous cleaning-woman ... he never could figure, not that it mattered either ... Everything he thought he had left behind, started again ... whispers, sniggers, people looking at him differently, their eyes wandering to his shoes during meetings ... Some suggested herbal and magical cures ... That was the last straw. After that, my friend gave up...'

'What do you mean "gave up"?'

'He accepted defeat at the hands of ugliness. He gave up all hopes of his life coming to fruition, of leading a meaningful life. Like others, he, too, merely moved files from one desk to another, from one office to the next. He threw away the photographs his parents had sent to him, gave up the flat he had been allotted and moved back into a paying-guest accommodation.'

I glanced at my watch and rapped on the table with my knuckles to attract the attention of a waiter drowsing by the wall. 'Tell me,' I asked, 'did it not occur to your friend to consult a plastic surgeon for his toe? Science has made such advances that surgeons give people entirely new faces; a toe can't be complicated to fix.'

The man with the sad eyes raised his head. Dark, unrelenting sadness was pooled in his eyes. 'What difference would plastic surgery make to my friend? Would it make him forget that such ugliness was a part of him? Would it make his parents forget it too and take him in their arms, caress him, call him by loving nicknames? Would he be able to make friends and talk and laugh with them uninhibitedly? Marry a woman and never cause her embarrassment? Would all ugliness disappear from his memory?'

The waiter came with the bills. The man with the sad eyes paid with crisp notes from an old wallet and rose. Involuntarily, my eyes gravitated towards his feet. He let out a sigh.

'The taint of ugliness never washes off ... never ... It is eternal, like the taint of mortality...'

THE QUEEN OF MAHIM

THE OLD BUILDING Kalindi lived in was just close enough to the Chembur train station for every autorickshaw to decline her fare but far enough to make the walk in the early monsoon heat unpleasant. Most mornings, after trying unsuccessfully to flag down an autorickshaw, she had no option but to walk, wending her way through people sleeping or squatting by the roadside, hawkers, newspaper vendors and piles of garbage. There was always a melee of commuters at the station, whatever be the time, and Kalindi struggled to board an early train to Nerul. But the penance did not end there. It was the Harbour line and trains were slow, trundling through Sanpada, Govandi, Mankhurd, through straggling slums, mould-stained buildings and mangroves, between rows of sleepy children defecating beside the tracks. The children occasionally threw pebbles at the passing trains which stung like wasps when they made contact with faces and necks, arms and bosoms. After the first time a stone grazed her cheek, Kalindi avoided window seats and endured the breathless heat inside the crowded compartment. It was all very different from the Bombay of roads curving along the sea, palm-shaded promenades and glitzy skyscrapers she had seen in movies back home. By the time she would reach her office in Nerul, she would be tired, her clothes crushed and sweat-stained.

The office, a squat, featureless building with a glass façade that glinted fiercely in the sun, stood among similar ones in the business park in Nerul. Despite the perpetual shortage of autorickshaws at the station, and bumpy, unpaved roads and ditches filled with stagnant rainwater, green with slow-rolling algae, at first Kalindi was very taken by this new office. After moving to Bombay, she had worked for a month at a trading company in an old mill-building close to Chembur. The building had a rickety lift with sliding doors that had to be pulled manually, narrow windows with glass covered in layers of dust, and cramped plywood cubicles strung out haphazardly, the ones furthest from the windows sinking into shadows even in the middle of the day. By contrast, the new office had shiny new lifts which opened and closed automatically, music playing while the lifts were in motion. People worked companionably side by side in the large, well-lit open-plan spaces on every floor. There were tall plants in white planters and glossy posters of clean-cut people in trim outfits with slogans like 'Efficiency, Effectiveness, Engagement' or 'Team, Tenacity, Target' emblazoned upon them in large font. Later, she felt a bit foolish when she realized that what she took for daylight was actually strip lighting installed in the false ceiling and the plants were all artificial. The music, too, grew stale with the same set of sitar chords playing over and over, all day, every day.

Several of her co-workers knew each other. They commuted together, took tea breaks calling out to each other and walked in the unpaved compound of the business park after lunch. They were not unfriendly and allowed her to join them at the communal table for lunch during which they made jokes she didn't understand and chatted about shift-timings and mothers-in-law. Sometimes they planned outings – to a popular movie or to Aksa Beach – which she felt too shy to join.

The work she did in the new office perplexed her. At her old workplace, she understood the purpose of her tasks. For example, she knew that she must record all invoices in the electronic ledger, reconcile and balance the accounts, and produce a report at the end of the day. If she didn't, the accountant would not be able to generate a trial balance with the accurate value of sales and purchases for that day. But here, at this new office, she couldn't form a clear idea of what the tasks she performed meant or what ends they were intended to achieve. Every day, she processed anonymized data and sent the results to distribution lists with names like 'Quality Control Audit Reporting', 'Risk and Resilience Audit Reporting', 'Standardized Operational Testing'. She did not have the slightest idea what the numbers she worked on signified. For all she knew, they could be the number of grains of sand on the Juhu beach or waves in the Arabian Sea.

She felt disoriented, as if she were walking on a dark night with a torch illuminating the spot immediately in front of her while all around remained immersed in darkness.

KALINDI FIRST NOTICED Vishakha at the communal lunch table. She was the only one at the table to order vegetable cutlets and manipulate her food with a knife and a fork in silence. Others ordered the day's specials – puri-bhaji and chole-bhature – and shared the dishes, taking food from each other's plates with their fingers, talking and laughing the whole time. A lively discussion was on about the possibility of being allowed to swap the Labour Day holiday for a day off during the Ganesh festival. Kalindi had only seen the Ganesh festival celebrations in Bollywood movies – heroes and heroines flanked by rows upon rows of gaudily dressed dancers, gyrating before the Ganesh idol, while drums beat and clouds of gulaal rose around them in colourful haze.

'There are pandals all over the city now,' someone commented. 'It has become the seasonal occupation for every unemployed good-for-nothing in the chawls and slums, an excuse to extort money from shopkeepers. What do "I kiss you, you kiss me" songs and boys and girls dancing got to do with Bappa?'

'Whatever you say, this is Bappa's time of the year. It is because of him that this city runs. Otherwise with the trains being late and onions costing sixty rupees a kilo, we'd all leave and only the Kolis would be left here, fishing for an hour a day and drinking moonshine all day long!'

'It would be better for the city if the Kolis would leave. We have a bunch boarding our train every morning and you can hardly breathe because of the stink.'

'And the noise they make! You can hear them up and down the length of the train!'

Vishakha raised grave eyes. 'More than anyone else, Bombay belongs to Kolis, they have always lived here.'

'You wouldn't speak for them if you had to live next to them,' one of the women commented.

There was a chorus of assents. Kalindi ducked her head and focused on her food. There was a Koliwada not far from where she lived and she had seen Koli women with baskets on their heads, walking with a freedom that startled her. One of them came to her building once in a while, a basket of fish on her head. She wore a red saree drawn between her thighs and tucked behind, like a man's dhoti. She was dark, like the bark of the mango tree under which she squatted and displayed her wares. Unlike the other vendors, she didn't engage in chit-chat or bargaining. Crouching beside her basket she barely glanced at the pale-complexioned, loose-fleshed housewives who stood before her with their string bags. Thrusting her finger into the mouth and gills of the fish to demonstrate its freshness, she called out its name and price in a high, scratchy voice. The green glass bangles on her bony arms jangled as she deftly cleaned and sliced the fish, wrapped it in bits of newspaper and tossed it into the open mouth of the bag held out by her customer, all in a flowing, practiced series of motions. Even after she left, her presence lingered under the tree. Her basket left a webbed mark in the dust like a secret sign and fish scales glimmered in the shade. Kalindi liked watching her and once had bought a fish from her even though she did not know how to cook it. Eventually she had put the pieces out for the cats in the neighbourhood.

The conversation about the Ganesh festival continued around her.

'Everyone prays to the Ganpati at Lalbagh, even the heroes and heroines,' someone said. 'I go every year. You should see the silks and gold he is decked up in. And the pandal is so beautiful you'd forget it is a temporary structure, made of cloth and bamboo, to be taken down after ten days.'

'Lalbagh cha raja is the true superstar of the festival! Let's all go together this time to see Bappa in Lalbagh.'

'If you really want to see Bappa in his glory, you should join the big procession on the tenth day. It takes all day and all night to reach Chowpatty from Dadar and people go crazy, dancing, throwing fistfuls of dry colours and tinsel. And when the idol finally reaches Chowpatty, you can't tell where the sea of people ends and the Arabian Sea begins.'

'Immersion?' Kalindi was startled into speaking. 'The idol is immersed in the sea? With all the clothes and jewels?'

'Of course not! If the silks and gold were thrown into the sea, slum kids from all over Bombay would be diving in after them! Everything is removed, even the metal weapons that Bappa holds.'

Kalindi imagined the majestic God with the elephant head, stripped of his rich silks and jewels, swaying helplessly over the surging, chanting crowds before slowly toppling into the grey sea, sinking into the murky depths to be eaten by fish.

'I don't even watch the procession go by from the terrace of our chawl. Just looking at the crowds makes me dizzy, people packed together like seeds in a pomegranate. The morning rush for the Virar Fast is nothing in comparison!'

'That's there. But if you want to get Bappa's blessings, you have to brave the crowds. Anyway, I'll go even if no one else does. I have to offer eleven coconuts to him.'

'But shouldn't you go with your husband? The prayers don't bear fruit unless husband and wife pray together.'

'Arre, for what she is asking, she needs to do other things with her husband than just pray together!'

Amidst the laughter that roiled the table and caused others to cast curious glances in their direction, Vishakha rose quietly and left.

'There goes the Queen of Mahim!' A woman raised her eyebrows and bobbled her head. 'Our talk was like thorns to her soft ears!'

There was laughter again. Kalindi looked down at her plate and remained silent, a slight, forced smile stretching her mouth.

As Labour Day drew near, Kalindi's colleagues talked about going to this pandal or that. Plans were firmed up, meeting points decided and home-made modaks promised. In the end, Kalindi decided not to swap the holiday for a day off during the Ganesh festival.

On the morning of the fourth day of the Ganesh festival, the office was nearly empty. She ran into Vishakha at the coffee machine. Setting her mug down on the counter, which for once wasn't marked with brown rings and spills, she waited. Moving to one side, Vishakha picked up Kalindi's mug and positioned it under the machine's nozzle. 'Latte or cappuccino?' she asked politely, finger poised over the buttons.

'Latte,' Kalindi muttered, though she did not know the difference and usually pressed a button at random. And as far as she could judge from the frothy, milky brown liquid that poured into her mug, the machine did not seem to differentiate between the two either. She watched Vishakha wipe her own cup thoroughly with a paper napkin before setting it down carefully on the counter and reaching for the sugar. Tearing the top of the small paper bag neatly, she tilted it with the slightest of motions and emptied the sugar into her cup. 'Your cup's overflowing,' she said glancing towards Kalindi. Blood rose to Kalindi's ears. She was so busy watching Vishakha that her cup had indeed run over. Vishakha passed her a paper napkin and helped her clean the mess. 'There's too much milk in your coffee now,' she said, smiling slightly. Still blushing, Kalindi shook her head. 'That's okay. I like it milky.'

That afternoon they walked into the cafeteria together, their shoes ringing loudly in the empty hall. A large number of staff were on leave and no hot food was being served that day. 'The cheese sandwiches are the only ones that are edible...' Vishakha pointed out the small triangles of bread covered in clear wrapping heaped on large platters. 'The ones with tomato get soggy unless the right kind of tomatoes are used and the juice drained out from the slices.'

The sandwiches were bland. Kalindi followed Vishakha's example and squeezed ketchup from plastic sachets over them. A group of men entered, laughing and talking among themselves, and examined the sandwiches critically. They shrugged their shoulders, throwing a fleeting glance at the two of them. 'Let's go down and get a proper Bombay sandwich. These ones are made for children!' There was a sandwich cart right outside the office. The man who ran it was always hard at work, slathering butter and green chutney generously over thick slices of bread, patting quantities of mashed potatoes between them and setting the sandwiches to toast over an open grill. Despite the dubious-looking butter and suspiciously bright colour of the chutney, the smell wafting from the grill invariably made Kalindi's mouth water.

'Proper sandwich,' Vishakha said, her nostrils puffed delicately and her mouth curled.

'You don't like Bombay sandwich?' Kalindi asked.

'Bombay sandwich is hardly a sandwich; just bread stuffed with potatoes,' Vishakha answered.

Kalindi stole a glance at her. She sat with her back straight, the yellow cotton kurta flowing down in perfect lines and throwing a golden glow on her pale, smooth face, picking at the food with her long, narrow fingers.

As if by tacit agreement, Kalindi stopped joining the others at the communal table in the cafeteria for lunch. Instead, she and Vishakha ate together. The lunch hour became enjoyable for her now and she looked forward to it. Instead of eating hurriedly and slipping away from the noisy table where her colleagues bantered and chatted, she lingered and ate slowly. Vishakha spoke little. Occasionally she recommended a dish or looked at Kalindi with the right corner of her mouth curled when a gust of loud laughter from the big table would reach them. She listened attentively as Kalindi, first shyly and then with increasing comfort, told her about her life back home in the small town she was born in and where she could not step out of her home without being hailed by the neighbours and asked where she was off to.

'It is a small place, very different from here. You can go anywhere in fifteen minutes – to the big market, to college or to a friend's house. Sometimes, when I am in the train returning from work and think about back home where all the streets either lead to the main market or to the old palace on the hill, it seems unreal that a place like that and a city like this can exist at the same time...'

Vishakha looked at her. Her eyes were shaped like almonds and tilted slightly, almost imperceptibly, upwards. They were unlike any other eyes that Kalindi had seen, their whites gleaming with a blue sheen, the lids the colour of new leaves with delicate veins showing pinkly. 'You don't like it here?'

'No, no, it's not that at all,' Kalindi replied quickly and added, 'after all, there isn't another city like Bombay. It is just that everything is so different here...'

'You really think so? That there is no other city like Bombay?'

Kalindi had used the phrase almost unthinkingly, so as to not appear critical of the city. She had heard the phrase often, people tacking it to the end when speaking about the city's inconveniences and hardships, punishing distances and crowds, the annual water-shortages during the summer months and flooding during monsoons. 'I haven't seen many cities,' she answered carefully. 'I am still getting used to things here.'

'It is not easy to get used to things in this city.' Vishakha frowned. 'And people make it all the more difficult. Anywhere else would be better than here.'

Kalindi was surprised. She had never heard Vishakha speak with such vehemence. 'You don't like Bombay? I thought you were from Bombay.'

Vishakha shook her head. 'I am from the hills.' Her eyes flitted away, skimming over the rows of desks, people pulling out chairs, adjusting monitors as the shift changed.

As she worked, Kalindi imagined Vishakha in the hills, dressed in a red and white outfit, her hair tied back with a woollen scarf, slowly walking up a green slope dotted with yellow flowers and barred with long, blue shadows of tall, spare trees, while a carrying mountain melody rose from somewhere in the distance. Later she realized that she had unwittingly borrowed the scene from a movie she had watched. She mentioned it to Vishakha at lunch one day. Vishakha smiled, the right side of her mouth curving deeper into her cheek than the left. 'You like watching Bollywood movies?'

'Yes, but now I wish I hadn't watched quite so many. Real Bombay is nothing like the Bombay of the movies. At least, Chembur isn't, nor is Sanpada or Mankhurd or Nerul.' Kalindi pursed her mouth and made a rueful face.

Vishakha's smile broadened.

'THE FUSE BLEW in my flat again last night,' Kalindi complained to Vishakha. 'This is the third time this month. It always blows up in the middle of the night and I have to wait until morning to get it fixed. If it happens one more time, I'll marry my cousin's brother-in-law. At least there would be someone to fix it at night!' She was joking. At her parents' insistence, she had taken a train one Sunday to Malad where her cousin lived with her family. The suburb was bustling with a weekend market. Her cousin's building, newly built but already weather-beaten, stood in a raw-looking patch of levelled dirt with a straggling row of shanties flung around it like a crumpled garland. The cousin was only a couple of years older than Kalindi but had been married off, while still in the first year of her graduation, to the taciturn man Kalindi greeted with her palms joined and who kept his eyes fixed at the television the whole evening, only speaking once to demand khari biscuits with his tea. After marriage, Kalindi's cousin had shown no interest in completing her degree and now had a two-year-old, with another on the way. She treated Kalindi with condescension and assured her that if the brother-in-law chose her, she, too, won't have to work. 'You'll live like the queen of your house instead of being harried at work,' she had said wiping the sweat off her forehead with the free end of her saree as she fried batches of savouries in the hot kitchen with the broken exhaust fan.

The very eligible brother-in-law was a pale young man with round shoulders and a slack stomach who had looked Kalindi up and down, slowly, a smile on his fleshy mouth, and talked exclusively about his degree in Chartered Accountancy and his new job the whole time Kalindi was there. Her parents were enthusiastic about the match. 'He liked you,' her mother said over the phone, exulting. 'Go again next Sunday. His mother would be there too.' Kalindi had refused. Her father had been furious. 'It was a mistake to allow you to leave home,' he had shouted. Despite her trembling legs and brimming eyes, Kalindi had held fast to her refusal. It had dawned upon her that her father could no longer force her to obey him, and the knowledge filled her with guilt and exhilaration at the same time.

The shadow of a frown crossed Vishakha's forehead. 'Do you like him?' she asked, her eyes resting on Kalindi with earnest scrutiny.

'I don't know.' Kalindi looked down at her palms, at the maze of criss-crossing, wavering lines etched into them. So much was beyond her comprehension. 'I've only met him once. Sometimes I think I should marry whomever my parents want me to.'

It was true. Every Sunday as she cleaned out her tiny flat, washed a week's worth of clothes, and cooked herself dal-rice, which she ate with the mango pickle she had brought from home, this thought occurred to her. She wondered what it would be like to share her meal and take the afternoon siesta with someone, to walk hand-in-hand down Marine Drive jostled by weekend crowds.

'What is he like, this cousin's brother-in-law?'

'He is ... he is a CA and works for a big company. He is thinking of buying a flat close to where my cousin lives. Two banks are willing to give him a loan on good terms.' Vishakha continued to gaze at her. Kalindi clasped her hands together and spoke slowly. 'His teeth were stained, and spittle flew from his mouth when he spoke. He put three spoonfuls of sugar in his tea. When I was leaving, he pressed up against me in the doorway. My cousin just looked away.' She remembered the stale tea-breath on her face and the crumbs in his moustache when he had laughed at her confusion.

They sat in silence gazing at the raggedy skyline of buildings under construction and a freeway, half-finished pillars sporting crane-heads or sprouting iron rods, visible through the glass walls that surrounded them.

'Perhaps it would be better if I just learn to fix the fuse myself,' Kalindi said after a while. Vishakha looked at her, startled. They both laughed, drawing curious glances.

RIGHT AT THE beginning of the monsoons, a cloudburst resulted in rains that paralysed the city, submerging railway tracks and flooding the streets, making it impossible for trains and buses to run. There was controlled panic and frenetic calling, people desperately looking for ways to return home to their families. Several of Kalindi's co-workers girded up their trousers, tucked their sarees around their waists and stepped out in the rain to find rides or walk home. For the first time Kalindi saw the advantage of not having anyone waiting for her back in the small apartment in Chembur, now impossibly far. She made a phone call to her parents and told them not to worry; she was safe in the office and would stay there until the tracks cleared. After the initial frenzy, she was surprised to see a holiday mood pervading the office. Computers were switched off and everyone stood around chatting, trading details of the devastation the rain was wrecking on the city. Many trooped to the cafeteria where tea and snacks were being served. Kalindi did not join them, she wasn't hungry. Also, she noticed that Vishakha had remained at her workstation all through the commotion. She had barely looked up when the announcement was made over the public announcement system about sleeping bags and dinner being provided to those who wished to stay in the office.

The sleeping bags were heaped up in one corner, their bright yellows and blues standing out against the grey-white walls. The plastic in which they were packed crackled under their fingers. A smell of rubber and cheap newness rose from the bags. Kalindi had slept in a sleeping bag only once on a school trip to Benares when they were put up in a hostel with not enough beds.

'These bags don't smell very good.' Vishakha joined her.

'No, they don't.' Kalindi wrinkled her nose. 'By tomorrow morning we will smell like them too.'

Vishakha let go of the sleeping bag she was holding and sniffed her fingers.

'At least these are new and still in their packaging,' Kalindi consoled herself, 'and not old or used ones.'

'These are not new. The bags are brought out of storage every monsoon and cleaned and packed away at the end of September,' Vishakha said. 'But we don't need to use them. I live close by. If you are okay with walking in the rain, we can be there in fifteen minutes.'

OUTSIDE, THE RAIN was still coming down heavily and the swollen rain clouds hung low over the buildings. Kalindi and Vishakha were drenched the moment they stepped out, their feet slipped in their plastic rain-shoes, clothes and hair stuck to their bodies. Water came up to their calves, but they did not roll up their leggings. 'A lot of this water is from the overflowing sewers...' Vishakha probed the ground with her rolled-up umbrella before each step. 'Sometimes people here open the manholes to speed up draining the water. There are stories of pedestrians disappearing down open manholes and found days later, washed up on a beach.'

They walked carefully through the waterlogged streets, stumbling over potholes and stones and debris. A mound of construction material – sodden bags of sand, heaped up gravel and cement blocks – rose like a minor peak from the muddy waters. Grabbing at each other's arms and shoulders for balance, they scrambled up its slippery sides and surveyed the area. Kalindi had wrapped her dupatta around her shoulders and chest so that her bra and breasts won't show through her wet tunic, but Vishakha had folded hers and stowed it in her bag. She stood with her long, slender body clearly outlined in her red kurta, a crimson tilak drawn against the grey-brown sky. Droplets hung from her lashes and ran down her face and into the hollow at the base of her neck, with the collar bones rising gently like wings on either side. The water eddied and lapped around the mound, and rain fell like fine needles on Kalindi's upturned face. She was filled with exhilaration.

'This place looks much better under water than otherwise, even if it is sewer water!' she called out. Vishakha looked at her, her mouth parted, the sound of rain beating down on corrugated iron roofs drowning the sound of her words.

KALINDI FOLLOWED VISHAKHA up the narrow stairs. Her clothes clung to her and hampered her at every step. 'I didn't know there were houses in Bombay.'

'This is hardly Bombay. There are still vadis and row houses here, and rents are low compared to the city.'

'Who lives downstairs?'

'No one. The people who own this house live elsewhere. They've closed up the ground floor.' Vishakha unlocked the door.

Kalindi was struck by how large and airy the flat was. There was a living room with a small balcony, two bedrooms and a proper kitchen, not just a slab and a sink like her own. The bathroom was big, too, with the area for washing clothes separated from the bathing area by a low cement wall. Kalindi stepped out of her soaking clothes and hurriedly poured water over herself straight from the water drum instead of first filling a bucket. Pulling on the cotton nightdress that Vishakha had lent her, she walked to the kitchen. Vishakha was making tea.

'The tea smells good.' Kalindi breathed in the spicy lemongrass fragrance.

'I have put some black pepper and chaipatta in the tea,' Vishakha said without turning. She, too, was wearing a nightie, but being taller than Kalindi, the dress skimmed her calves, and her pale legs and bare feet shone like glass.

Kalindi glanced around. Rain was splattering on the eaves and throwing a fine spray into the balcony. 'This flat is so big. You must have a good agent to find you this kind of place. Mine's so small that after the bed and a chair, there's no room for anything else, not even me! And the rent is a third of my salary.'

Vishakha looked over her shoulder and smiled. 'The rents are not so high in this area.'

'You are lucky. Everything is so expensive in this city, and people only like to rent to families and vegetarians, no one wants single women. How did you manage to find this place?'

'Like you said, perhaps I am lucky.' Vishakha turned off the gas and covered the pot.

'I wish some of your luck would rub off on me.' Kalindi thought of her tiny, one-room apartment with its single window covered with an iron grille and opening on to a rubbish-filled back alley.

Vishakha sieved the tea into two large mugs and handed one to Kalindi. 'You'll have biscuits with your tea?' She reached for a steel container.

They sat in the small balcony and ate sweet biscuits dipped in tea. The rain showed no sign of abating. The front steps of the house were completely submerged, and they could see a thin, shimmering film of water spreading across the verandah on the ground floor. 'I haven't seen rain like this ever. It looks like someone has turned the world's largest faucet on and forgotten to turn it off.' Kalindi broke a biscuit into half. 'It must remind you of your home.'

Vishakha was looking intently at the row of ants carrying crumbs. She moved her foot out of their way and looked at Kalindi, her eyes blank. 'What?'

'The rain. It rains a lot in the mountains, doesn't it?'

'Oh yes.' Vishakha crumbled her biscuit and dribbled the crumbs on to the floor. A new row of ants formed around them.

Kalindi followed Vishakha's eyes and watched the ants carry the crumbs that seemed too large for their tiny bodies in a seemingly endless loop, the ants at the back of the line following those in the front. 'These ants are like us, doing the same thing over and over,' she observed.

Vishakha raised her wide eyes to her. 'Yes, isn't it? I got so fed up with excel sheets and numbers that I applied for a transfer to Pune. There are more product lines there.'

'So, when are you going?' Kalindi asked slowly.

'That was a few months ago. I am not going now.' Vishakha smiled. 'I don't mind it here so much now.'

BY EVENING, THE rain had ceased, but the streets were still under water and the train service hadn't resumed. Kalindi and Vishakha cooked dinner together. Kalindi garnished the boiled lentils with garlic, ginger and green chillies, and Vishakha sauteed potatoes with cumin and coriander. 'At home, no one eats onions except my father,' Kalindi commented as Vishakha chopped onions. 'My mother won't let me eat them because of the smell.' Vishakha smiled and sprinkled the onions with tart chat masala.

They ate sitting cross-legged, plates balanced on their laps, on a cotton durrie Vishakha had spread in the living room. 'It is so good to eat a proper meal in the middle of the week,' Kalindi sighed as they finished and carried their plates back to the kitchen. 'Most days I just eat bread and milk.'

Vishakha raised her eyebrows. 'Why?'

'It takes me over an hour to reach Chembur, and by the time I reach home I am so tired, I just want to lie down and watch TV,' Kalindi explained. She scrubbed and rinsed the plates in the sink while Vishakha put away the leftovers in plastic containers. 'I should look for a place around here. Perhaps your agent can help me find a flat here?'

Vishakha wiped down the kitchen slab and bent to check if the gas knob was turned off. 'How about living here?' She straightened up. 'There's plenty of room, and I don't think the landlord would mind.'

'Really? Are you sure? That would be fantastic!' Kalindi almost skipped with joy. 'We can split the rent and other things and share the housework. I am okay at cleaning and quite good at eating.'

Vishakha laughed.

KALINDI WOKE UP, her own breath rasping in her ears. She had fallen asleep lying flat on her back, her hands pressing down on her chest, and had dreamt strange, fragmented dreams of repeatedly falling over while boarding a train and landing into something soft and yielding – a heap of flowers, swampy mud, a downy sleeping bag. Soundlessly, she turned to her side. Light from the street lamp lay in yellow, vertical bars over Vishakha. She was sleeping with her arms thrown out, hair spread in a dark wave over the pillow, mouth slightly open. Her nightdress had ridden up to her thighs and her chest rose and fell rapidly. Kalindi was used to sharing beds, sleeping in a cramped space, wedged between tightly curled and covered bodies of sisters, cousins and aunts. The spaciousness of Vishakha's double bed, the abandon of her sleeping body seemed luxurious to her. She stretched her legs and lay at ease, watching the grey monsoon dawn lighten the room, the glow from the street lamps fade to a watered paleness. Vishakha turned in her sleep and threw her leg over Kalindi.

Kalindi gave notice to her landlord. He lived in a building close by with his wife and two adult sons and came over to convey his dismay. The agent had charged him a month's rent as fee, he complained, and now he would need to pay again, plus lose rent until another tenant was found.

'There were many people who wanted to rent this flat, but I gave it to you. I thought, you are like my daughter, you are alone in this city, this is a good building, you'll be safe here. And now it is not even a year and you say you want to leave. This is the reason people don't rent to unmarried girls, you can never be sure with them. They are not stable.'

The tenancy agreement provided for termination with a month's notice. Still, Kalindi apologized. 'It was okay when my office was in Dadar, but now my office is very far and it takes me over one hour one way...'

'Everywhere is far, this is Mumbai.' He cast a keen look around. 'There's a crack in the partition and some plaster has fallen from the ceiling. I'll have to deduct the cost of repair from the deposit if you leave.' He threw her a look. 'You are getting married?' Kalindi shook her head. He paused at the door. 'Anyway, you think it over. It is not easy to get a good place in this area with the station only fifteen minutes away.'

'My landlord is upset. He is threatening to dock my deposit for some made-up reason,' Kalindi told Vishakha over lunch.

'He had himself insisted that the lease should have a break clause with a month's notice and now he is complaining that I am leaving too soon.'

'He has no right to complain. If he causes trouble, let me know. I have a lawyer who is helping me over something. Anyway, your landlord has a month to find another tenant.'

'The agent told me that he wanted the break clause because he was looking for a match for his son and would've asked me to vacate as soon as his son got married. He never expected me to give notice.'

'There's still time. He might still be able to fix his son's marriage.'

'That's what I said to the agent! I said he should focus on getting his son married instead of wasting his time on threatening me, but that's no longer an option it seems. The son has married a Muslim girl, and my landlord has disowned him.'

'So first he lost his son and now he is losing his tenant.' Vishakha smiled archly. 'And both for good reasons.'

Kalindi smiled too. 'And who knows this might all work out well for him. He is so stingy that he might reconcile with his son so that the flat doesn't remain empty!'

Vishakha laughed, moisture gathering like dewdrops in the corners of her eyes.

'WE ARE ALL surprised to see the Queen of Mahim actually laughing and chatting with you!' The woman colleague who talked the most and laughed the loudest at the lunch table nudged Kalindi with her elbow, her eyes dancing. There was no one in the pantry except the two of them. 'Tell me, how have you managed to achieve that? Others can hardly elicit a word from her. Talking to her is like talking to a wall.'

Kalindi rinsed her water bottle and smiled the smile that made her temples and jaws ache.

'You are not so different from her, but at least you smile instead of getting offended if anyone so much as breathes in your direction! I bet you have secrets that you tell each other!' She nudged Kalindi again, jogging her arm as she tried to fill her bottle.

Kalindi kept her smile intact. 'I am such a boring person, Mrs Dhoole, what secrets could I have?'

'That's true, you haven't lived long enough to have secrets yet, but one can never tell! Look at the Queen of Mahim. She is not that much older than you!'

Kalindi screwed the cap on the bottle. 'Why do you call her the Queen of Mahim?'

'Because that's who she thinks she is! I have known her for years, my in-laws' place is right next to the chawl she lived in in Mahim. She always acted as if everyone there was beneath her' – Mrs Dhoole pointed her chubby chin up and looked down her nose – 'never mixed with anyone. It was college and then off to the community centre with her. She'd spend all evening watching "Learn English" videos or reading magazines, even during Navratri when the other girls would be rehearsing garba or making flower-chains for the goddess.'

'Mahim?' Kalindi was puzzled. 'Mahim ... in Bombay?'

'I don't know of any other Mahim!'

'But she—' Kalindi bit back the next word and began again, '—I thought she was from the hills...'

'Because of her eyes?' Mrs Dhoole placed each of her two index fingers on her temples and pulled the skin up, laughing. 'The kids in the chawl used to tease her and call her a frog-eater, but the fact is the only hill she has ever been to is Matheran on a school trip!' She came closer and lowered her voice: 'The fact is her mother was from the hills near Nepal, and before Vishakha's father married her, she worked in Kamathipura.' She narrowed her eyes and nodded significantly. 'She was a working woman there. Everyone knows about it.'

Her voice scraped at Kalindi like a straw-broom. She stared blankly. 'Kamathipura?'

'Oh ho, I forget you are not from Mumbai. It is the red-light area, you know.' Mrs Dhoole gave Kalindi a sidelong glance and rocked her head from side to side in a dance-like movement. 'She worked there for a Madam. The father was no better, a troublemaker all his life – union leader he called himself, but all he did was cause trouble right to his dying day. He used to frequent Kamathipura and brought Vishakha's mother back with him one day' – Mrs Dhoole widened her eyes and wrinkled her small nose – 'just like that. No wedding, no ceremony, no nothing. Some say they married in a temple, but who knows what's true, what's not, when it comes to that man? Even his death was shady. Some claim he was murdered by the Kamathipura dada when he was returning from a dharna or a strike or something. And despite all this, our queen gives herself airs...'

Kalindi stood rooted. She was revolted by the way Mrs Dhoole whispered, smacking her lips, and closed one eye. Yet she felt unable to move. It was like watching a repulsive worm slowly emerge from a dark hole. A couple of people entered the pantry, and one of them, a woman, came up to Mrs Dhoole.

'We were talking about the Queen of Mahim!' Mrs Dhoole explained, nodding with a loathsome significance. Kalindi's stomach turned.

'Oh ho, what has she done now? Only a couple of weeks ago her uncle and aunty were complaining that she has got herself a lawyer and is not dropping the property case. Just imagine, suing her own uncle.' The woman wrinkled her brow deeply, causing her large stick-on bindi to come partly unstuck.

'Where did she get a lawyer from? Lawyers cost money!'

'You know where she'd get money from for this kind of a stunt. She is lucky to have that doctor crazy enough about her to pander to her every whim.'

'That's true, she is lucky,' Mrs Dhoole said, nodding. 'Luckier than some who are better than her. Who could have known that things would go this far with the doctor? He is such a respectable man, comes from a good family, married and with grown-up daughters too.' She turned towards Kalindi, her eyes glinting: 'Tell me, has she told you what's the position now? Is the doctor planning to divorce his wife and marry her?'

'What a silly question to ask,' the other woman chided Mrs Dhoole. 'Why would he marry her when he has her anyway? He is not a fool, and now with the mother, too, dead, it is not as if there's anyone who would question him. Not that her mother would have said anything anyway, she wasn't too fussy about marriage herself! What do you think?' She, too, turned towards Kalindi. 'You must have met the doctor. Did you get any sense where this is heading from his behaviour? That's his parents' house that she lives in, by the way. His father had clinics here and in Vashi. He was quite well known around here.'

Kalindi shook her head. 'No...' Her voice sounded small in her own ears. 'No, I haven't...'

'No?' The other woman raised her eyebrows and her bindi wobbled. 'I guess he might not get the time to visit her so often now. I heard he spends more time in Pune these days, he is building a hospital there.'

'He used to come almost every day back when her mother was sick and even after she passed away, until her uncle objected. You remember how she fought with her uncle?' Mrs Dhoole looked at the other woman and mimicked Vishakha shrilly: '"You can't tell me what to do, he paid my college fees when you would not give me a penny, I have a share in this house, these rooms belonged to my ajoba..."' She rocked her head. 'Such an ungrateful girl. The uncle could have kicked them out of the chawl after her father died. Instead, he let them live there, even bought her mother a sewing machine so she could sew garments and supplement the pension she got from the government, and this was how she repaid him.'

'I must say the mother was very good at tailoring, no one could sew blouses like her—' The other woman reached a hand and straightened the chain of flowers tucked in her hair. 'And she used to be always at it, bent over that second-hand machine that had to be propped up against the wall because its stand was broken.'

'That's true. Whatever she did before, the fact is, after the husband's death she lived like a pious widow. I guess going by that, there's hope our queen would reform, too, when she is fifty!'

THE EVENING SHIFT staff began trickling in, but Kalindi remained at her workstation. Vishakha logged off from her computer, picked up her handbag and walked over to her. They had planned to shop at the mall together that evening. Vishakha wanted to buy new curtains and a mirror.

'Are you ready?' She placed her hand on the back of Kalindi's chair. 'The mall won't be so crowded since it is the middle of the week. We can eat at Biryani Durbar afterwards.'

Kalindi kept her eyes on the screen of her computer. 'I ran into Mrs Dhoole this afternoon ... She said ... several things...'

There was a moment's silence. Then Vishakha turned slowly and left.

KALINDI INFORMED HER landlord that she had changed her mind and would like to stay on. 'That's right, that's a good decision you are making. You'll not find another place as good as this at this rent anywhere in Chembur,' he repeated.

'He called me and chewed me out. Said he'll never again rent to a single woman,' her agent informed her. 'It is always one day this and the other day that with them, can't make up their minds. You be watchful,' he warned her. 'He is keeping an eye out for a good tenant. If he finds one, he'll give you notice. Call me if you want to find another place. Don't go to anyone else, like you did the last time.'

Kalindi continued to eat lunch with Vishakha at the small table. She didn't want to return to the communal table to be grilled by Mrs Dhoole and others. Why Vishakha chose to eat with her, she could not say. The table was small enough for their knees to occasionally touch or eyes to flit across to each other. They both moved their limbs and looked away. Very little was said during lunch, and Kalindi went back to her old habit of eating quickly, her head bent over her plate.

Monsoon had settled into a familiar rhythm – continuous rain for a few days, followed by a dry spell – when Vishakha switched to the later shift. Kalindi rarely saw her. She came to work after Kalindi finished her shift. Kalindi worked on her reports and ate lunch by herself. She kept her eyes averted from the group at the communal table and avoided Mrs Dhoole and others. Once while walking towards the station, she thought she saw Vishakha in a car, a man in the driving seat beside her.

One evening, just as Kalindi was getting ready to leave, Vishakha walked up to her. She placed a tiffin box on her table. 'I brought you some food,' she said softly, 'dal, rice and potatoes.'

Kalindi glanced at the tiffin carrier. She could smell the freshly roasted cumin and coriander. Saliva slowly gathered in her mouth. 'Thanks, but I have food at home. I don't want it to go waste.'

Vishakha nodded and picked up the box. It left a faint, moist ring on the smooth metal surface.

IT WAS LUNCHTIME. Nothing seemed appetizing to Kalindi. She watched the clouds, billowing layers of them rolling over from somewhere beyond her sight and darkening the day while the dosa on her plate lost its crispness and turned limp. Mrs Dhoole called out to her.

'Come, join us. Leave that dosa, today's special is misal.' Reluctantly, Kalindi walked over to the large table. 'Why do you eat alone now?' Mrs Dhoole said jocularly as Kalindi pulled a chair and sat down. 'Now that the Queen of Mahim has got a transfer to Pune, there is no disloyalty in sitting with us!' Kalindi blinked, the smile hanging from her lips like a heavy, clumsy weight, threatening to slip any moment.

'So, it seems like she is hell-bent on breaking the doctor's family. I heard she is living in his house there in Pune,' Mrs Dhoole continued. 'Just think, living with him, like his wife, when he is there for the hospital work.' Mrs Dhoole looked at her keenly, smiling with delight the whole time. 'She didn't tell you she was going to Pune, did she?'

Kalindi rose and walked out of the cafeteria.

THE SATSUMA PLANT

T̲he Satsuma plant was a gift.

One afternoon a peon had walked into Meena's office, his arms wrapped around a large potted plant. He had lowered the planter carefully in the corner under the window on the far side from her desk. Dusting his hands, he had handed her a note.

'I saw this Satsuma orange plant at the nursery yesterday and remembered you,' it read. 'I was told the plant needs open space to grow into a tree but could certainly thrive and bear fruit in the right kind of pot. I liked the idea of gifting this plant from faraway Japan to you for, though you've never spoken much about your time in Japan, I have a feeling it must have been memorable. I hope this plant will help release those memories and make room for new ones. Isn't there something promising and springlike about orange trees?'

Meena had curled her mouth. The Satsuma would never come into fruit here, in these long, interminable summers, the earth cracked with dry heat, the sky seared white. The Satsuma orange was a child of the cold – the colder the weather, the sweeter the fruit. She had torn up the note and dropped its fragments into the dustbin, resolving to kill any false sense of intimacy that he might have acquired. It shouldn't be difficult to remind him that he was just a colleague with whom she had taught a seminar and talked about the quality of papers turned in by students over cups of bad coffee. She had avoided him thereafter, spending her free time in her own office and bringing tea from home instead of going to the cafeteria.

But it wasn't possible to avoid the plant crouched in a corner of her office. She watered it occasionally, but did not care for it in any other way – never turning or refreshing the soil, and allowing the dry leaves to accumulate in the planter. The bottle of organic liquid fertilizer which he had thoughtfully sent along with the plant, gathered dust, as did the unopened bag of potting soil. But the plant, sturdy and leaf-laden, had remained stoically green, though fruitless. Its citrusy smell penetrated everywhere. It wafted into the corridor through the open door, causing passing students to stop and breathe deeply. The fragrance made them forget the test that hadn't gone well, the lover who hadn't called in days, the world that wasn't waiting for them outside the university. The breeze sometimes carried the smell upwards to the dean's offices. On such days, the dean quoted Faiz's poetry and told everyone that economics was guesswork dressed up with numbers, and that he wished someone had told him so thirty years ago when he enrolled for an economics course just because the model boy in his neighbourhood had done so.

When Meena returned to her office after long days of teaching classes and departmental meetings, the fragrance of the Satsuma plant waited for her like a trap. It made her grab her bag and flee to her small flat at the other end of the campus. Every night she tried to wash the smell out of her hair, her skin, her memory, but it returned in her dreams. The barren Satsuma plant bore fruit in her dreams, trembling under their weight. When she tried to pluck a fruit, she realized they were made of metal, covered in a corrosive paint. They burned holes in the ground as they fell from her scalded fingers, steam rose from the holes, nothing could be seen except the mountains that towered like beasts of stone rearing their angry heads high. She emerged from the steam to find herself in the fruit-filled aisles of a large supermarket.

'Look, such lovely oranges!' someone said in her voice.

'Not oranges, these are mikan, the honey citrus. They become sweeter the colder the weather gets! You'll only find them here in Japan, Meenu-chan.'

The orange spheres, piled impossibly high in the wooden fruit barrows all around, began to topple like marigolds. She escaped through a doorway into a large kitchen. The sharp, fresh smell of peeled oranges enveloped her. 'These are found all over the world. I have seen Satsuma orange orchards in California. The "only in Japan" is hokum. People here think everything from seasons to flowers only happen in Japan. Open your mouth.' The fingers lingered inside her mouth, the orange tasting sweet, oh so sweet, too sweet.

A very sad voice whispered, 'How could you, Meenu-chan?'

The oranges burst, a bright stream of juice flooded everything, everything drowned in the brilliant rising stream, until she awoke gasping, struggling to breathe.

A FEW WEEKS later, he knocked at her office door. Meena had just finished her office hours, poured and drunk the last dregs of tea from the teapot, and was enjoying the first moments of quiet ease in her day.

'Good afternoon. You are impossible to find these days. If I was of a suspicious mind, I'd think you were avoiding me.' He was laughing but his eyes regarded her searchingly. 'I see the plant has added about a hundred per cent to the aesthetics of your office, though I don't remember being thanked for it!'

Meena looked at him evenly. 'You'd like to take it back?'

His head jerked up in surprise. 'Ouch, that wasn't nice.'

Meena stretched her lips in a smile. 'Yes, it wasn't,' she agreed. 'I can't be nice for long.'

He stood at the door looking down at her. 'I don't understand. What has happened? I thought we were friends, we had such a good time together…'

'We led a seminar and graded papers together.'

'Was that all? Is that how you remember it?'

The smile remained on Meena's lips like the straight edge of a knife. 'I don't remember it at all,' she replied.

He turned on his heel and left.

Later that day, Meena wrote to the dean: 'I am not sure that it would be useful to hold another joint seminar on

Women in Indian and Japanese Classics next term. It is too important a topic to just pick up in occasional seminars, and I think the seminar last term served its purpose of creating interest and awareness. Instead, I'd like to think along the lines of designing an independent course module on the topic.'

MEENA'S MOBILE RANG the minute she entered her office, as if the caller knew she had just finished teaching her last class and was free to face fate. It was her younger sister. She sounded strangely muffled. There was a hum of voices in the background.

'Ma passed away...' her voice faltered. 'The funeral is tomorrow morning. Ma didn't want us to inform you, but Didi and I ... You didn't get to see Papa either, and now Ma, too, is gone...' Her throat filled up.

'I'll be there by the morning.'

Back in her apartment, Meena packed a bag. She had learned of her father's death from the newspaper. There was an obituary and a notice of a prayer meeting. 'The renowned scholar and professor emeritus passed away at his home peacefully,' it read. 'He will be greatly missed by his students, colleagues, and all the cats in the university he fed and cared for. Classes at the university are suspended in his honour. He is survived by his wife and two daughters.'

Two daughters. Meena had sat frozen, the newspaper falling from her numb hands on to her lap. Two daughters. They had remembered to erase her from the family even at such a time. She had called her elder sister.

'Meenu, Papa left so suddenly...' She had wept quietly. 'Ma was adamant, I couldn't do anything ... I can't talk now ... The whole city's here for the prayer meeting...'

She had learned later that her father had died in his favourite spot in the garden, under the fine-leaved gooseberry tree. He had been watching the sunset as usual, and the servant who had come to call him in had found him dead, his unseeing eyes still trained at the horizon, a cat curled in his lap. Meena didn't know whether he had thought of her before he died, or had regretted that the only time he had spoken to her in the last ten years was to tell her not to call her younger sister again. She did not know whether he remembered her as a child, playing beside him as he sat reading under the gooseberry tree, shaking it to send showers of green leaves and green marbled fruits on him. She didn't know anything and now, would never know.

AFTER THE FUNERAL, Meena stood apart from everyone as relatives embraced her sisters, patted their husbands on the back. 'They are orphans now, the poor girls,' they cried. 'Now you are their everything – father, mother, husband, keeper. The poor orphaned girls ... How will they carry this mountain of grief for the rest of their lives?' Some of them glanced at her. 'You should mend your ways now that your makers are no more,' they observed acidly. 'You gave them so much pain while they lived, they never ate a morsel nor drank a mouthful without the thought of you turning it bitter for them.' Meena remained silent, her eyes fixed on the rose and marigold petals which had fallen from her mother's bier and lay scattered everywhere.

'Ma had to bear the brunt of everything,' her elder sister said as they spread beddings on the floor in the front room where a large photograph of her mother stood on a low marble table, a wilting rose garland and another of sandalwood beads adorning it. 'You heard everyone yourself this morning ... Ma had to listen to them every day. The things they would say to Ma at every family gathering – Meena has brought such shame upon you, how will you marry the younger one off now? What will become of your good name? Everyone knows the learned professor, how difficult it must be for him to face people with this shame ... You can't imagine how they tormented her.'

'She could have refused to see them, just as she refused to see me all these years,' Meena said in a brittle voice.

Her sister shook her head as she poured oil in the large diya burning before their mother's photo, the lamp that was to burn undimmed for a period of thirteen days until her soul left this realm. 'How hard you are, Meenu ... But you were always this way, never really caring for anyone, always doing what you wanted. You never thought from Ma-Papa's side, never asked them to forgive you for all the trouble you caused here.' Meena's chest swelled; she felt suffocated but remained silent. 'I could never understand why you were always so stubborn,' her sister said. 'Keep an eye on the diya until I come back.'

Meena sat on the bare floor, her back against the wall, gazing at her mother's photograph. The eyes in the photo were glancing away from her, the lips were folded upon each other. Her full cheeks did not have even a hint of the dimple that appeared when she smiled, the pretty dimple which always gave Ma away when she was pretending to be angry.

'She was in the hospital until the day before...' Her younger sister came and sat down beside her. 'We brought her home yesterday because she didn't want to stay in the hospital any longer and the doctors said there was nothing more ... The cancer...' She sniffed and wiped her raw-looking nose. 'You won't believe Meenu di, she was so thin her bangles would fall off, but her face was unchanged, her complexion was like kundan the day she died. You saw yourself how beautiful she looked, Meenu di...' Tears brimmed in her eyes, so like their mother's. Meena looked away, her dry eyes smarted as if she had walked through a sandstorm. She stroked her sister's bowed head as she sobbed.

'Where is Ma's big green trunk?' she asked more to distract her sister than from any real wish to see it.

'Ma gave it away to the man who delivers milk and newspapers. She said she had no use for it, and it was rusting. You know, Meenu di, the first time Ma was admitted to the hospital, we opened it to air the sarees and things Ma had collected for you, and everything inside had been eaten by silverfish. Ma hadn't opened it in years. You should have seen how Didi cried to see the silks and ojharias that Ma had bought for you turned to powder.'

Meena imagined a cloud of dust rise from the opened trunk – all that remained of the beautiful sarees embellished with gold and silver threads, with fine appliqué of golden tissue, with intricate beadwork and silk embroidery. She had never worn those sarees meant for her wedding, childbirth, the sixteen-day-long Teej festival celebrated in shravan. Her mother had allowed them to become the food of voracious insects, had not cared for them as she did for her own sarees which she aired every few months even during her illness. While those meant for Meena turned to dust, hers were layered with dried neem leaves for protection against bugs, sandalwood sachets tucked among their folds like always. The scent of dry leaves and sandalwood was the smell of festival days for Meena, of bustle and a busy hum, and Ma radiant in an elaborate saree.

Her sister wiped her cheeks and leaned against Meena's shoulder. 'We are sitting like this after so many years, Meenu di. I used to snuggle up to you all the time. You would complain that I was crowding you, but I would still stick to you and you'd push and say I was like a leech. Do you remember?'

Meena placed her arm around her sister. 'I remember.' Her sister was four years younger to her, and Meena had found out about her marriage from a school friend she had run into at an airport. She had bought a pair of pearl and coral earrings as a wedding present for her but was at a loss about where to send them. In the end, she had sent the earrings to her elder sister. A few months later, her younger sister had called. She was in a hurry and spoke in a low voice. Meena could hear the sounds of bustle around her. 'It has been mad here,' she had said. 'We are still doing the wedding rounds. Today there's dinner at Bhua ji's. I am wearing the earrings you sent, Meenu di. I'll call you when no one's around and we'll talk.' She hadn't called back.

'What happened to that Japanese girl, Meenu di? The one, you know, your ... your girlfriend?'

'She died,' Meena said quietly.

'Died? How? She was so young. Was she in an accident?'

Yes, she was, Meena wanted to say, *Yuri was in an accident, and so was I*. 'No, she killed herself.'

'What?' Her sister sat up straight. 'You mean suicide? My God. It must have been horrible for you, Di. You ... you lived with her, no?'

'Yes, but I wasn't there that day.'

'My God...' she repeated, shuddering. 'She seemed such a quiet person too. What happened? Where were you when she died?'

'I ... We had had some issues. I was at a friend's place that day.'

'What kind of issues? I thought you ... loved her and wanted to be with her. You weren't breaking up with her, were you?'

'It wasn't that simple. I ... I wanted to tell Yuri about ... about my friend ... but things just got out of hand.'

'Who is this friend? Are you still with her?'

Meena averted her eyes. 'No, I am not with him any more.'

'Him? Your friend was a man?' She turned towards Meena. 'But ... you said you can't marry Prakash because you ... you liked that girl ... I don't understand ... You did all this,' she made a sweeping gesture with her arm, as if to include everything – their parents' absence, the emptiness in the house, the distance between them, 'all this to Ma-Papa, to us, to Prakash, for that girl, and then you cheated on her with a man? What's wrong with you, Meenu di? What are you?' Meena remained silent.

That night and every night she remained in her parents' house, Meena dreamt the same dream. The neighbours next door were celebrating a festival noisily, blowing conch shells, setting off fireworks. She went up to her one true love and asked him to hold her. Her clothes fell away from her body that was made of sharp flint. It lacerated the arms of her true love. She could see her father and mother across the street, in a house which was like a conservatory, all glass and heat. Their backs were turned towards her. She hurriedly opened her mother's trunk to take out some clothes and cover her nakedness, but someone had heaped coals in it. Smoke rose from the trunk, the pink lotuses painted on its lid wilted in the heat. A shock of small, flame-coloured oranges tumbled down from the Satsuma orange tree. They rolled everywhere. She stepped on a fruit, and the blood of the Satsuma orange stained her bare feet. She woke up trembling, sweat rolling down her face and neck, chills running up and down her limbs.

At the end of the thirteen days of rituals, she packed her bag. No one asked her to stay back.

MEENA WAS WORKING late, getting through the tasks that had piled up during her absence, when her phone rang. It was her elder sister. 'I wanted to let you know about the will, Meenu. We didn't get a chance to talk about it. Ma-Papa had drawn up a simple one; they didn't leave anything for you.' Meena picked up a pen and put it down again. She glanced at the document open on her laptop and adjusted the desk-lamp. 'We don't think it is right that you are left out this way, so we've decided to split the house, shares, jewellery that Ma left between the three of us,' her sister continued. 'Are you there, Meena?'

'Yes, I am here, Didi,' Meena said hoarsely and cleared her throat. 'I don't want anything.'

'You've hurt Ma-Papa enough when they were alive, living with that girl and breaking the match they fixed for you. I won't give you a cause to reproach them now that they are gone. A third belongs to you. If you don't want it, give it away to charity, do whatever you want. I have emailed you a copy of the will and statement of assets that was in Ma's safe and an agreement about the three-way division. I only had your old email address. Check it and message me if you haven't got the documents. I have to go now, I have surgeries lined up early tomorrow morning.'

Meena sat in silence. Outside, the day drew to a close. The sky framed in her window turned from a soiled red to ashen, the edges of the horizon bleeding colour long after it drained from the rest of the sky.

'Hey, I was just passing by and saw the light in your office. Just want to say I am so sorry to hear about your mother...'

Meena raised her head to look at him. Her cheeks glistened with tears.

'Hey...' He reached her in two strides. 'Please don't cry. I am so sorry, so sorry...' All the unshed tears from the past weeks streamed silently from Meena's eyes. 'Hey, hey...' He bent over her. 'It's okay, it's okay...' he spoke softly and, raising her from her chair, held her close. 'These things ... one's never prepared for them, but it will get better, I promise it will.' He tucked the strands of hair sticking to her face behind her ears and touched her forehead with his lips folding her closer and closer. Meena felt the tremor in his chest as his fingers stroked her face, slowly sliding down her neck. He kissed her on the temples, on her wet eyes, her soft mouth. She allowed his lips to linger, his fingers to trail further and further. 'Meena...' His hand caressed her back, tracing the long furrow down its length. 'Meena ... come home with me.'

Meena glanced at the Satsuma plant in the corner. Its unmoving leaves suffused the evening with their smell. She moved away from him. 'I still have some things to finish here.'

'Can't they wait?' He touched her fine hair.

'No, I have to clear the backlog.'

'Finish and call me then. I will wait. Okay?'

She nodded.

AFTER WRAPPING UP her work, Meena logged into her personal email. She hadn't checked it for a while, and it was teeming with spam. Japan Rail was still sending her emails after all these years, as was a popular izakaya in Ginza, a clothes boutique in Shinjuku. Smiling wryly, she had begun to delete the emails when she saw one that bore the Kyoto University domain name. His email, sent a month ago.

> *I don't know whether you still check this old email. Still, this is the only one I have, so write here I must.*
>
> *It has been years, so many that I thought I was allowed to forget that one brief year, truncated by tragedy, that we had spent together. I returned to Kyoto this autumn. Autumn is a good time to forget, to let everything flare in brilliant colours one final time and then extinguish after the turbulence of spring and summer. I was certain I had shed my memories and thought it would be fitting to go back, to see this city again, untouched by our brief joy, our sudden pain, just as I saw it the first time. But I was wrong. Memories are not like leaves that fall in autumn, they are like shadows. Shadows wax and wane with the seasons, but they never leave. There's no bidding goodbye to shadows. They walk with you. They walked with me through Kyoto, along the quiet-flowing Kamo and up Arashiyama.*
>
> *I wonder where you are, whether you, too, are walking in the shadows or if you have been able to fix yourself in the unrelenting glare of the present. I ought to wish that you left the shadows behind, but I don't want to. Meena, there is a comfort in shadows, a slow, lingering comfort that can hold you and soothe you. If you perchance read this email, know that I am back in Japan, in Kyoto, and will remain*

here, every day hoping that you'd emerge from the Admin block and follow me across the quad. That's it. That's all I am hoping for.

Meena read the email again and again until the words merged and turned into fluctuating lines across the screen, the kind that zigzag on hospital monitors. Finally, she rose and walked stiffly to the Satsuma plant. She tried to move the planter, but it was too heavy for her. Grabbing some old newspapers, she spread them on the floor. Then she began scooping out the potting soil with her bare hands while her phone rang again and again. Soon her hands were covered in peat moss and compost. Mud crusted under her nails, her clothes were stained with the brown mixture, but she kept digging until the roots of the Satsuma were visible. She seized the sturdy trunk of the plant and shook it loose. Dragging its leafy mass to the dustbin, she began stuffing the plant into it, breaking the long, glossy leaves and cracking the branches. The room welled with the overwhelming smell of the Satsuma plant being butchered.

'I am sorry,' she panted forcing the plant into the metal dustbin, 'I am sorry.'

ACKNOWLEDGEMENTS

THE STORIES BEGAN a long while back, dreamt of by a fish swimming in briny waters, thought up by a goh lizard burrowing in the arid sands, plucked from the blowing wind by a black kite. And as I was translating them into words, struggling, uncertain, I received help, generous and selfless – from Siddhartha Gigoo who was the first reader of many of these; Prabhat Ranjan bhaiya who encouraged me when I most needed it; my son, Yashodhar, who energized me with his frank, at times too frank, opinions on my work; my editor, Rahul Soni, who read, advised and selected with care, and listened to my doubts and writer's insecurities ad nauseum; Rinita Banerjee, my copy editor, whose patience and thoroughness was exemplary; and my publisher, Udayan Mitra, whose belief in my work has held me up; my father, Dr Surendra Upadhyay, who gave me all my words, and mother, Puja Upadhyay, who gave all of herself; my father-in-law and mother-in-law, Krishan Kumar Sharma and Girija Sharma; my sister, sisters-in-law, brothers-in-law, nieces, nephews, cousins, who created an affectionate and nurturing environment; and my husband, Vikas Sharma, with whom I saw the world in all its colours and shades, without fear, with hope and faith. Towards them, my gratitude is unbounded, inexpressible, eternal.

ABOUT THE AUTHOR

ANUKRTI UPADHYAY writes fiction and poetry in both English and Hindi. Her Hindi works include a collection of short stories titled *Japani Sarai* (2019) and the novel *Neena Aunty* (2021). Among her English works are the twin novellas, *Daura* and *Bhaunri* (2019), and her novel *Kintsugi* (2020); the latter won her the prestigious Sushila Devi Award 2021 for the best work of fiction written by a woman author. Her writings have also appeared in numerous literary journals such as *The Bombay Review*, *The Bangalore Review* and *The Bilingual Window*. Anukrti has post-graduate degrees in management and literature, and a graduate degree in law. She has previously worked for the global investment banks Goldman Sachs and UBS, in Hong Kong and India, and currently works with Wildlife Conservation Trust, a conservation think tank. She divides her time between Mumbai and the rest of the world, and when not counting trees and birds, she can be found ingratiating herself with every cat and dog in the vicinity.

30 Years *of*
HarperCollins *Publishers* India

At HarperCollins, we believe in telling the best stories and finding the widest possible readership for our books in every format possible. We started publishing 30 years ago; a great deal has changed since then, but what has remained constant is the passion with which our authors write their books, the love with which readers receive them, and the sheer joy and excitement that we as publishers feel in being a part of the publishing process.

Over the years, we've had the pleasure of publishing some of the finest writing from the subcontinent and around the world, and some of the biggest bestsellers in India's publishing history. Our books and authors have won a phenomenal range of awards, and we ourselves have been named Publisher of the Year the greatest number of times. But nothing has meant more to us than the fact that millions of people have read the books we published, and somewhere, a book of ours might have made a difference.

As we step into our fourth decade, we go back to that one word – a word which has been a driving force for us all these years.

Read.

Harper Collins | 4th | HARPER PERENNIAL | HARPER BUSINESS | HARPER BLACK | हार्पर हिन्दी

HarperCollins *Children'sBooks* | HARPER DESIGN | HARPER VANTAGE | Harper Sport